NANCY DREW

girl detective ®

#11

Monkey Wrench Blues

STEFAN PETRUCHA & SARAH KINNEY • Writers
SHO MURASE • Artist
with 3D CG elements and color by CARLOS JOSE GUZMAN
Based on the series by
CAROLYN KEENE

PAPERCUTZ™
New York

Monkey Wrench Blues
STEFAN PETRUCHA & SARAH KINNEY – Writers
SHO MURASE – Artist
with 3D CG elements and color by CARLOS JOSE GUZMAN
BRYAN SENKA – Letterer
JIM SALICRUP
Editor-in-Chief

ISBN 13: 978-1-59707-076-8 paperback edition
ISBN 10: 1-59707-076-9 paperback edition
ISBN 13: 978-1-59707-077-5 hardcover edition
ISBN 10: 1-59707-077-7 hardcover edition

Printed in China.
Distributed by Holtzbrinck Publishers.

10   9   8   7   6   5   4   3   2   1

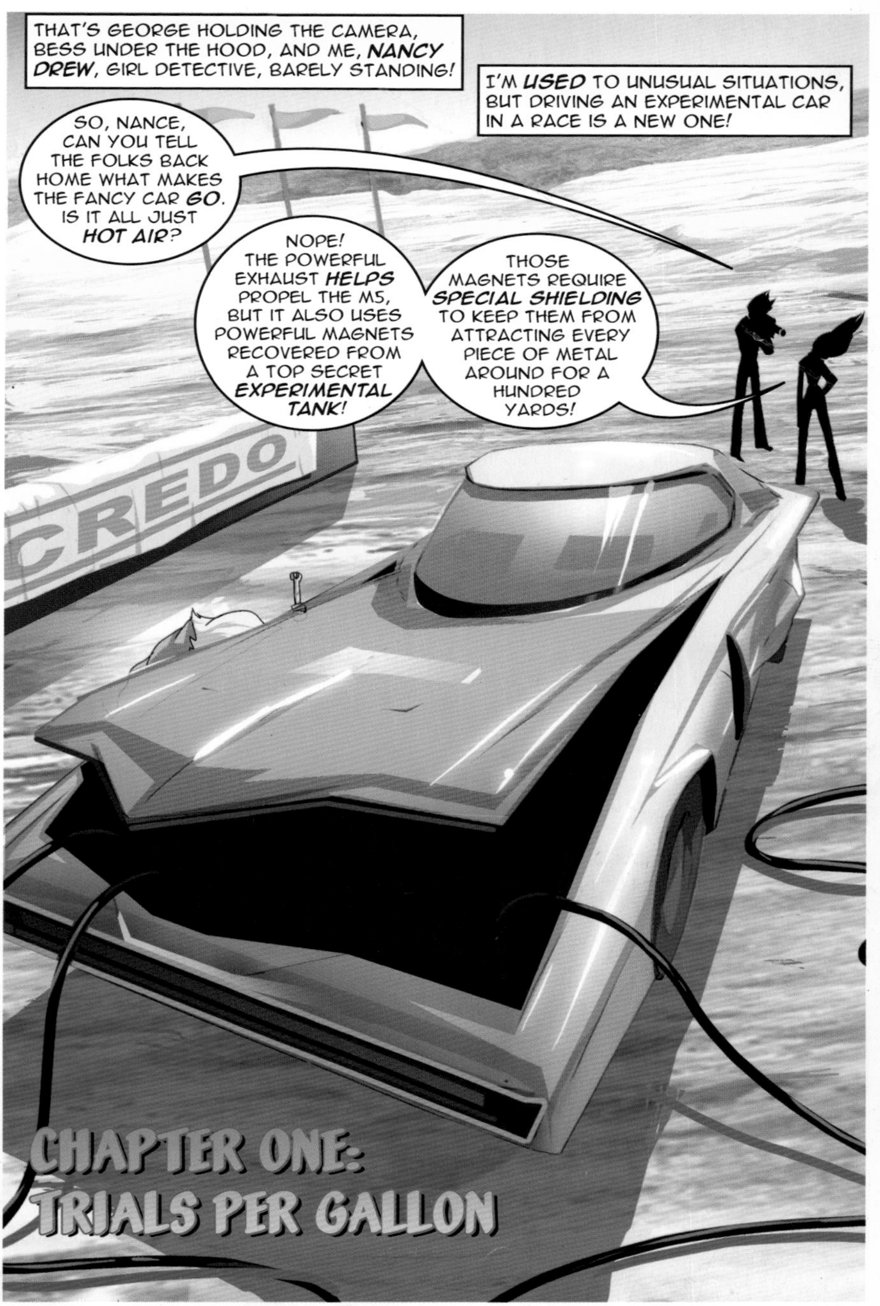
THAT'S GEORGE HOLDING THE CAMERA, BESS UNDER THE HOOD, AND ME, NANCY DREW, GIRL DETECTIVE, BARELY STANDING!
I'M USED TO UNUSUAL SITUATIONS, BUT DRIVING AN EXPERIMENTAL CAR IN A RACE IS A NEW ONE!
SO, NANCE, CAN YOU TELL THE FOLKS BACK HOME WHAT MAKES THE FANCY CAR GO. IS IT ALL JUST HOT AIR?
NOPE! THE POWERFUL EXHAUST HELPS PROPEL THE M5, BUT IT ALSO USES POWERFUL MAGNETS RECOVERED FROM A TOP SECRET EXPERIMENTAL TANK!
THOSE MAGNETS REQUIRE SPECIAL SHIELDING TO KEEP THEM FROM ATTRACTING EVERY PIECE OF METAL AROUND FOR A HUNDRED YARDS!
CREDO
CHAPTER ONE: TRIALS PER GALLON

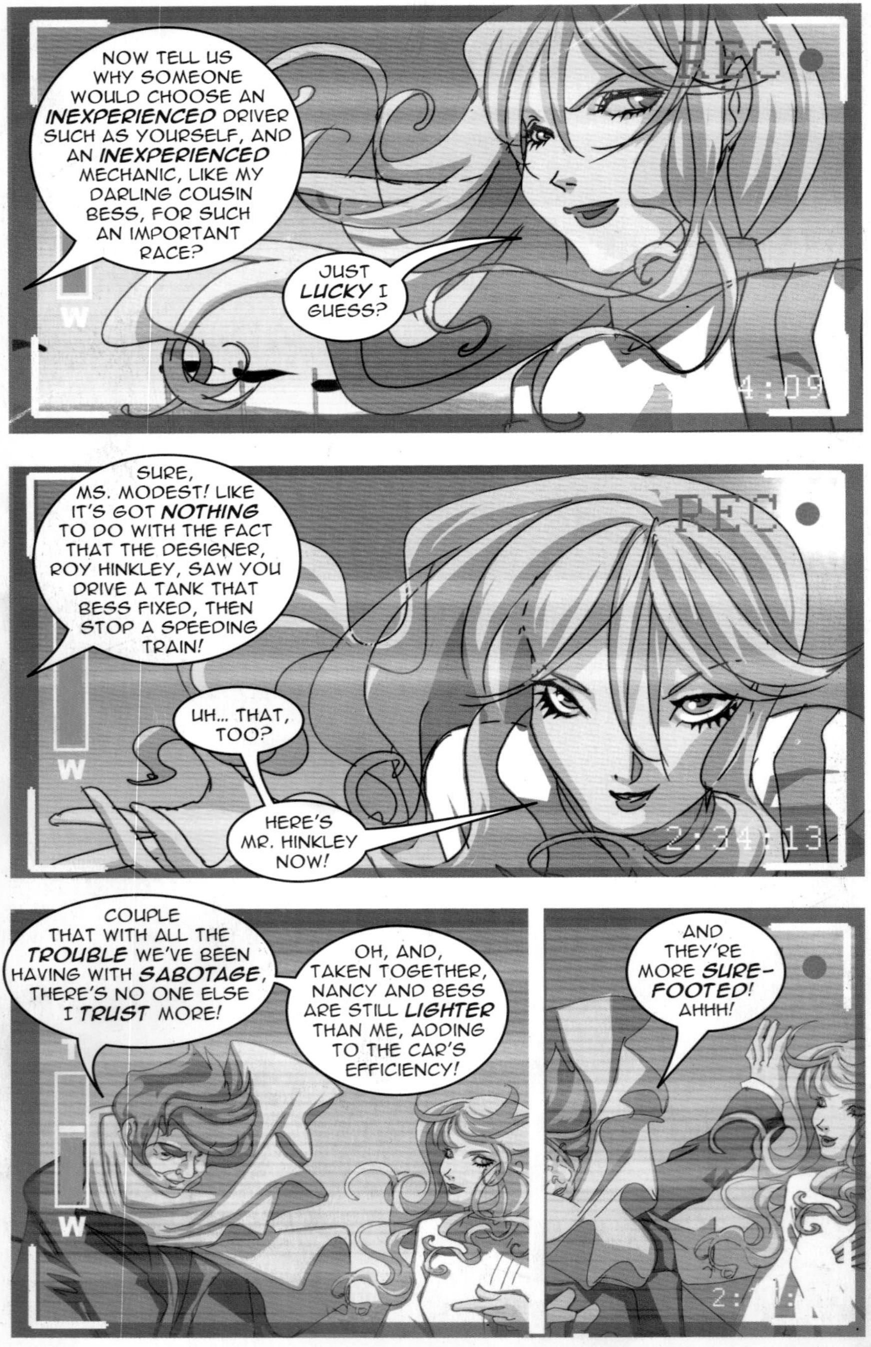
NOW TELL US WHY SOMEONE WOULD CHOOSE AN INEXPERIENCED DRIVER SUCH AS YOURSELF, AND AN INEXPERIENCED MECHANIC, LIKE MY DARLING COUSIN BESS, FOR SUCH AN IMPORTANT RACE?
JUST LUCKY I GUESS?
SURE, MS. MODEST! LIKE IT'S GOT NOTHING TO DO WITH THE FACT THAT THE DESIGNER, ROY HINKLEY, SAW YOU DRIVE A TANK THAT BESS FIXED, THEN STOP A SPEEDING TRAIN!
UH... THAT, TOO?
HERE'S MR. HINKLEY NOW!
COUPLE THAT WITH ALL THE TROUBLE WE'VE BEEN HAVING WITH SABOTAGE, THERE'S NO ONE ELSE I TRUST MORE!
OH, AND, TAKEN TOGETHER, NANCY AND BESS ARE STILL LIGHTER THAN ME, ADDING TO THE CAR'S EFFICIENCY!
AND THEY'RE MORE SURE-FOOTED! AHHH!

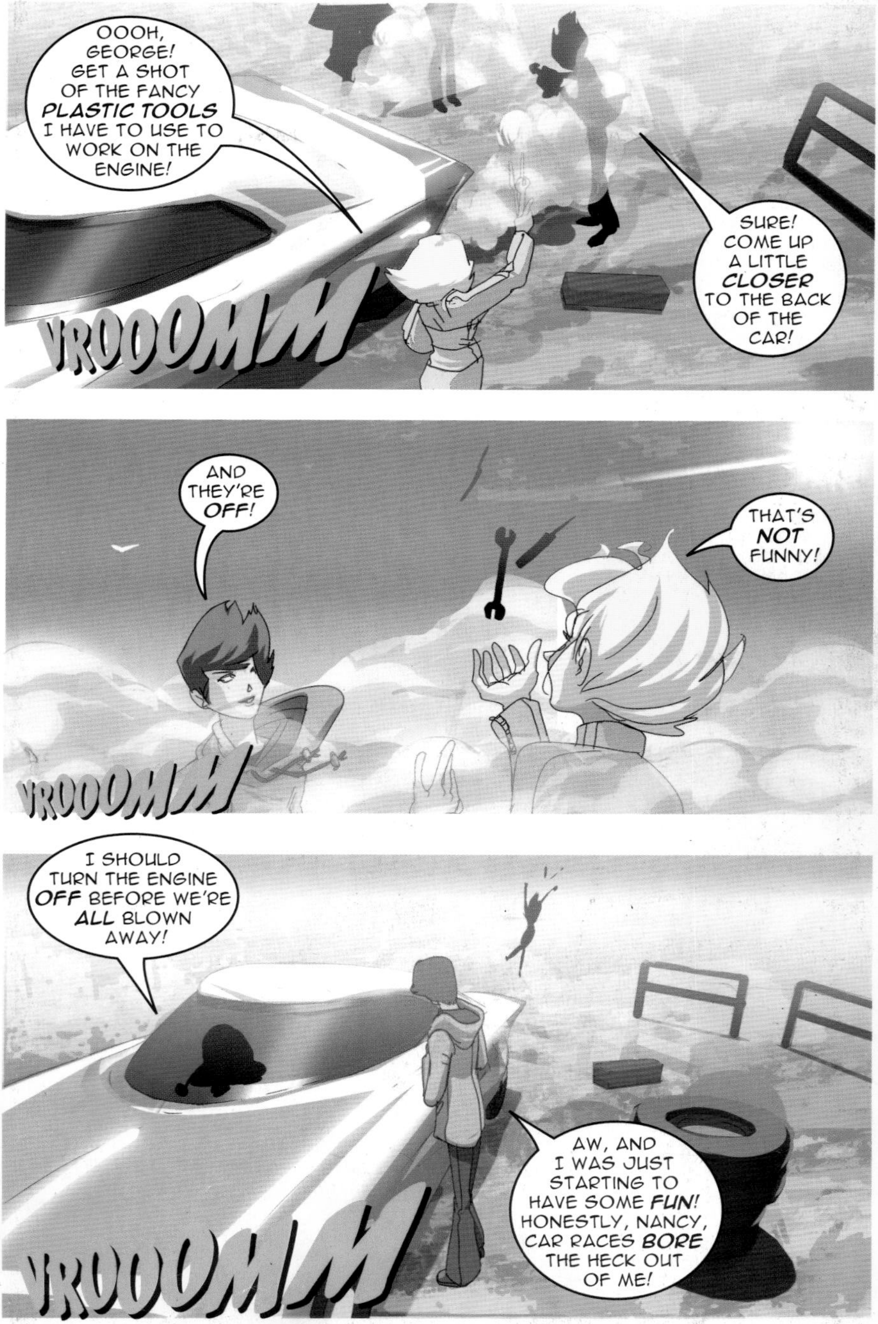
OOOH, GEORGE! GET A SHOT OF THE FANCY PLASTIC TOOLS I HAVE TO USE TO WORK ON THE ENGINE!
SURE! COME UP A LITTLE CLOSER TO THE BACK OF THE CAR!
VROOOMM
AND THEY'RE OFF!
THAT'S NOT FUNNY!
VROOOMM
I SHOULD TURN THE ENGINE OFF BEFORE WE'RE ALL BLOWN AWAY!
AW, AND I WAS JUST STARTING TO HAVE SOME FUN! HONESTLY, NANCY, CAR RACES BORE THE HECK OUT OF ME!
VROOOMM

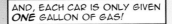

GEORGE MIGHT BE BORED, BUT NOT ME! THEN AGAIN, *I'M* THE ONE WHO'S GOING TO BE DRIVING!

IN AN EFFORT TO REPLICATE ACTUAL DRIVING CONDITIONS, THIS GOVERNMENT-SPONSORED RACE GOES THROUGH THREE DIFFERENT TYPES OF TERRAIN – DIRT, MOUNTAIN AND DESERT!

AND, EACH CAR IS ONLY GIVEN *ONE* GALLON OF GAS!

WHOEVER MAKES IT OVER THE FINISH-LINE FIRST WINS A *HUGE* GOVERNMENT DEVELOPMENT CONTRACT.

THAT'S THE MONEY ROY HINKLEY AND HIS SPONSOR, ENTREPRENEUR *RALPH CREDO* NEED TO BRING THE CAR TO PRODUCTION!

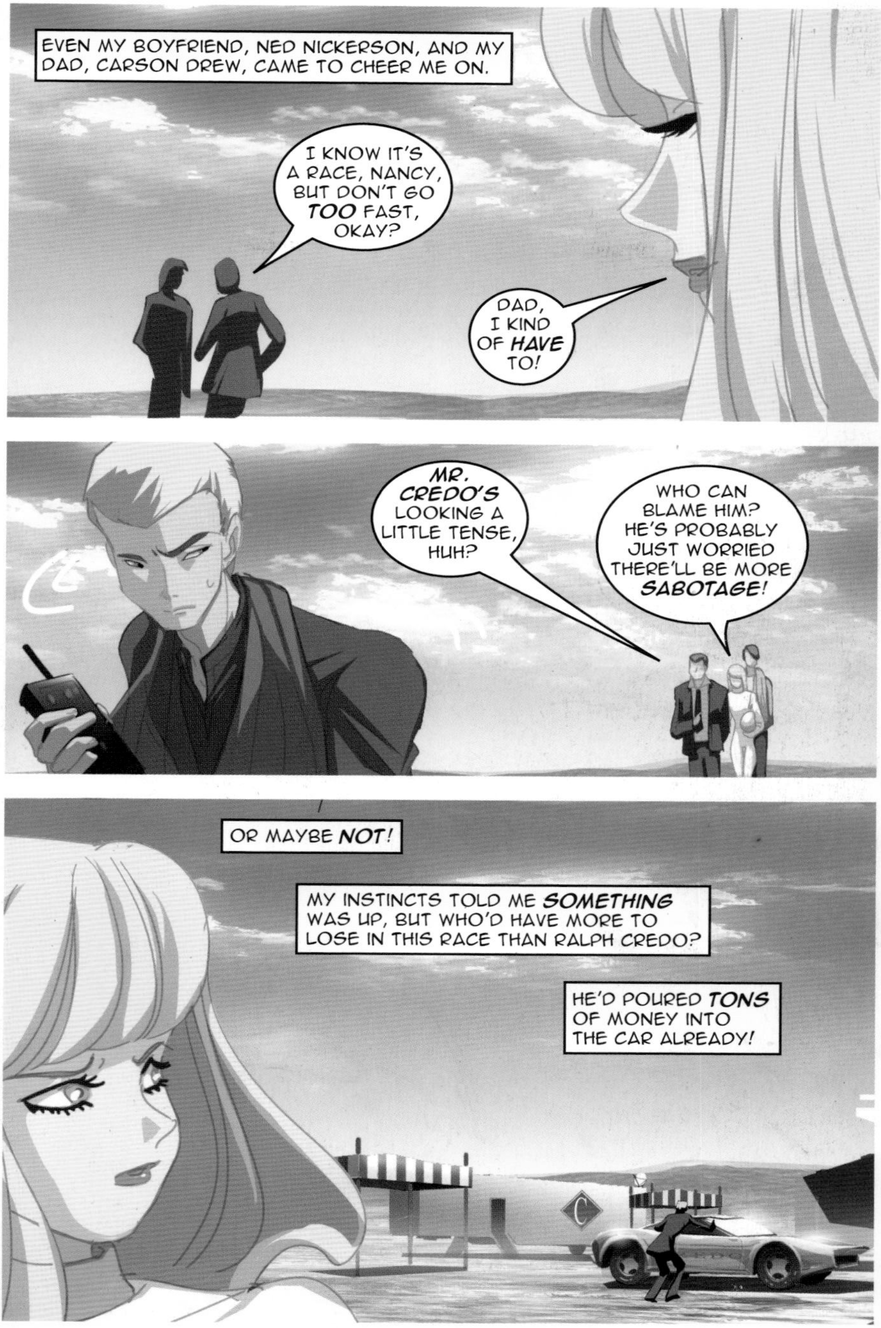
EVEN MY BOYFRIEND, NED NICKERSON, AND MY DAD, CARSON DREW, CAME TO CHEER ME ON.
I KNOW IT'S A RACE, NANCY, BUT DON'T GO TOO FAST, OKAY?
DAD, I KIND OF HAVE TO!
MR. CREDO'S LOOKING A LITTLE TENSE, HUH?
WHO CAN BLAME HIM? HE'S PROBABLY JUST WORRIED THERE'LL BE MORE SABOTAGE!
OR MAYBE NOT!
MY INSTINCTS TOLD ME SOMETHING WAS UP, BUT WHO'D HAVE MORE TO LOSE IN THIS RACE THAN RALPH CREDO?
HE'D POURED TONS OF MONEY INTO THE CAR ALREADY!

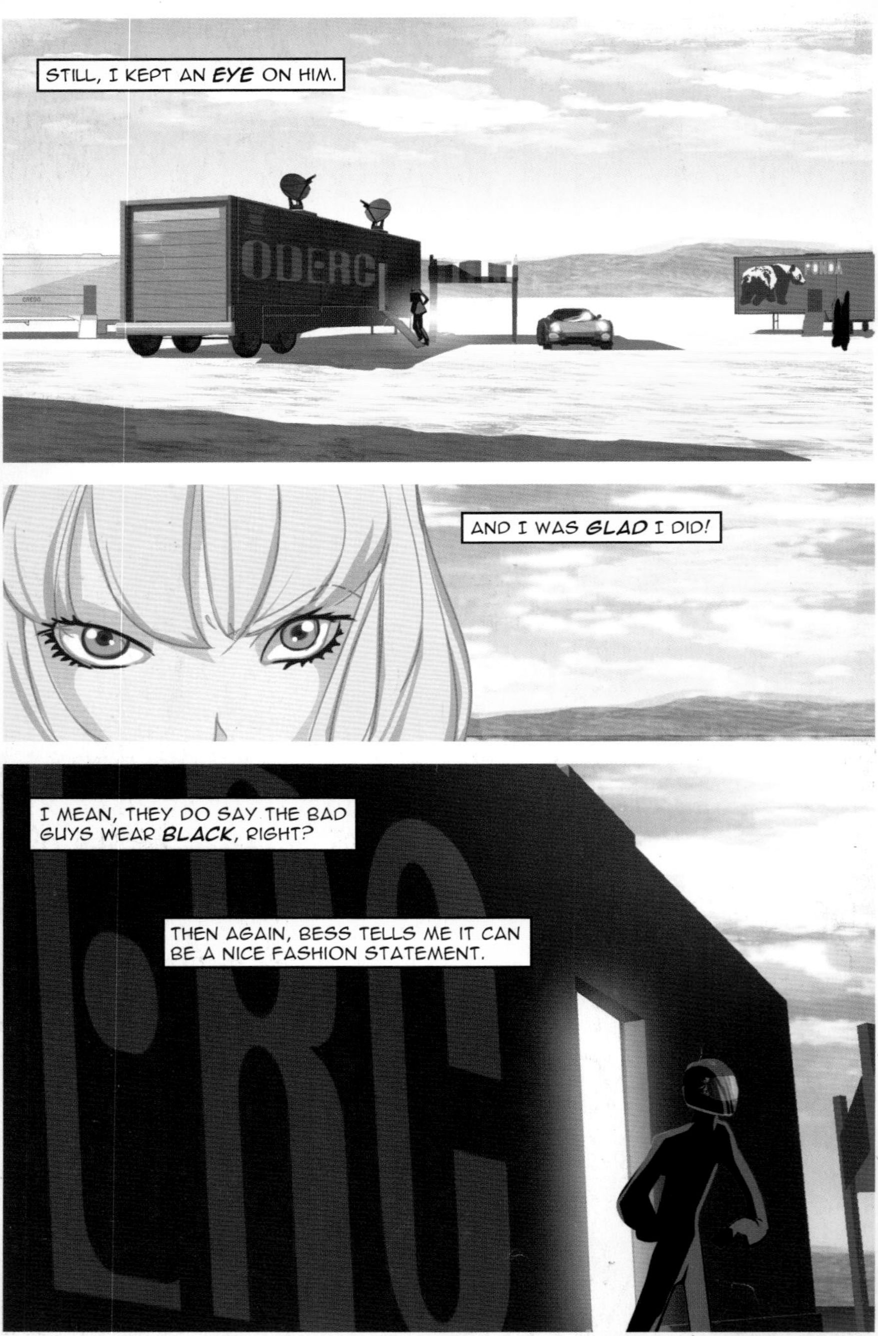
STILL, I KEPT AN EYE ON HIM.
ODERC
AND I WAS GLAD I DID!
I MEAN, THEY DO SAY THE BAD GUYS WEAR BLACK, RIGHT?
THEN AGAIN, BESS TELLS ME IT CAN BE A NICE FASHION STATEMENT.

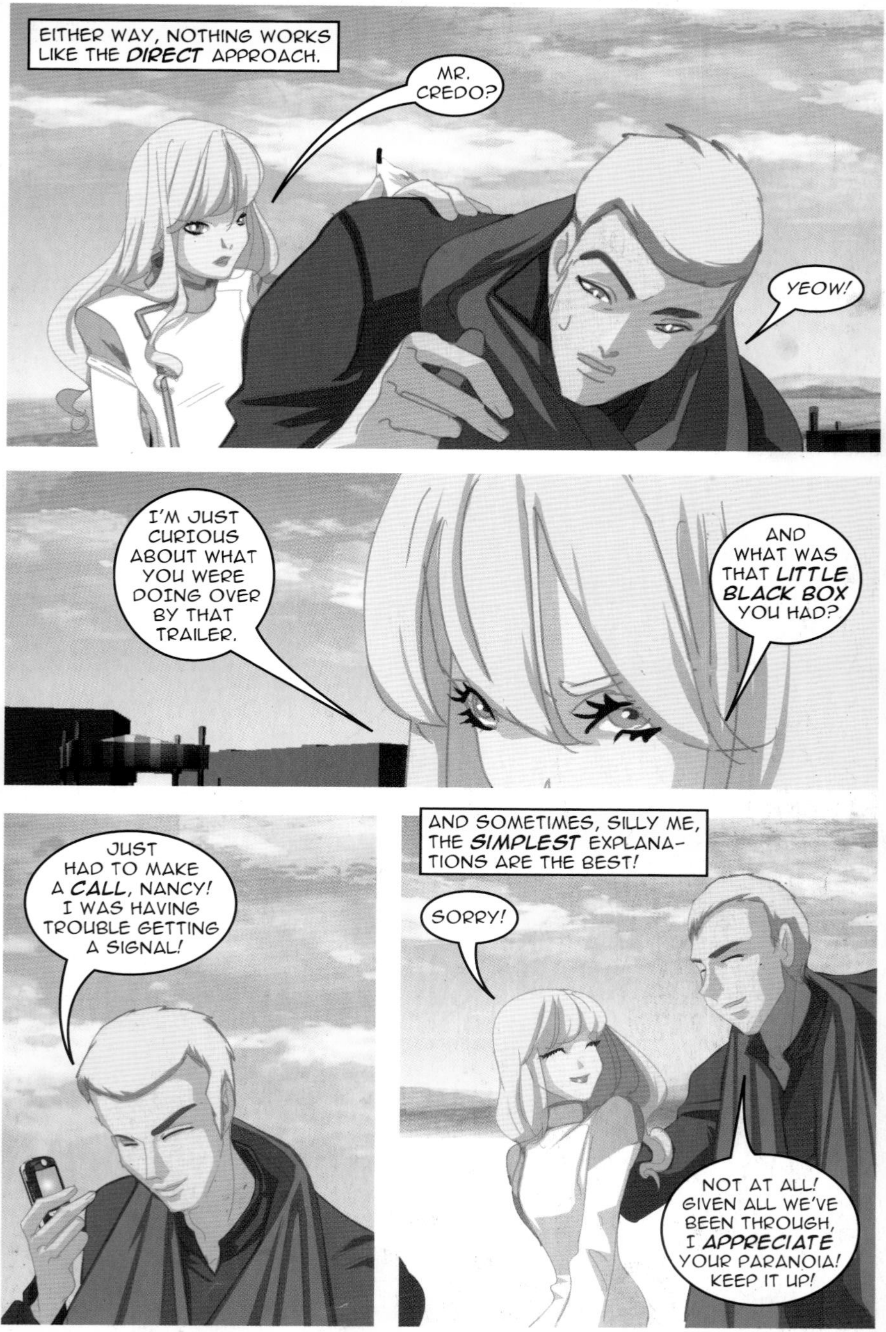
EITHER WAY, NOTHING WORKS LIKE THE DIRECT APPROACH.
MR. CREDO?
YEOW!
I'M JUST CURIOUS ABOUT WHAT YOU WERE DOING OVER BY THAT TRAILER.
AND WHAT WAS THAT LITTLE BLACK BOX YOU HAD?
JUST HAD TO MAKE A CALL, NANCY! I WAS HAVING TROUBLE GETTING A SIGNAL!
AND SOMETIMES, SILLY ME, THE SIMPLEST EXPLANATIONS ARE THE BEST!
SORRY!
NOT AT ALL! GIVEN ALL WE'VE BEEN THROUGH, I APPRECIATE YOUR PARANOIA! KEEP IT UP!

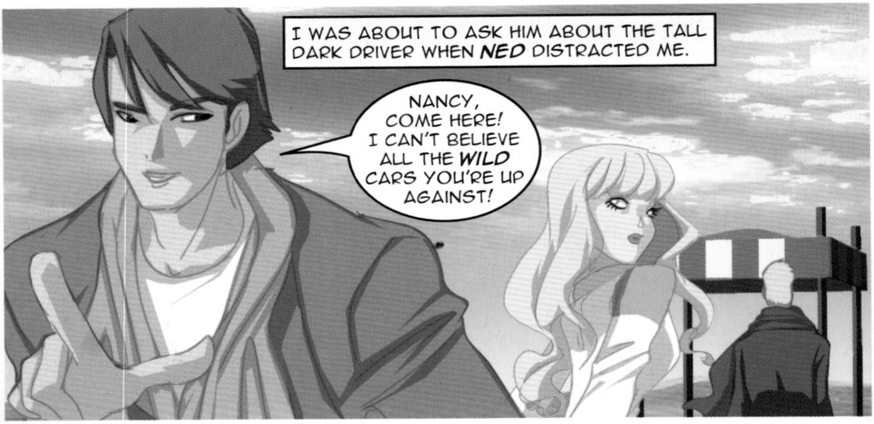
I WAS ABOUT TO ASK HIM ABOUT THE TALL DARK DRIVER WHEN *NED* DISTRACTED ME.
NANCY, COME HERE! I CAN'T BELIEVE ALL THE *WILD* CARS YOU'RE UP AGAINST!

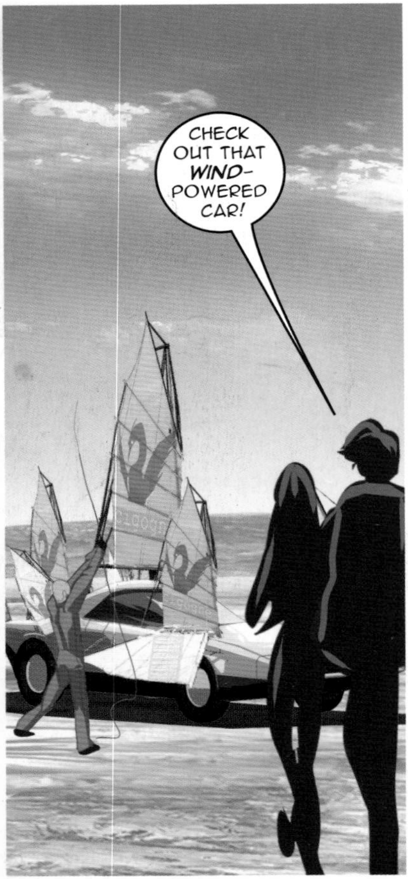
CHECK OUT THAT *WIND*-POWERED CAR!

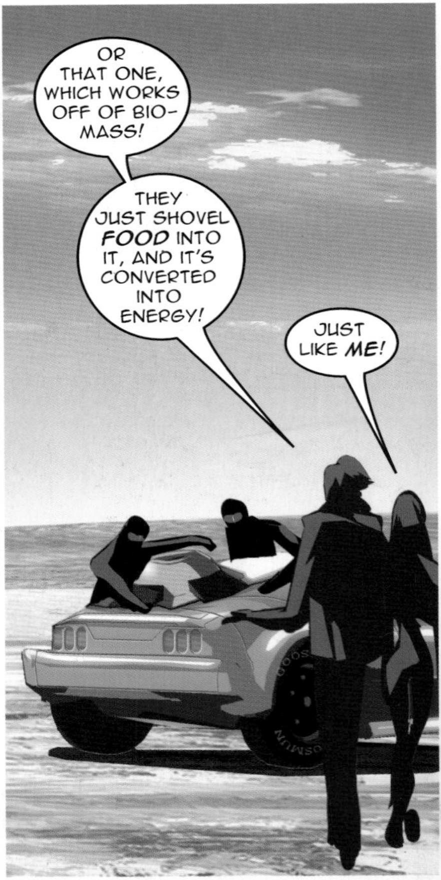
OR THAT ONE, WHICH WORKS OFF OF BIO-MASS!
THEY JUST SHOVEL *FOOD* INTO IT, AND IT'S CONVERTED INTO ENERGY!
JUST LIKE *ME*!

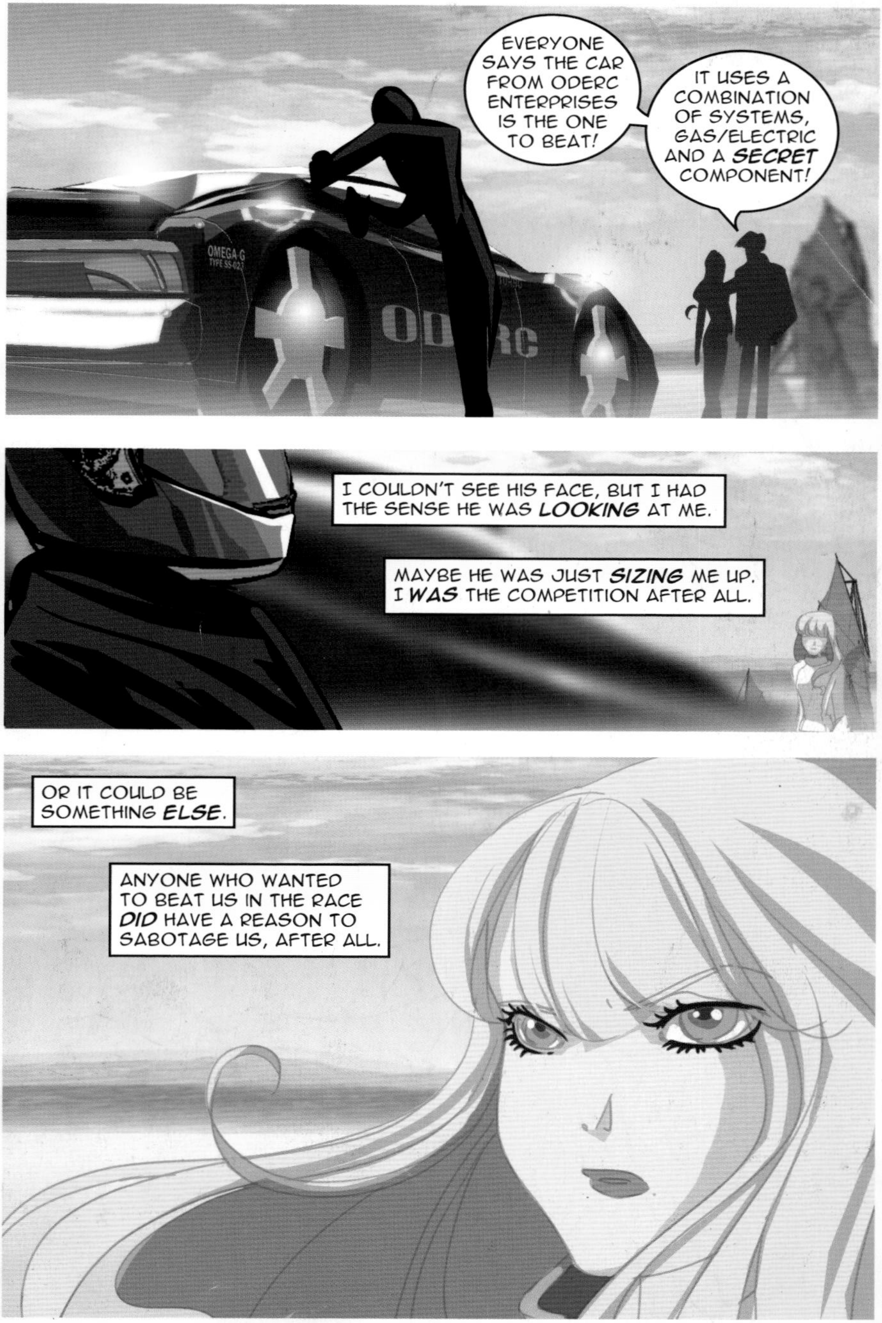
EVERYONE SAYS THE CAR FROM ODERC ENTERPRISES IS THE ONE TO BEAT!
IT USES A COMBINATION OF SYSTEMS, GAS/ELECTRIC AND A *SECRET* COMPONENT!
OMEGA-G
I COULDN'T SEE HIS FACE, BUT I HAD THE SENSE HE WAS *LOOKING* AT ME.
MAYBE HE WAS JUST *SIZING* ME UP. I *WAS* THE COMPETITION AFTER ALL.
OR IT COULD BE SOMETHING *ELSE*.
ANYONE WHO WANTED TO BEAT US IN THE RACE *DID* HAVE A REASON TO SABOTAGE US, AFTER ALL.

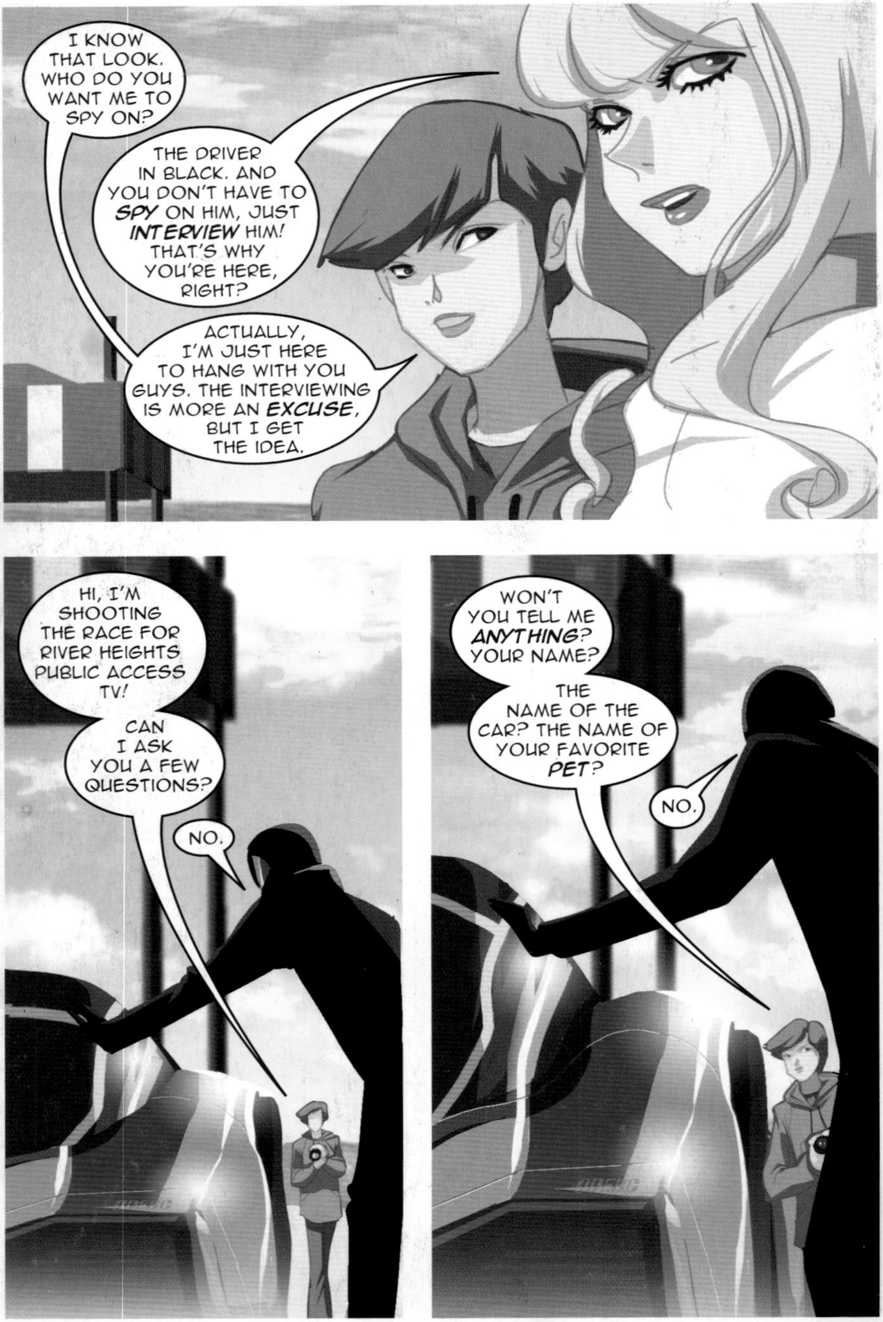
I KNOW THAT LOOK. WHO DO YOU WANT ME TO SPY ON?
THE DRIVER IN BLACK. AND YOU DON'T HAVE TO *SPY* ON HIM, JUST *INTERVIEW* HIM! THAT'S WHY YOU'RE HERE, RIGHT?
ACTUALLY, I'M JUST HERE TO HANG WITH YOU GUYS. THE INTERVIEWING IS MORE AN *EXCUSE*, BUT I GET THE IDEA.
HI, I'M SHOOTING THE RACE FOR RIVER HEIGHTS PUBLIC ACCESS TV!
CAN I ASK YOU A FEW QUESTIONS?
NO.
WON'T YOU TELL ME *ANYTHING*? YOUR NAME?
THE NAME OF THE CAR? THE NAME OF YOUR FAVORITE *PET*?
NO.

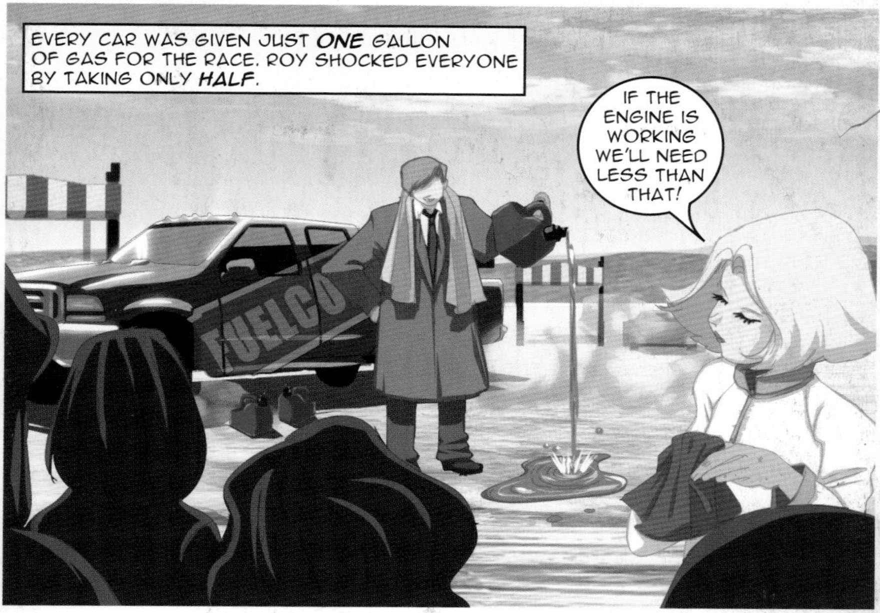
EVERY CAR WAS GIVEN JUST ONE GALLON OF GAS FOR THE RACE. ROY SHOCKED EVERYONE BY TAKING ONLY HALF.
IF THE ENGINE IS WORKING WE'LL NEED LESS THAN THAT!
FUELCO

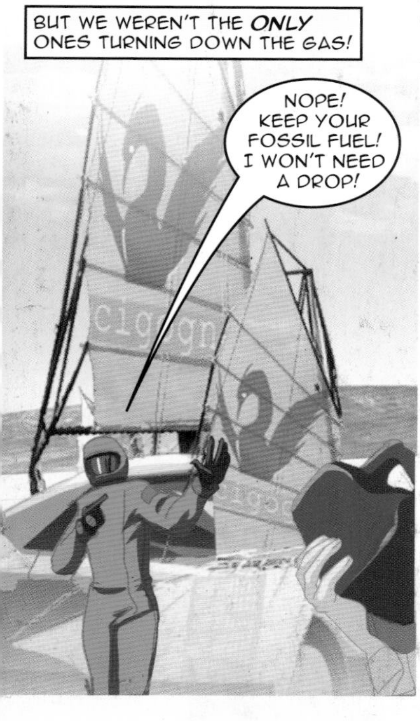
BUT WE WEREN'T THE ONLY ONES TURNING DOWN THE GAS!
NOPE! KEEP YOUR FOSSIL FUEL! I WON'T NEED A DROP!

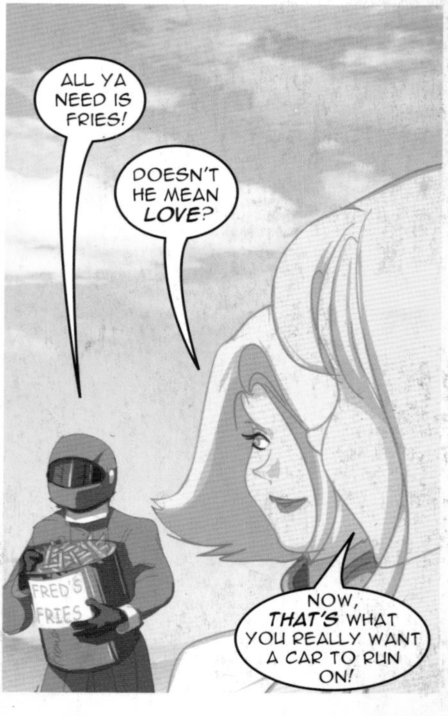
ALL YA NEED IS FRIES!
DOESN'T HE MEAN LOVE?
FRED'S FRIES
NOW, THAT'S WHAT YOU REALLY WANT A CAR TO RUN ON!

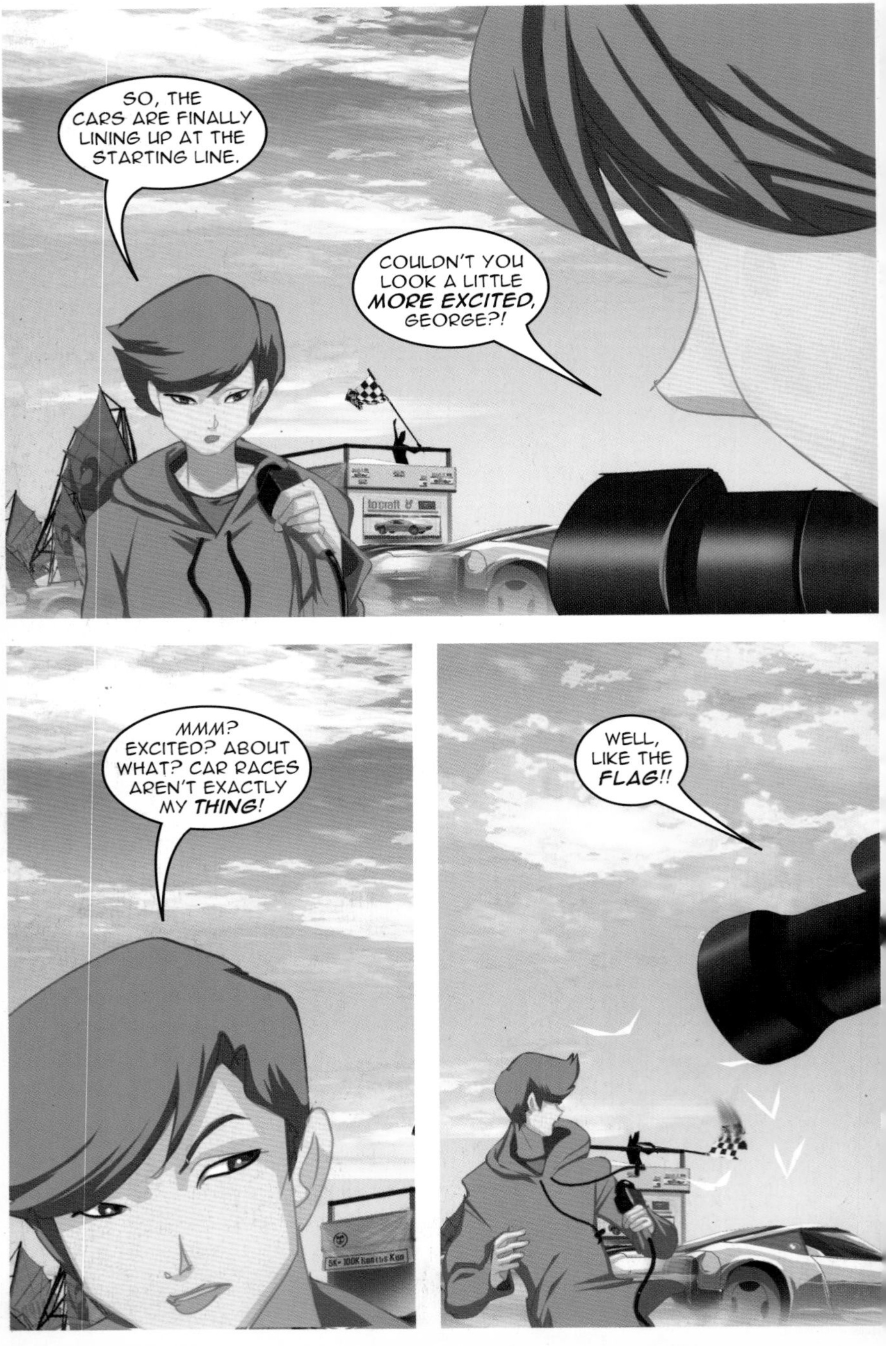
SO, THE CARS ARE FINALLY LINING UP AT THE STARTING LINE.
COULDN'T YOU LOOK A LITTLE *MORE EXCITED*, GEORGE?!
MMM? EXCITED? ABOUT WHAT? CAR RACES AREN'T EXACTLY MY *THING*!
WELL, LIKE THE *FLAG*!!

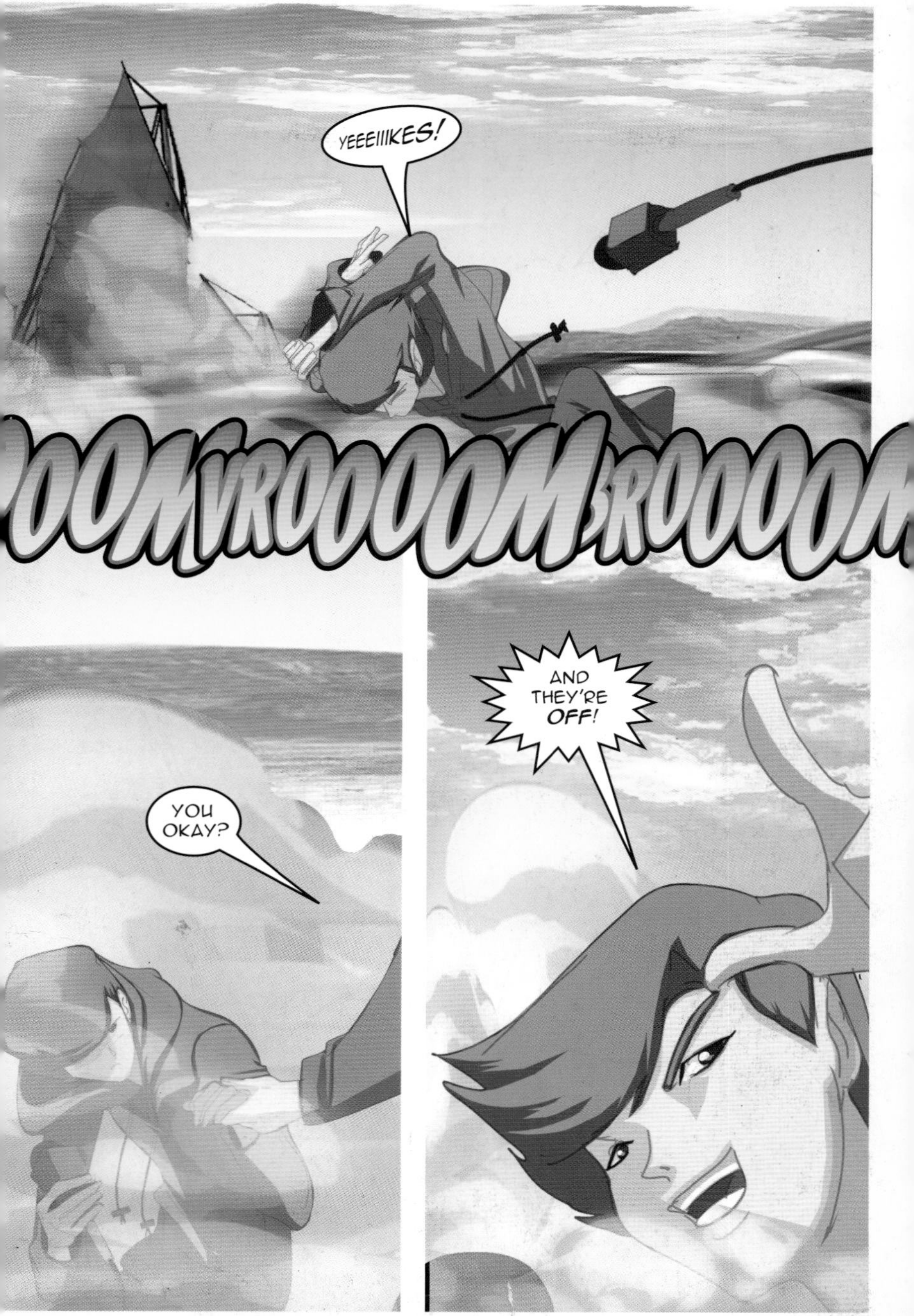
YEEEIIIKES!
OOM VROOOOOM BROOOOOM
YOU OKAY?
AND THEY'RE OFF!

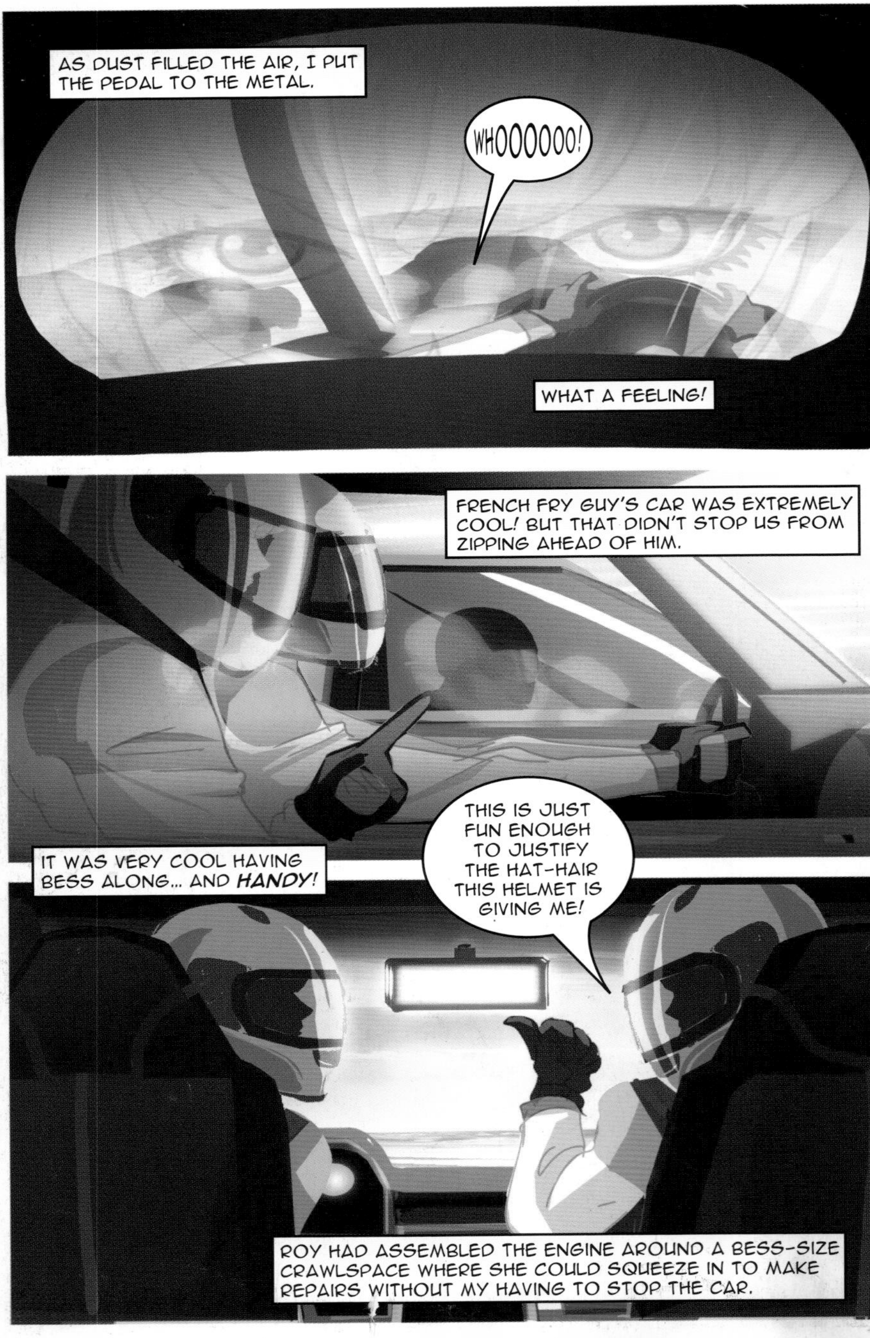
AS DUST FILLED THE AIR, I PUT THE PEDAL TO THE METAL.
WHOOOOOO!
WHAT A FEELING!
FRENCH FRY GUY'S CAR WAS EXTREMELY COOL! BUT THAT DIDN'T STOP US FROM ZIPPING AHEAD OF HIM.
IT WAS VERY COOL HAVING BESS ALONG... AND *HANDY*!
THIS IS JUST FUN ENOUGH TO JUSTIFY THE HAT-HAIR THIS HELMET IS GIVING ME!
ROY HAD ASSEMBLED THE ENGINE AROUND A BESS-SIZE CRAWLSPACE WHERE SHE COULD SQUEEZE IN TO MAKE REPAIRS WITHOUT MY HAVING TO STOP THE CAR.

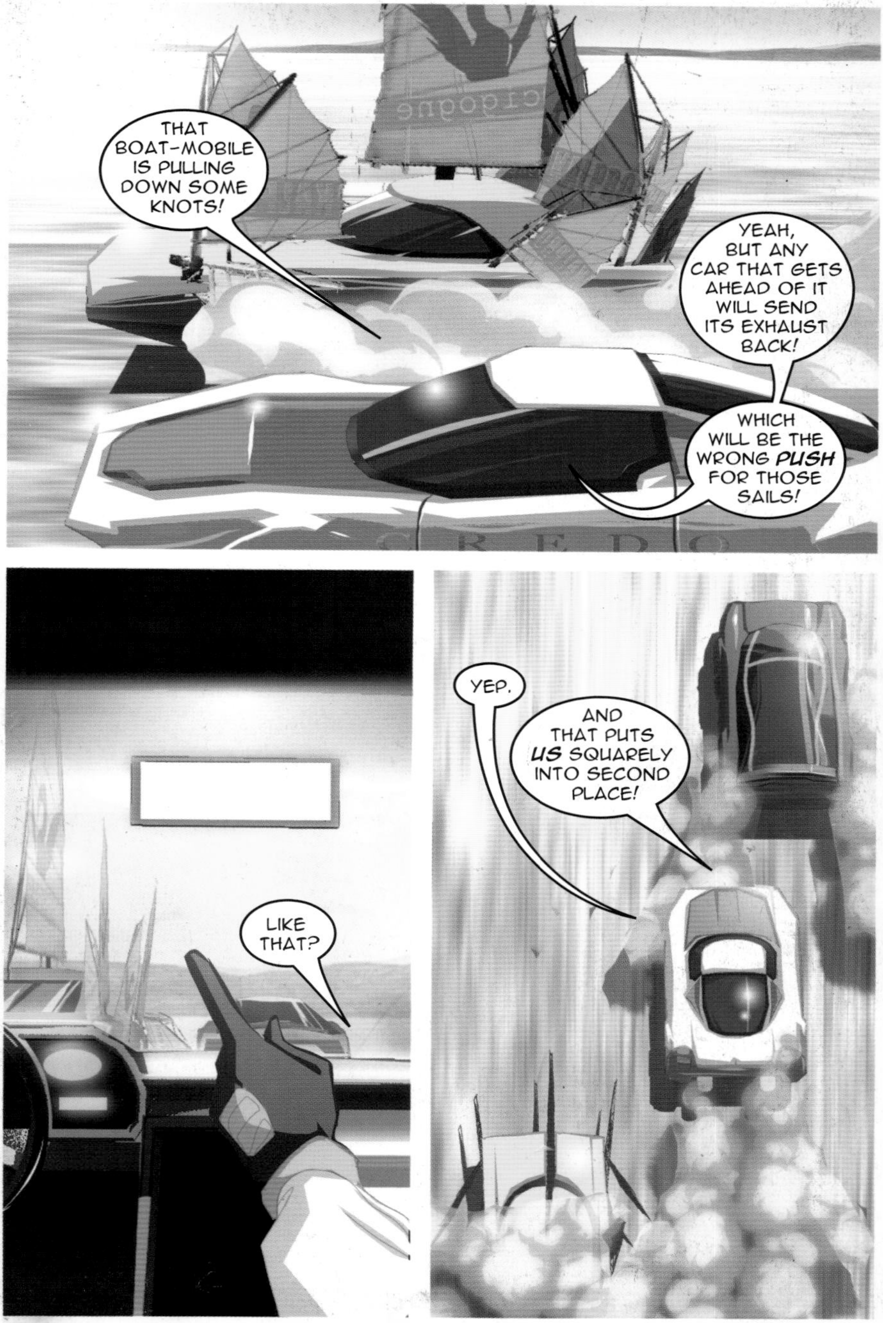
THAT BOAT-MOBILE IS PULLING DOWN SOME KNOTS!
YEAH, BUT ANY CAR THAT GETS AHEAD OF IT WILL SEND ITS EXHAUST BACK!
WHICH WILL BE THE WRONG ***PUSH*** FOR THOSE SAILS!
LIKE THAT?
YEP.
AND THAT PUTS ***US*** SQUARELY INTO SECOND PLACE!

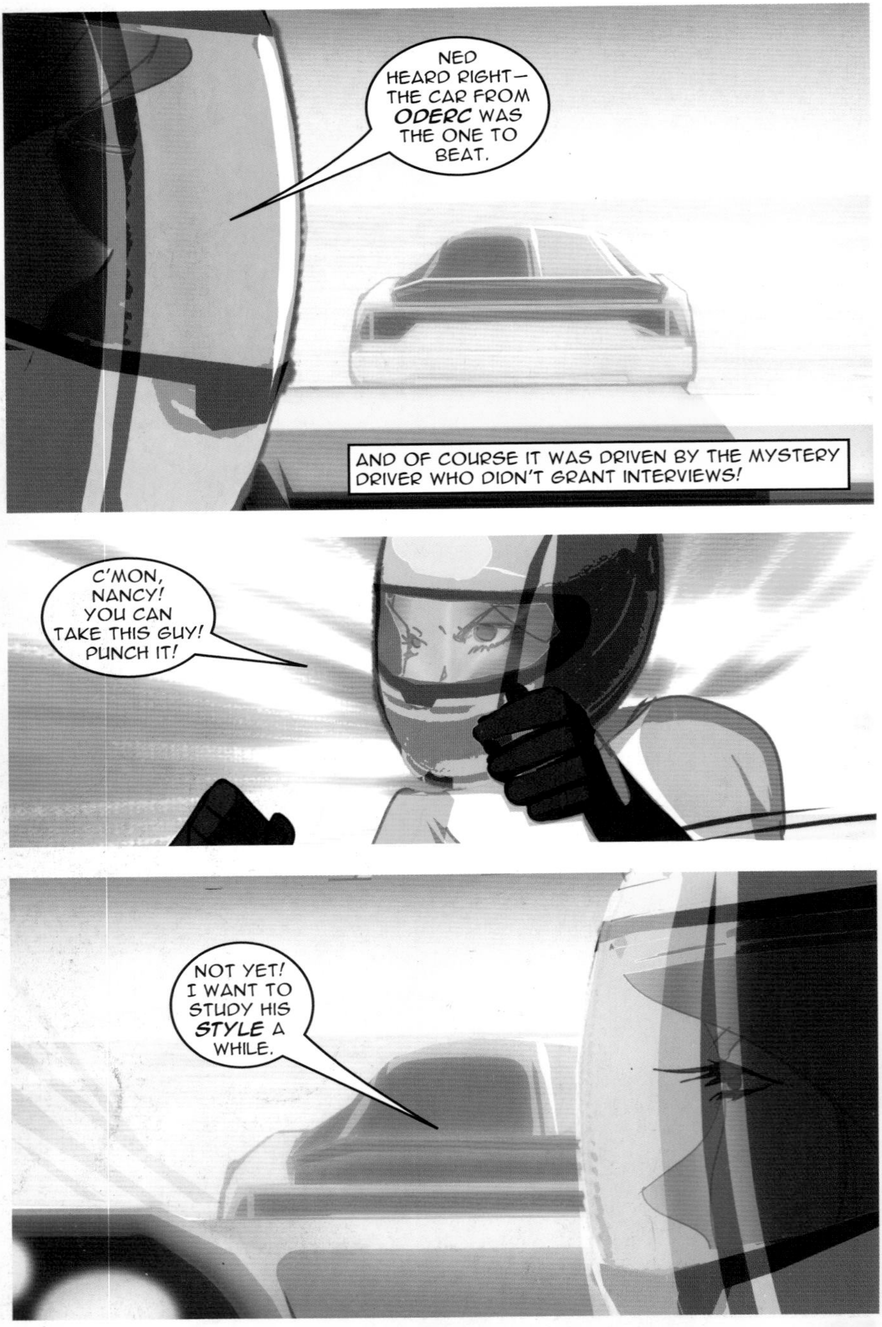
NED HEARD RIGHT— THE CAR FROM ODERC WAS THE ONE TO BEAT.
AND OF COURSE IT WAS DRIVEN BY THE MYSTERY DRIVER WHO DIDN'T GRANT INTERVIEWS!
C'MON, NANCY! YOU CAN TAKE THIS GUY! PUNCH IT!
NOT YET! I WANT TO STUDY HIS STYLE A WHILE.

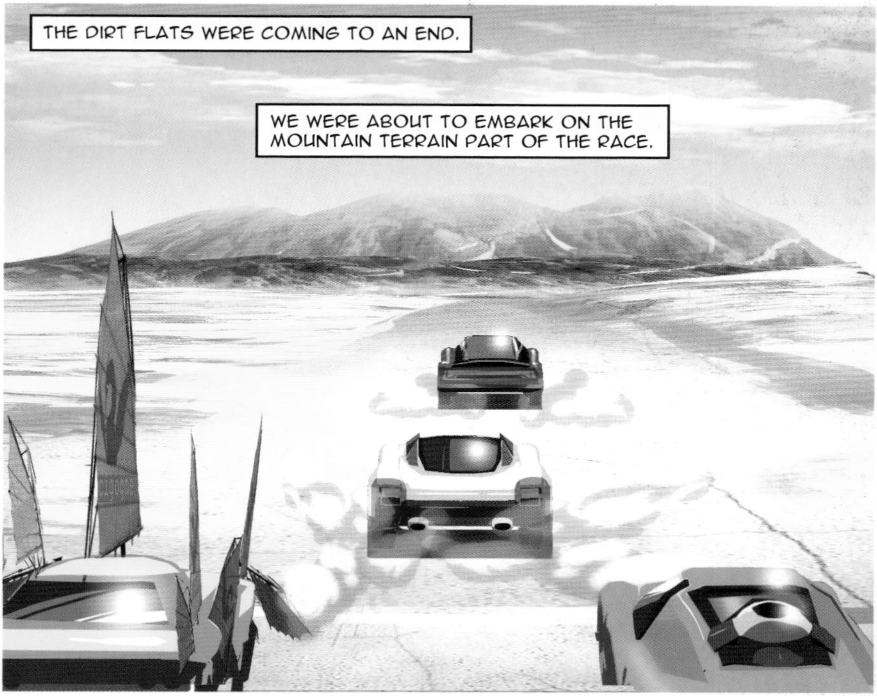
THE DIRT FLATS WERE COMING TO AN END.
WE WERE ABOUT TO EMBARK ON THE MOUNTAIN TERRAIN PART OF THE RACE.

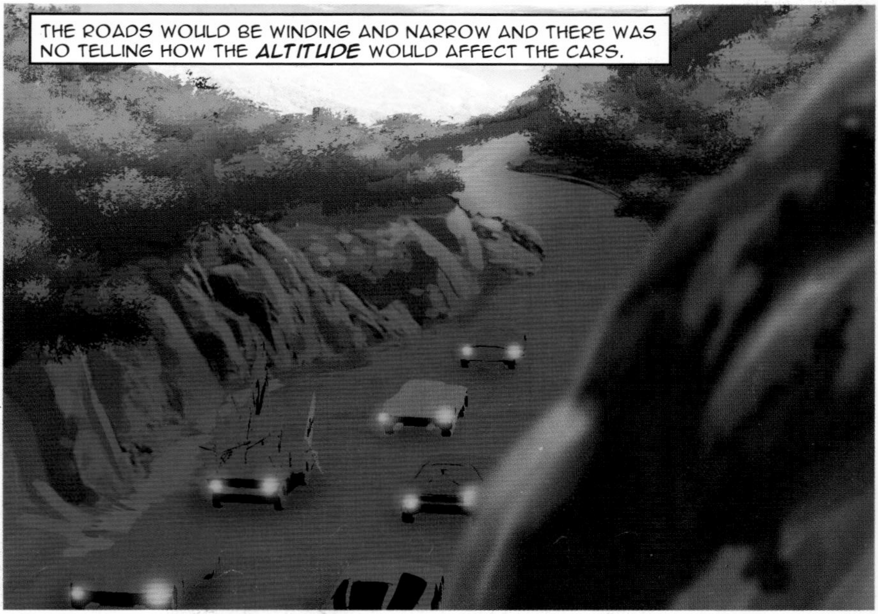
THE ROADS WOULD BE WINDING AND NARROW AND THERE WAS NO TELLING HOW THE *ALTITUDE* WOULD AFFECT THE CARS.

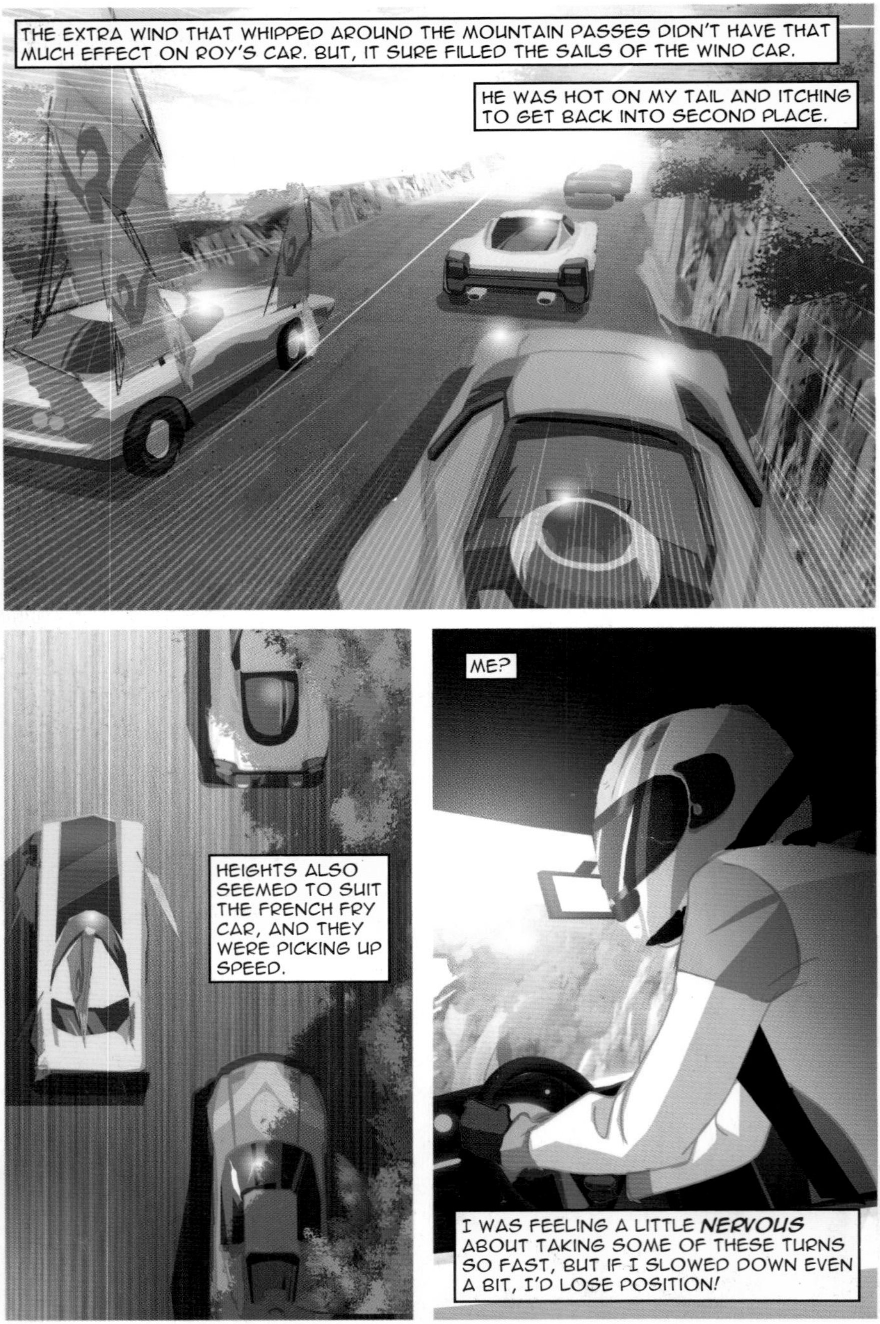
THE EXTRA WIND THAT WHIPPED AROUND THE MOUNTAIN PASSES DIDN'T HAVE THAT MUCH EFFECT ON ROY'S CAR. BUT, IT SURE FILLED THE SAILS OF THE WIND CAR.
HE WAS HOT ON MY TAIL AND ITCHING TO GET BACK INTO SECOND PLACE.
HEIGHTS ALSO SEEMED TO SUIT THE FRENCH FRY CAR, AND THEY WERE PICKING UP SPEED.
ME?
I WAS FEELING A LITTLE ***NERVOUS*** ABOUT TAKING SOME OF THESE TURNS SO FAST, BUT IF I SLOWED DOWN EVEN A BIT, I'D LOSE POSITION!

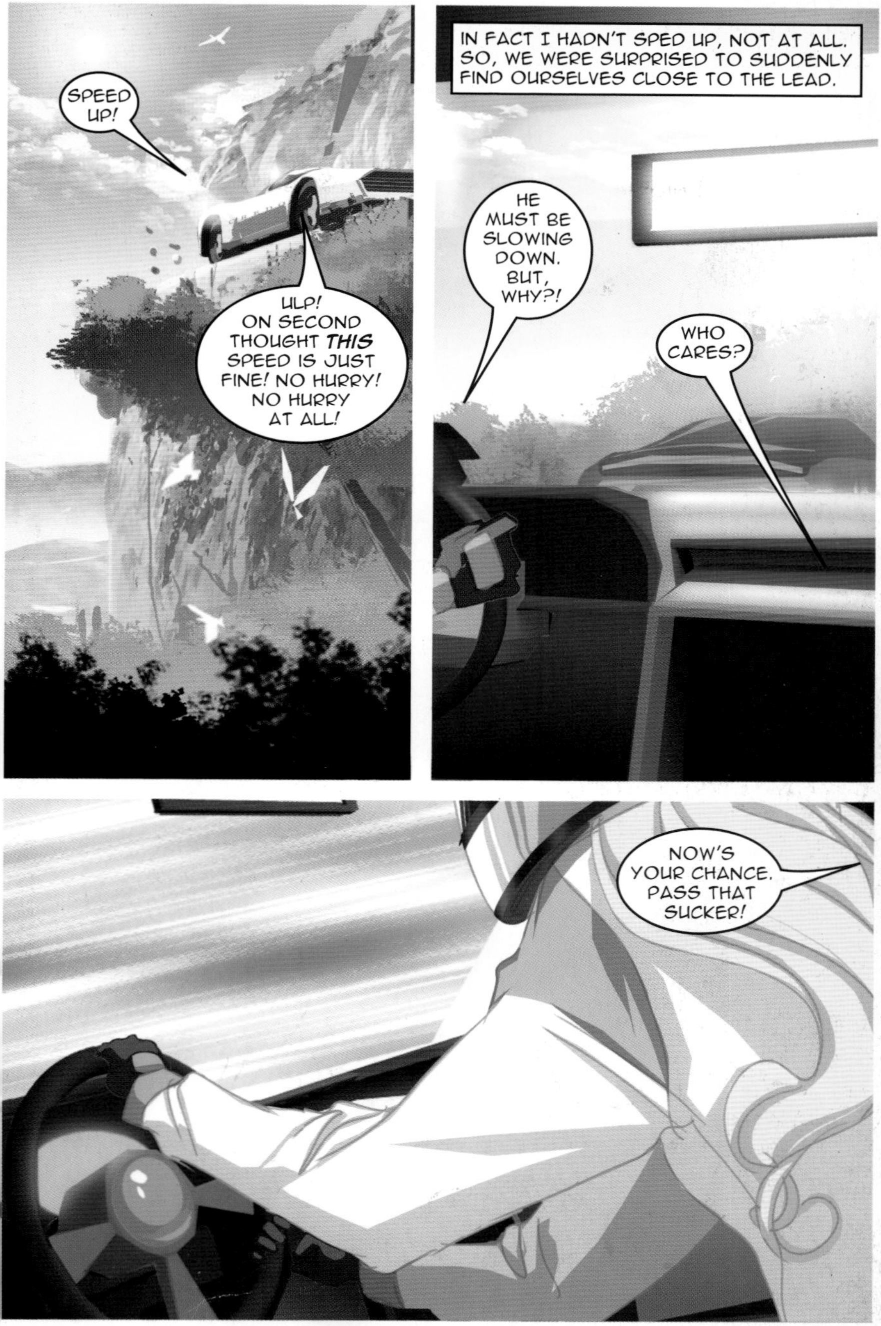
SPEED UP!
ULP! ON SECOND THOUGHT *THIS* SPEED IS JUST FINE! NO HURRY! NO HURRY AT ALL!
IN FACT I HADN'T SPED UP, NOT AT ALL. SO, WE WERE SURPRISED TO SUDDENLY FIND OURSELVES CLOSE TO THE LEAD.
HE MUST BE SLOWING DOWN. BUT, WHY?!
WHO CARES?
NOW'S YOUR CHANCE. PASS THAT SUCKER!

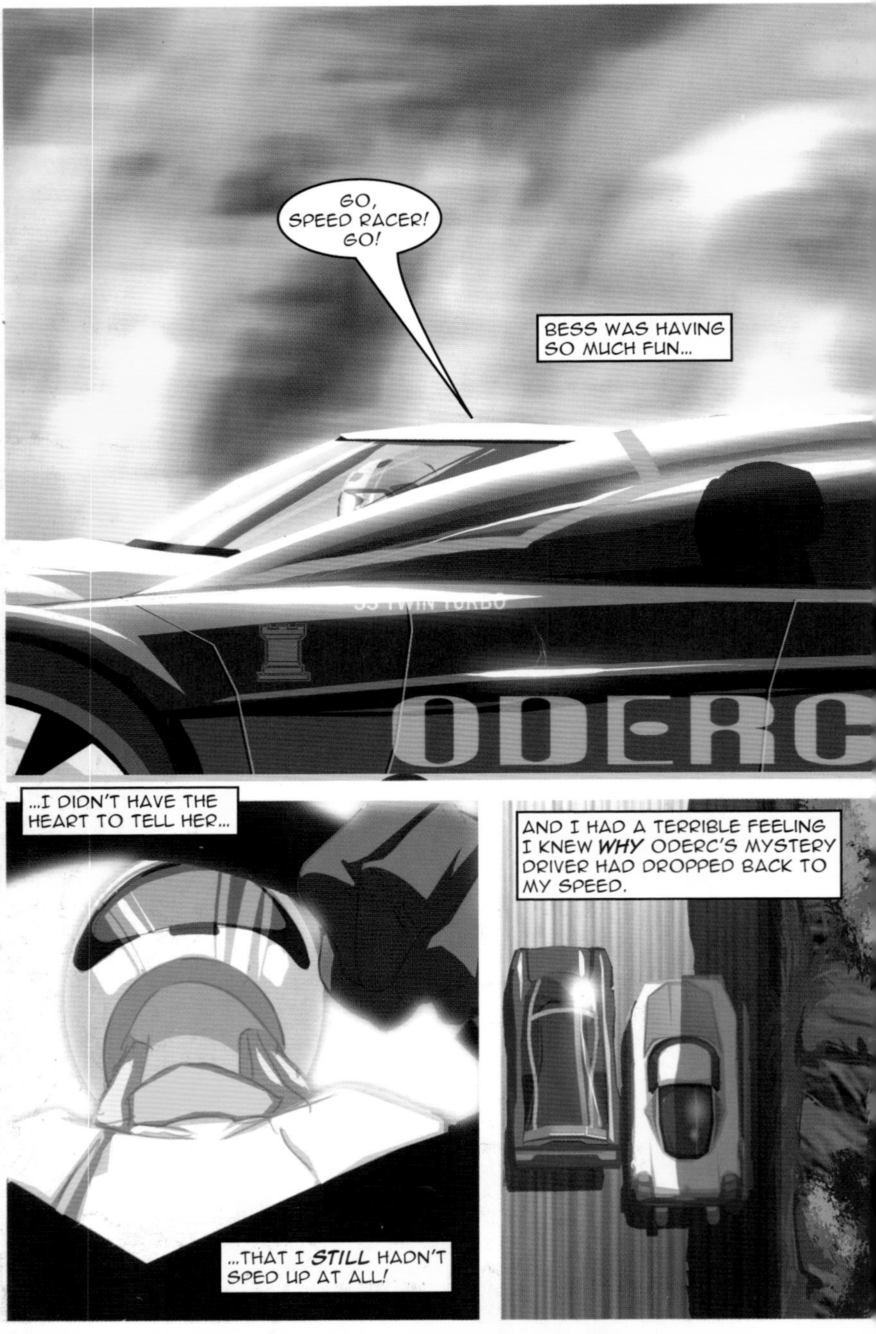
GO, SPEED RACER! GO!
BESS WAS HAVING SO MUCH FUN...
ODERC
...I DIDN'T HAVE THE HEART TO TELL HER...
...THAT I *STILL* HADN'T SPED UP AT ALL!
AND I HAD A TERRIBLE FEELING I KNEW *WHY* ODERC'S MYSTERY DRIVER HAD DROPPED BACK TO MY SPEED.

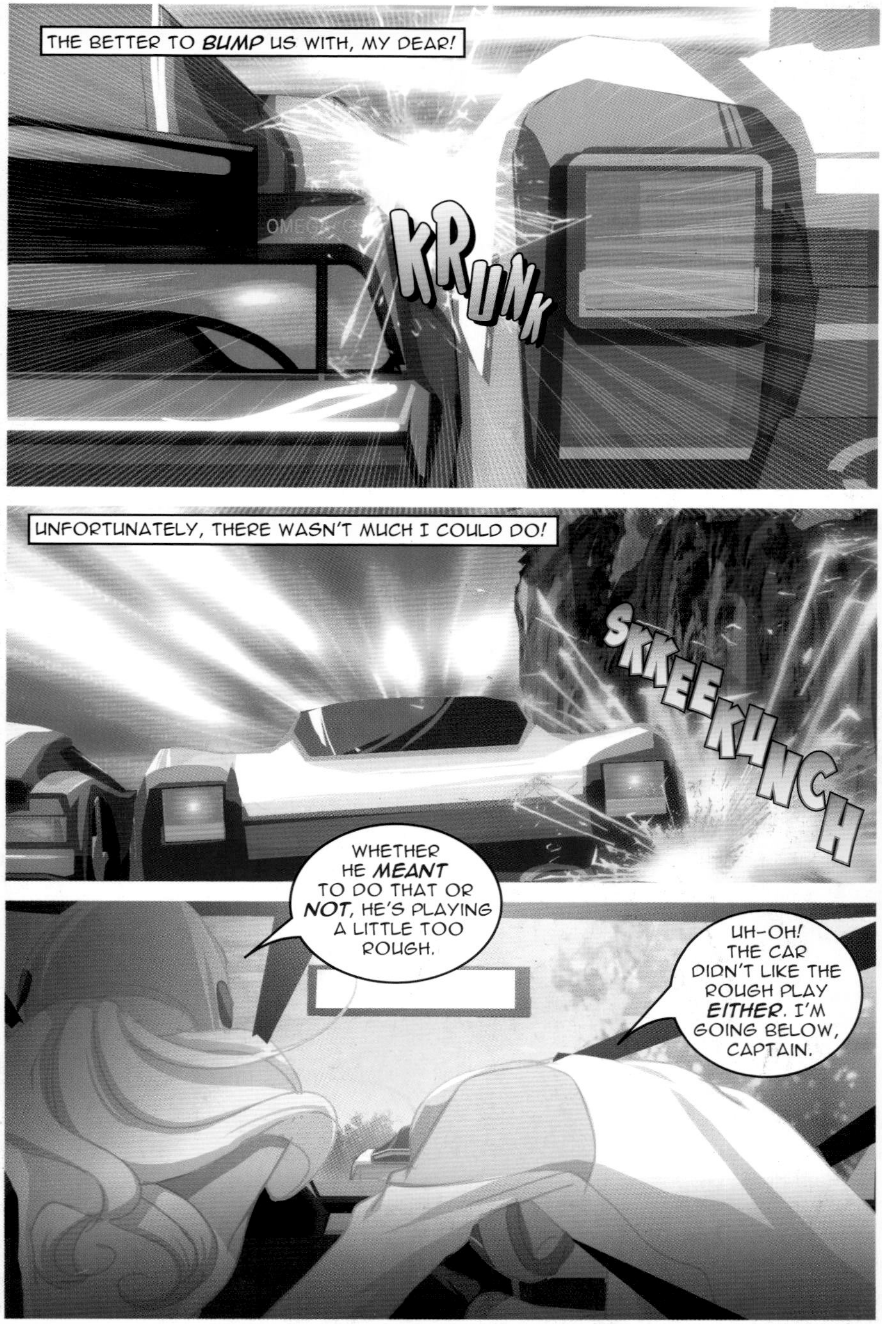
THE BETTER TO *BUMP* US WITH, MY DEAR!
KRUNK
UNFORTUNATELY, THERE WASN'T MUCH I COULD DO!
SKKEEKUNCH
WHETHER HE *MEANT* TO DO THAT OR *NOT*, HE'S PLAYING A LITTLE TOO ROUGH.
UH-OH! THE CAR DIDN'T LIKE THE ROUGH PLAY *EITHER*. I'M GOING BELOW, CAPTAIN.

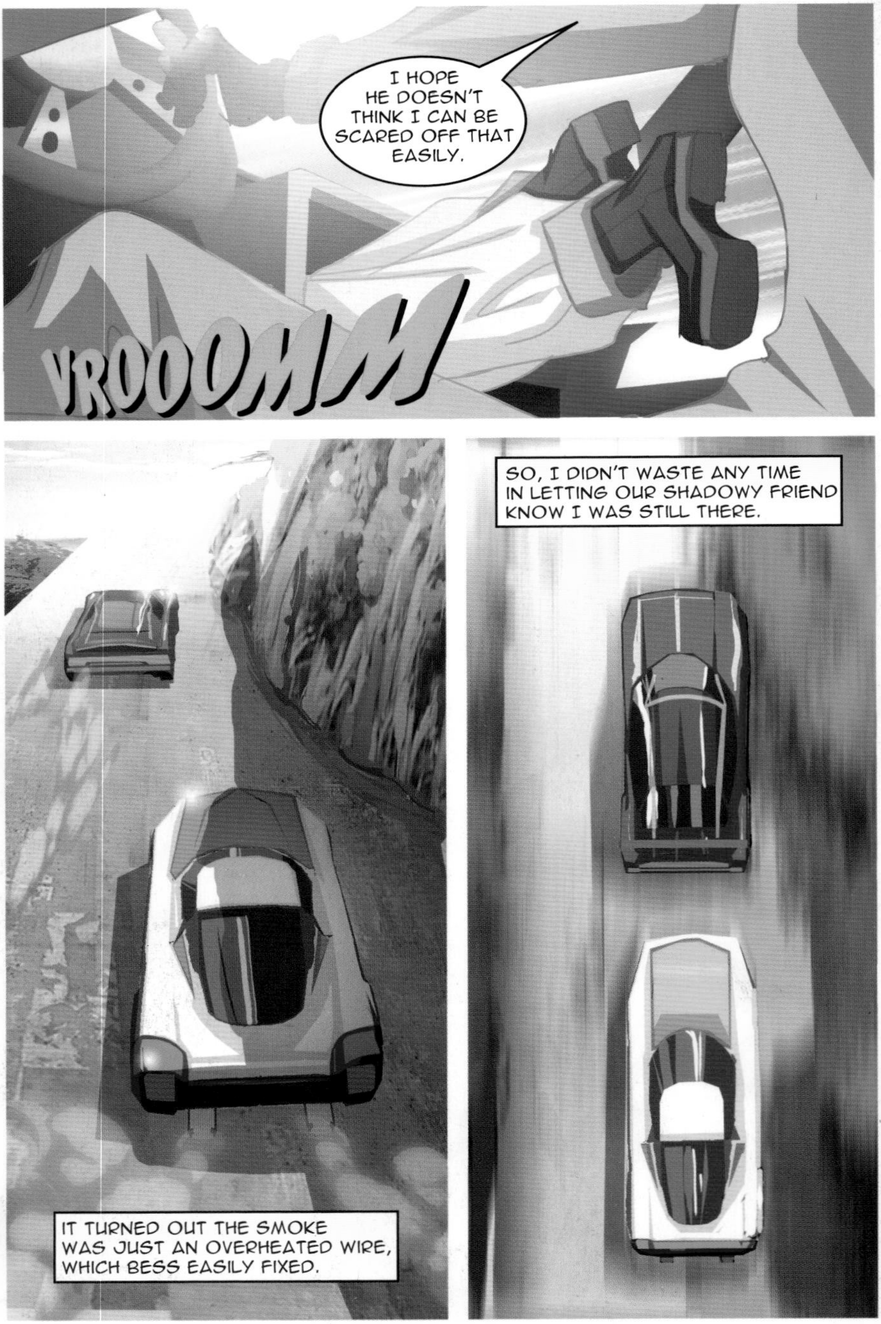
I HOPE HE DOESN'T THINK I CAN BE SCARED OFF THAT EASILY.
VROOOMM
IT TURNED OUT THE SMOKE WAS JUST AN OVERHEATED WIRE, WHICH BESS EASILY FIXED.
SO, I DIDN'T WASTE ANY TIME IN LETTING OUR SHADOWY FRIEND KNOW I WAS STILL THERE.

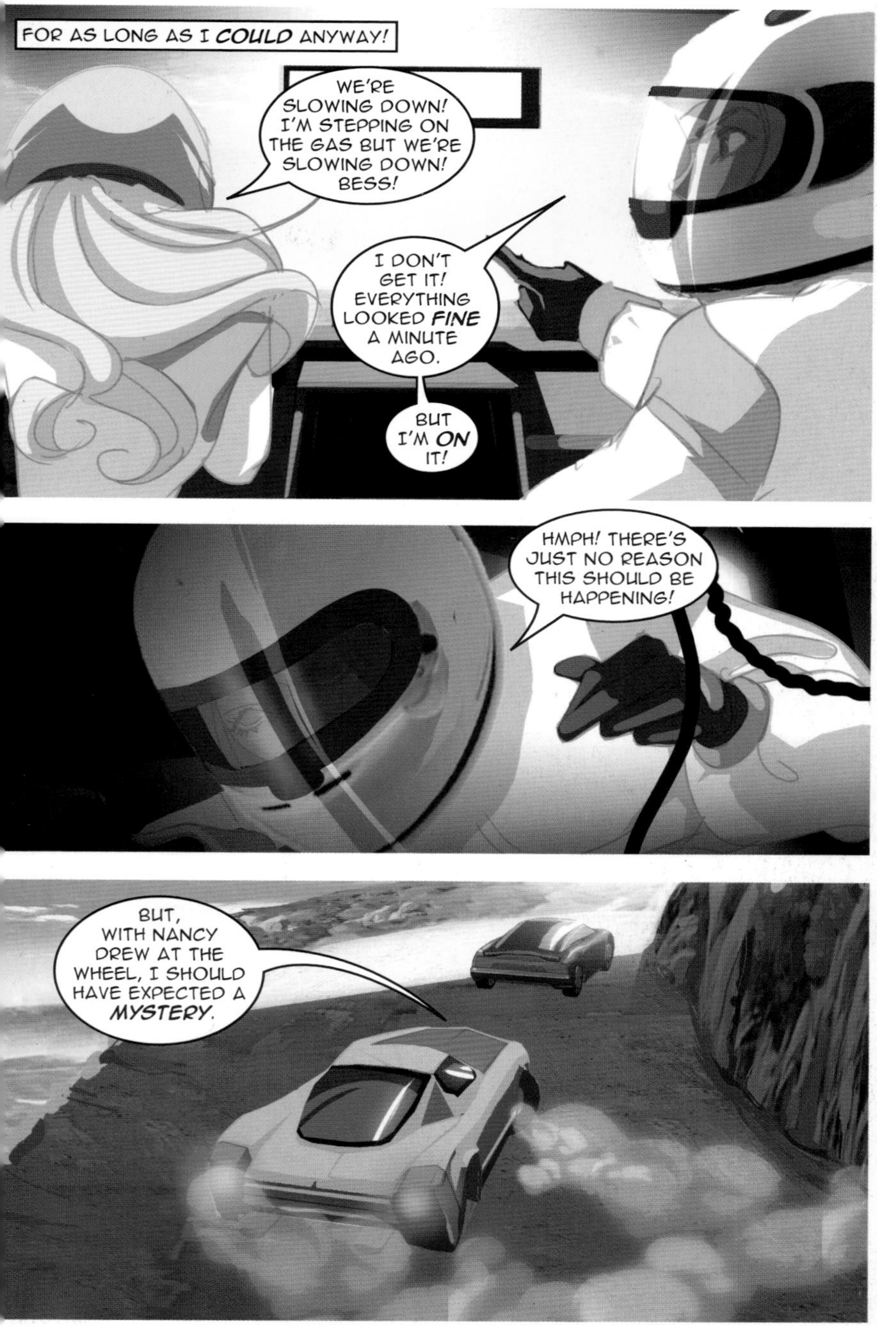
FOR AS LONG AS I COULD ANYWAY!
WE'RE SLOWING DOWN! I'M STEPPING ON THE GAS BUT WE'RE SLOWING DOWN! BESS!
I DON'T GET IT! EVERYTHING LOOKED FINE A MINUTE AGO.
BUT I'M ON IT!
HMPH! THERE'S JUST NO REASON THIS SHOULD BE HAPPENING!
BUT, WITH NANCY DREW AT THE WHEEL, I SHOULD HAVE EXPECTED A MYSTERY.

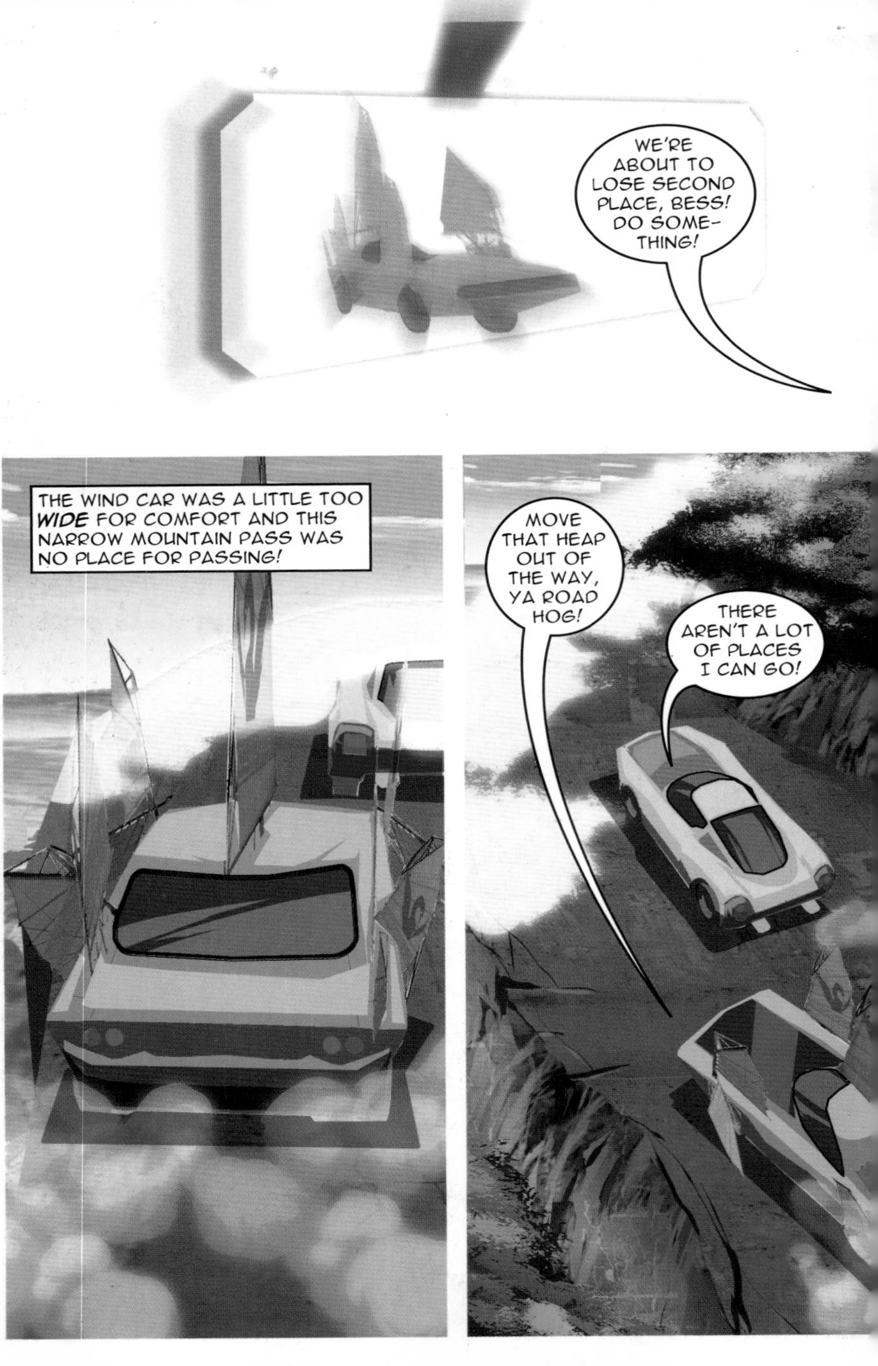
WE'RE ABOUT TO LOSE SECOND PLACE, BESS! DO SOME-THING!
THE WIND CAR WAS A LITTLE TOO WIDE FOR COMFORT AND THIS NARROW MOUNTAIN PASS WAS NO PLACE FOR PASSING!
MOVE THAT HEAP OUT OF THE WAY, YA ROAD HOG!
THERE AREN'T A LOT OF PLACES I CAN GO!

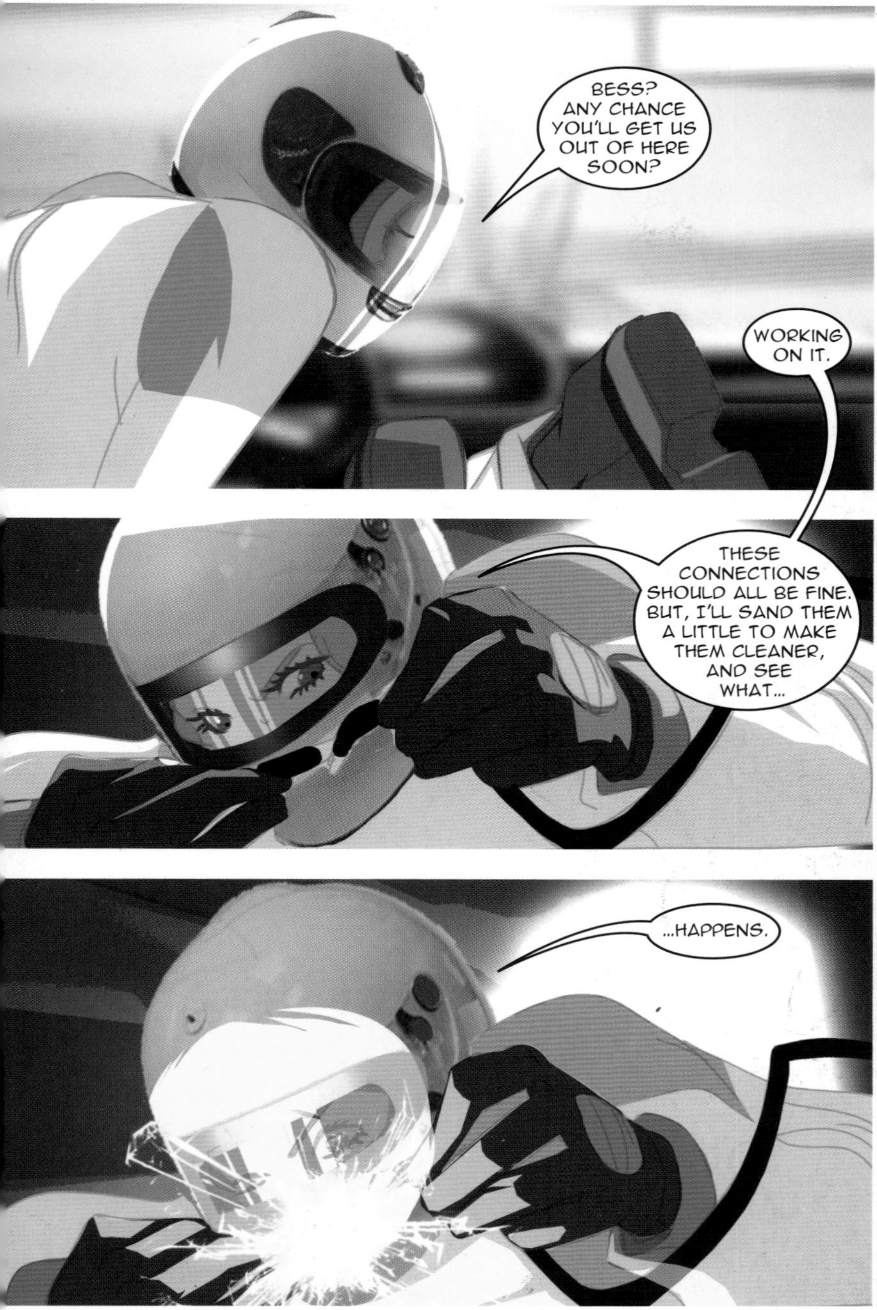
BESS? ANY CHANCE YOU'LL GET US OUT OF HERE SOON?
WORKING ON IT.
THESE CONNECTIONS SHOULD ALL BE FINE. BUT, I'LL SAND THEM A LITTLE TO MAKE THEM CLEANER, AND SEE WHAT...
...HAPPENS.

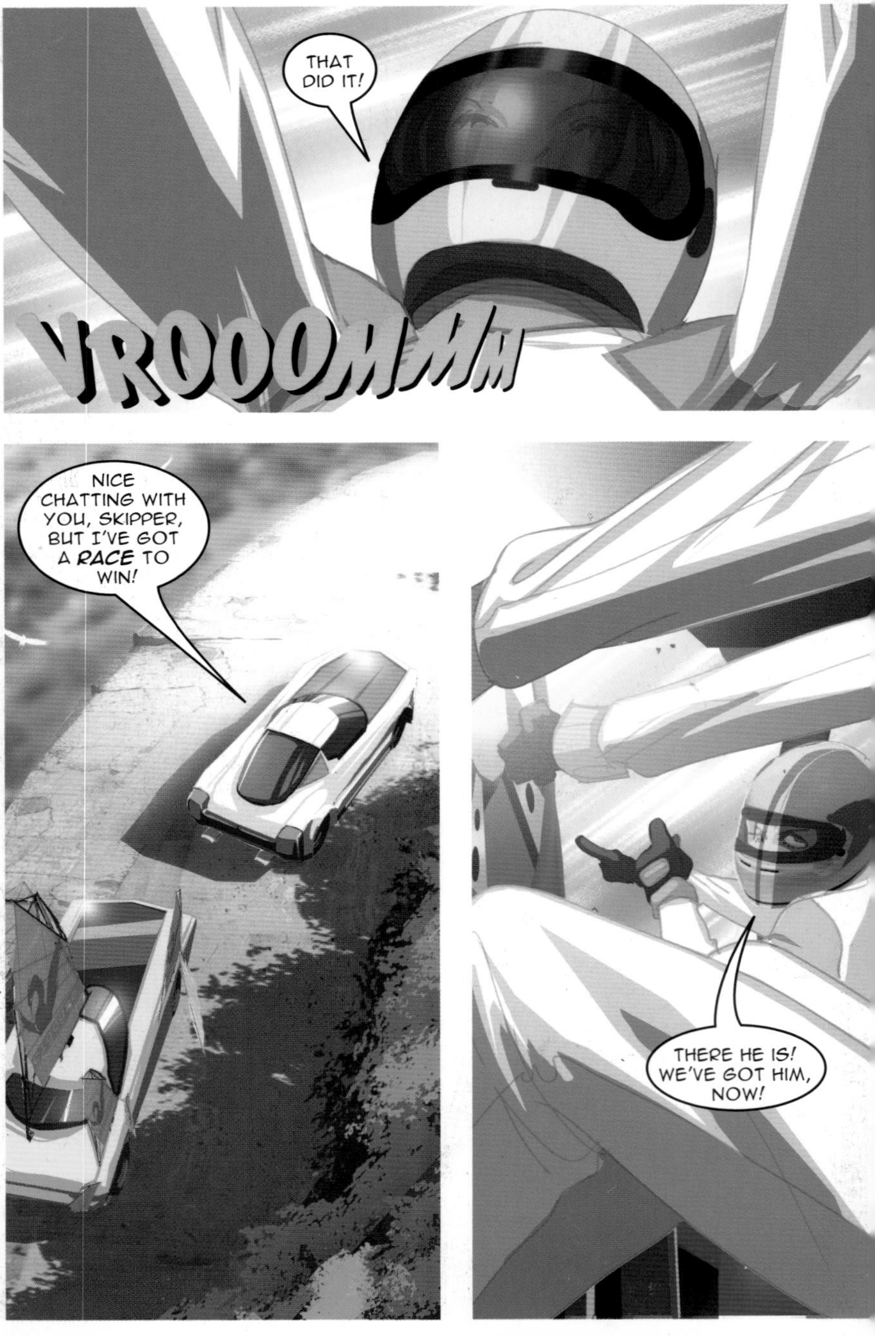
THAT DID IT!
VROOOMMM
NICE CHATTING WITH YOU, SKIPPER, BUT I'VE GOT A RACE TO WIN!
THERE HE IS! WE'VE GOT HIM, NOW!

HUH?! WHO'S GOT *WHO*?!

YOU'LL NEVER GET AROUND HIM! STOP!

SLAAMM

I GUESS I DIDN'T REALIZE JUST HOW *FAST* I WAS GOING...

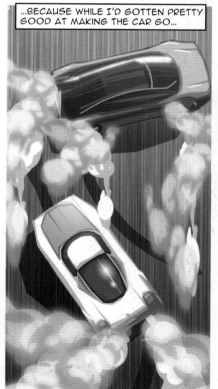

...BECAUSE WHILE I'D GOTTEN PRETTY GOOD AT MAKING THE CAR GO...

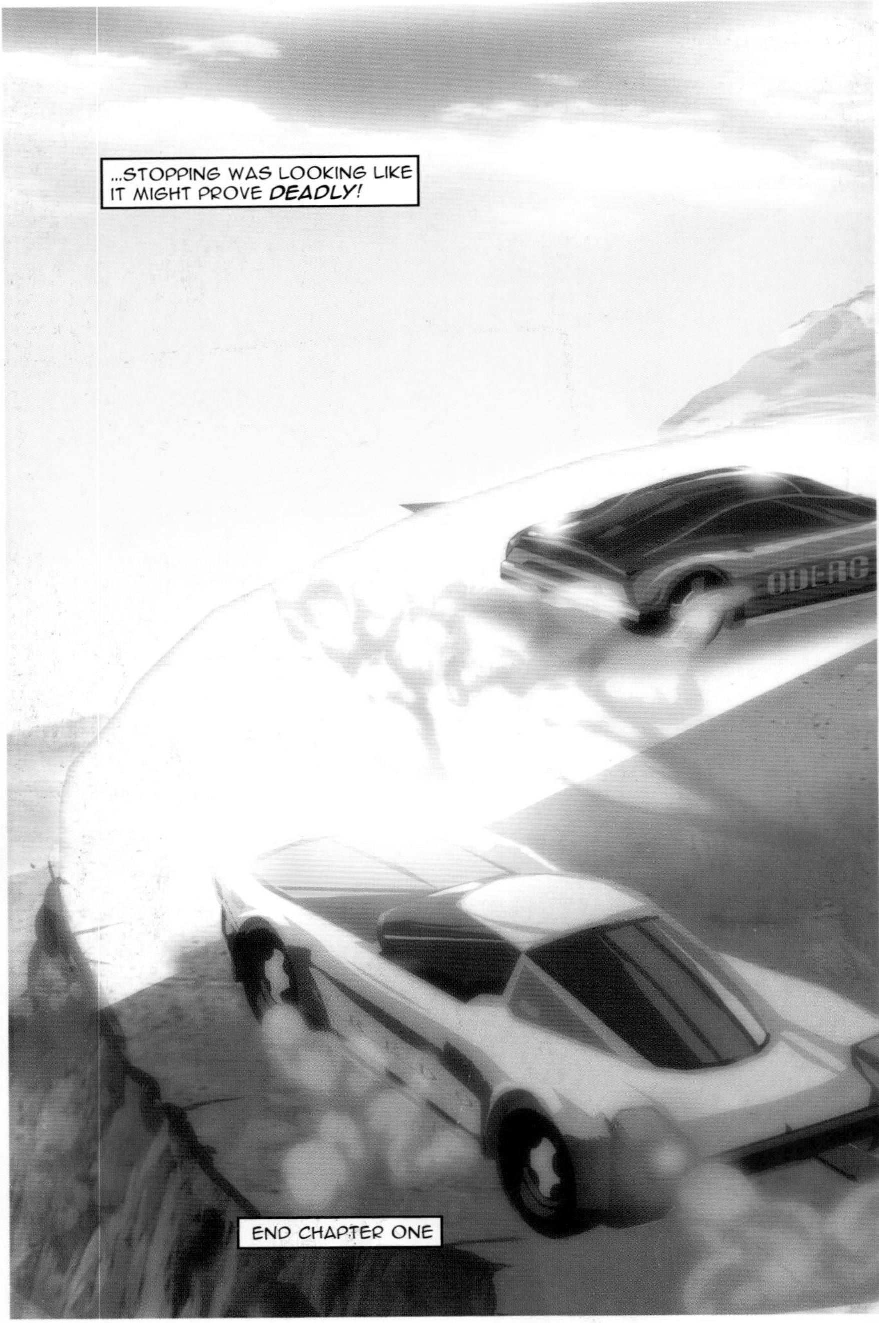
...STOPPING WAS LOOKING LIKE IT MIGHT PROVE *DEADLY*!
END CHAPTER ONE

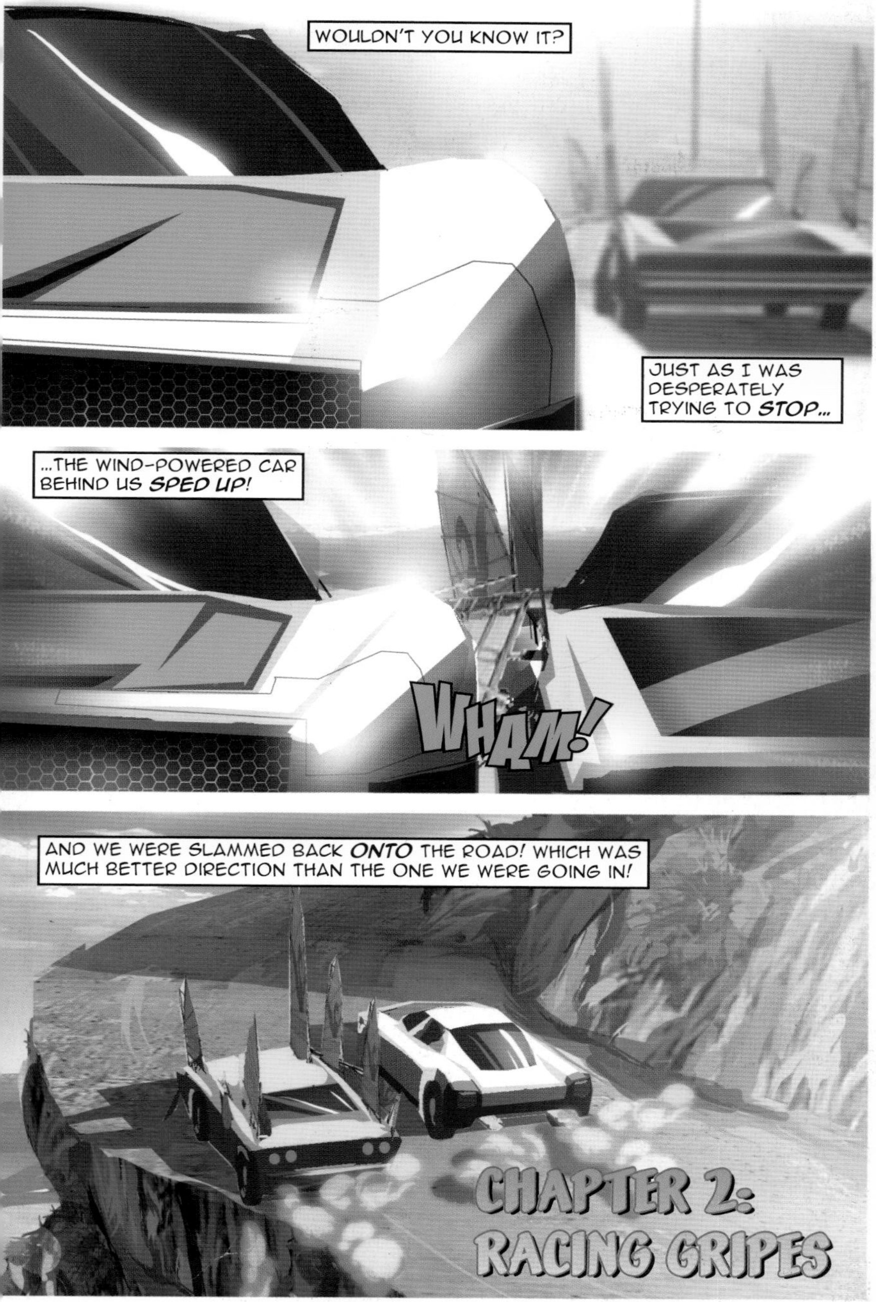
WOULDN'T YOU KNOW IT?
JUST AS I WAS DESPERATELY TRYING TO STOP...
...THE WIND-POWERED CAR BEHIND US SPED UP!
WHAM!
AND WE WERE SLAMMED BACK ONTO THE ROAD! WHICH WAS MUCH BETTER DIRECTION THAN THE ONE WE WERE GOING IN!
CHAPTER 2: RACING GRIPES

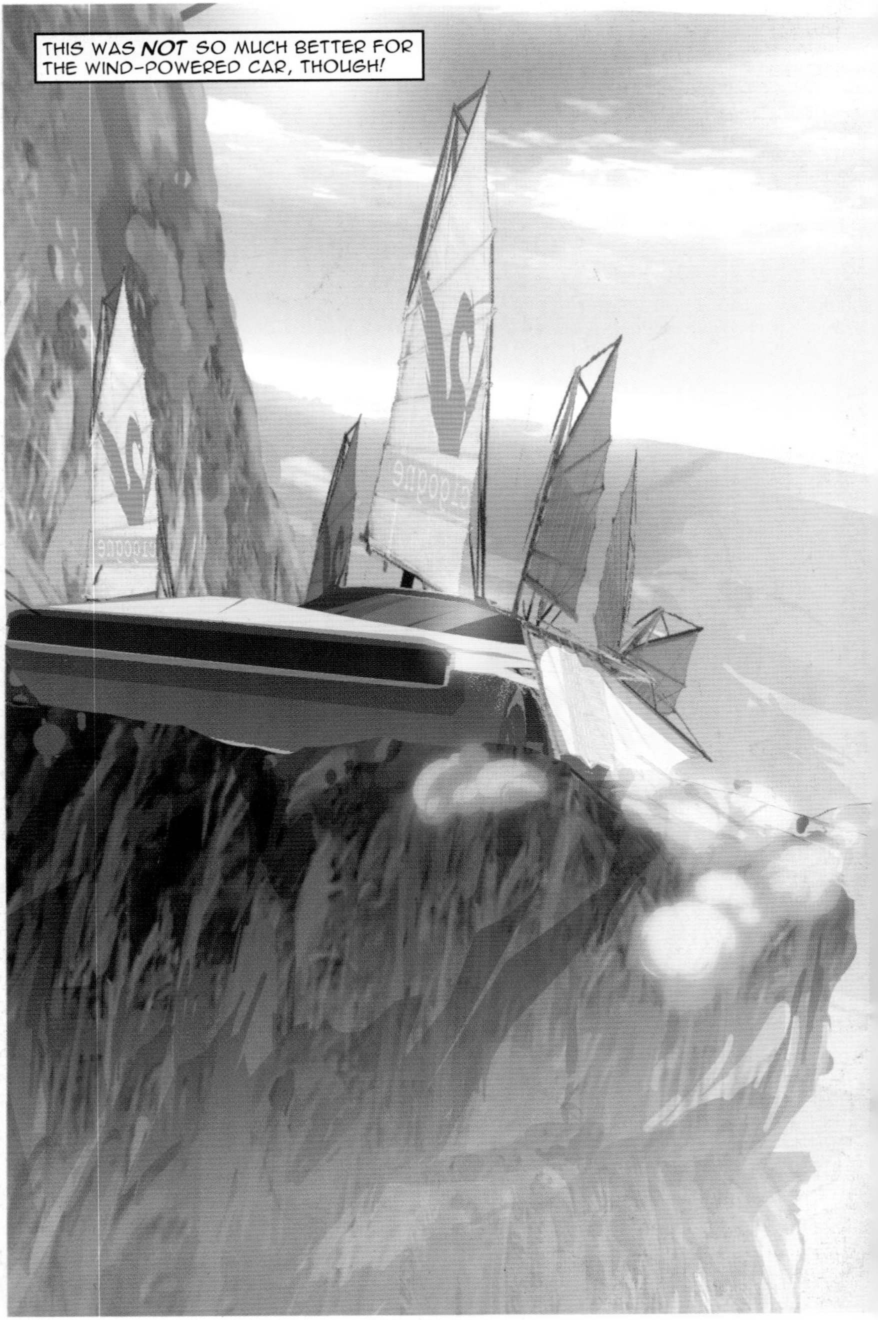
THIS WAS **NOT** SO MUCH BETTER FOR THE WIND-POWERED CAR, THOUGH!

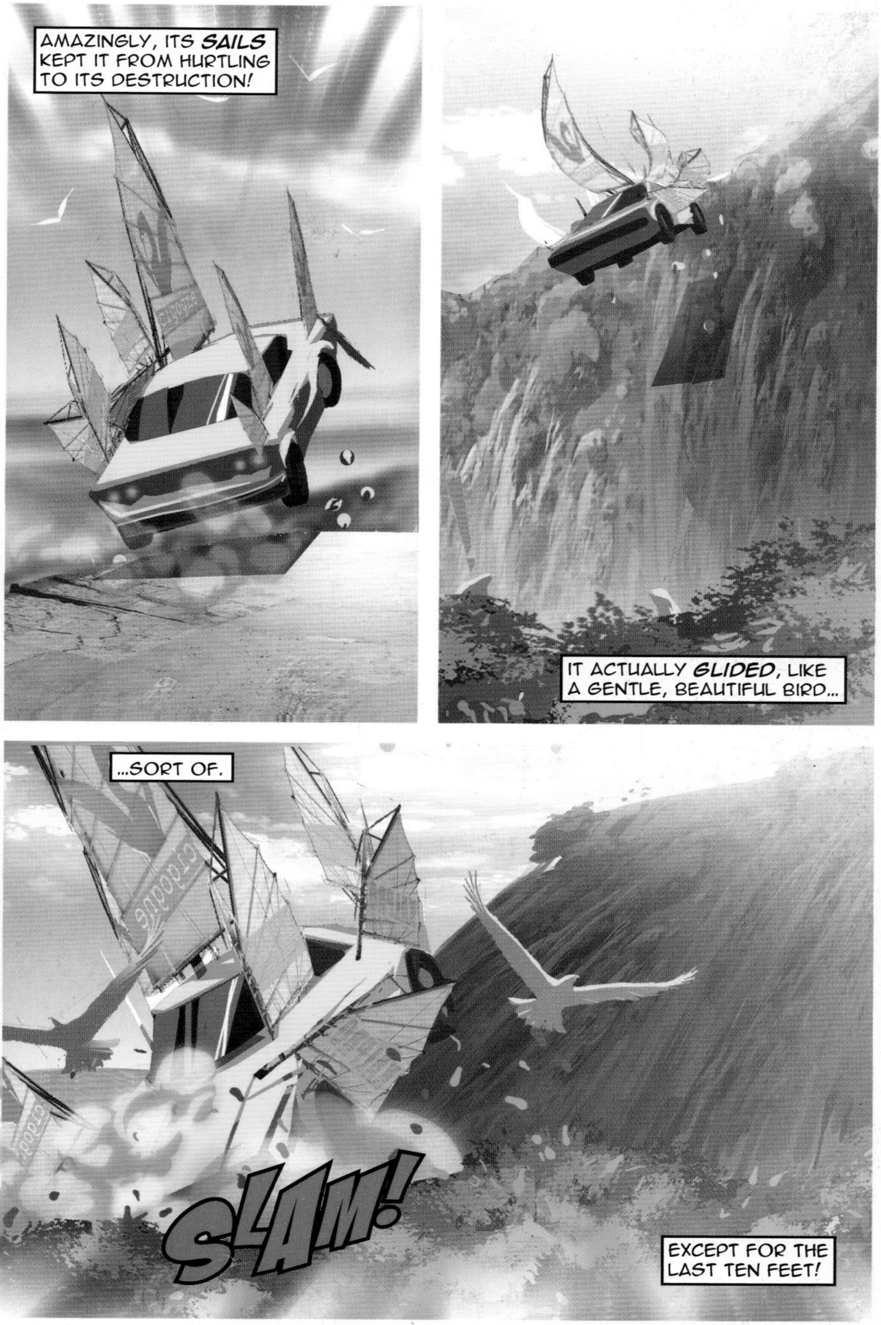
AMAZINGLY, ITS SAILS KEPT IT FROM HURTLING TO ITS DESTRUCTION!
IT ACTUALLY GLIDED, LIKE A GENTLE, BEAUTIFUL BIRD...
...SORT OF.
SLAM!
EXCEPT FOR THE LAST TEN FEET!

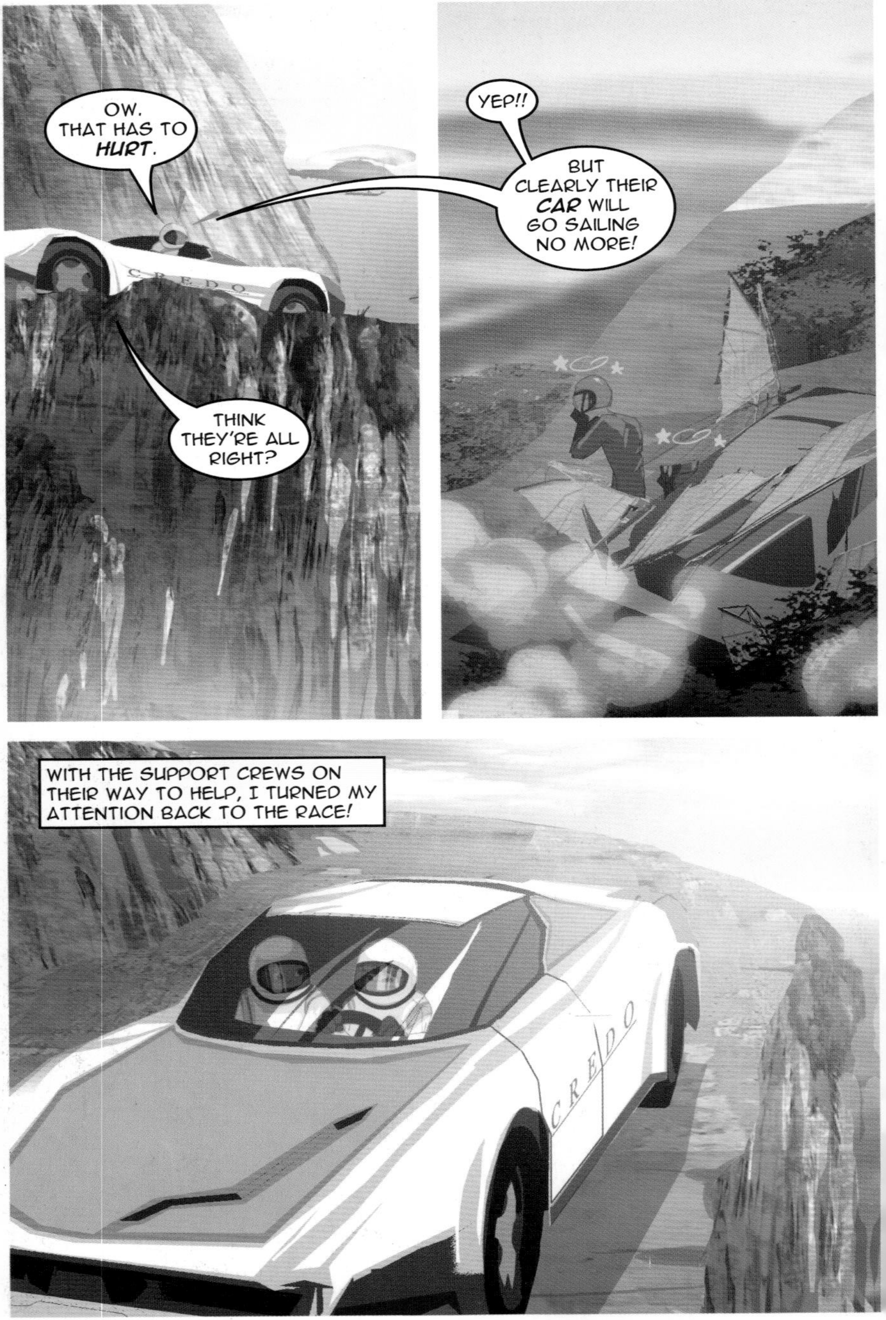
OW. THAT HAS TO HURT.
THINK THEY'RE ALL RIGHT?
YEP!!
BUT CLEARLY THEIR CAR WILL GO SAILING NO MORE!
CREDO
WITH THE SUPPORT CREWS ON THEIR WAY TO HELP, I TURNED MY ATTENTION BACK TO THE RACE!
CREDO

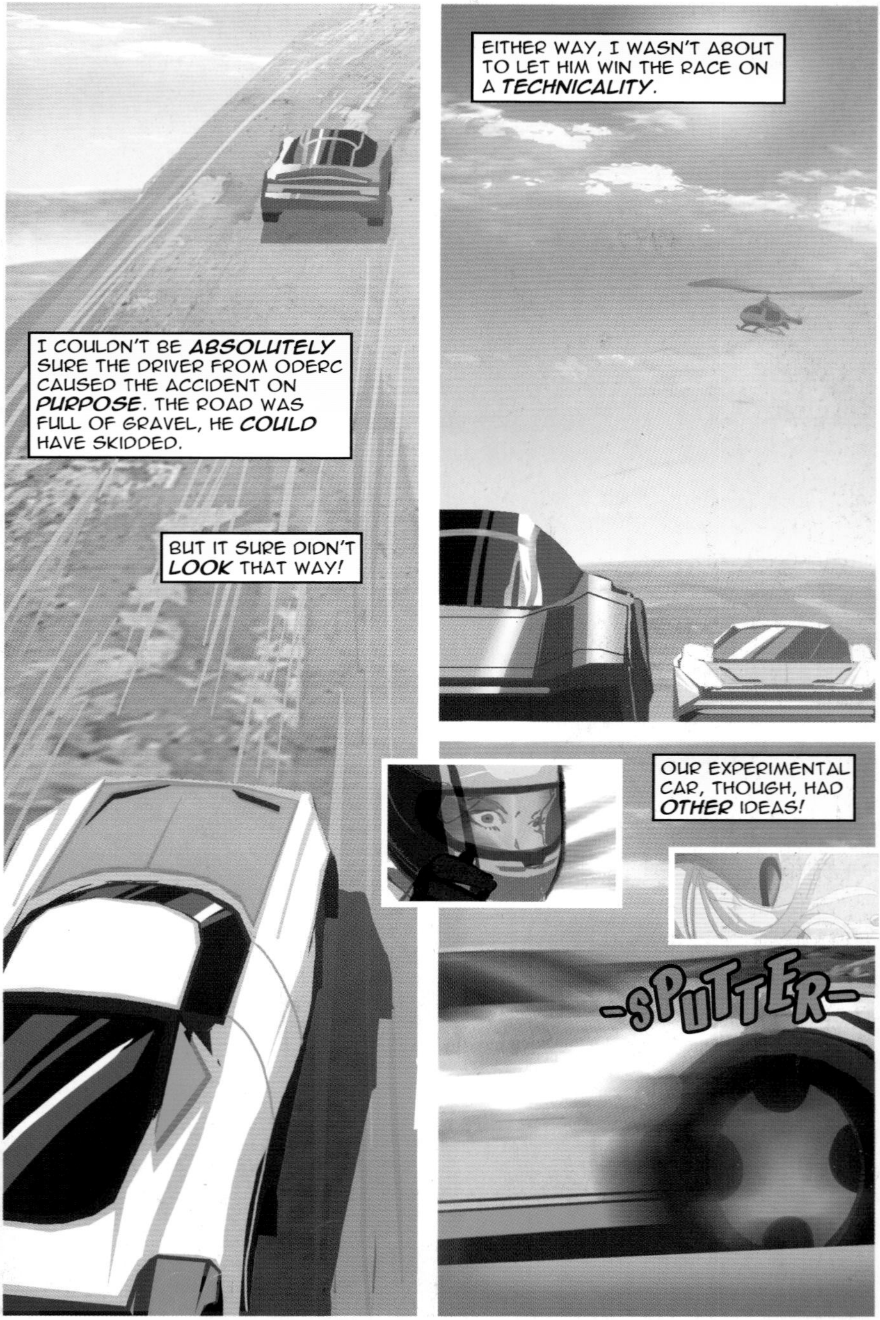
I COULDN'T BE ABSOLUTELY SURE THE DRIVER FROM ODERC CAUSED THE ACCIDENT ON PURPOSE. THE ROAD WAS FULL OF GRAVEL, HE COULD HAVE SKIDDED.
BUT IT SURE DIDN'T LOOK THAT WAY!
EITHER WAY, I WASN'T ABOUT TO LET HIM WIN THE RACE ON A TECHNICALITY.
OUR EXPERIMENTAL CAR, THOUGH, HAD OTHER IDEAS!
-SPUTTER-

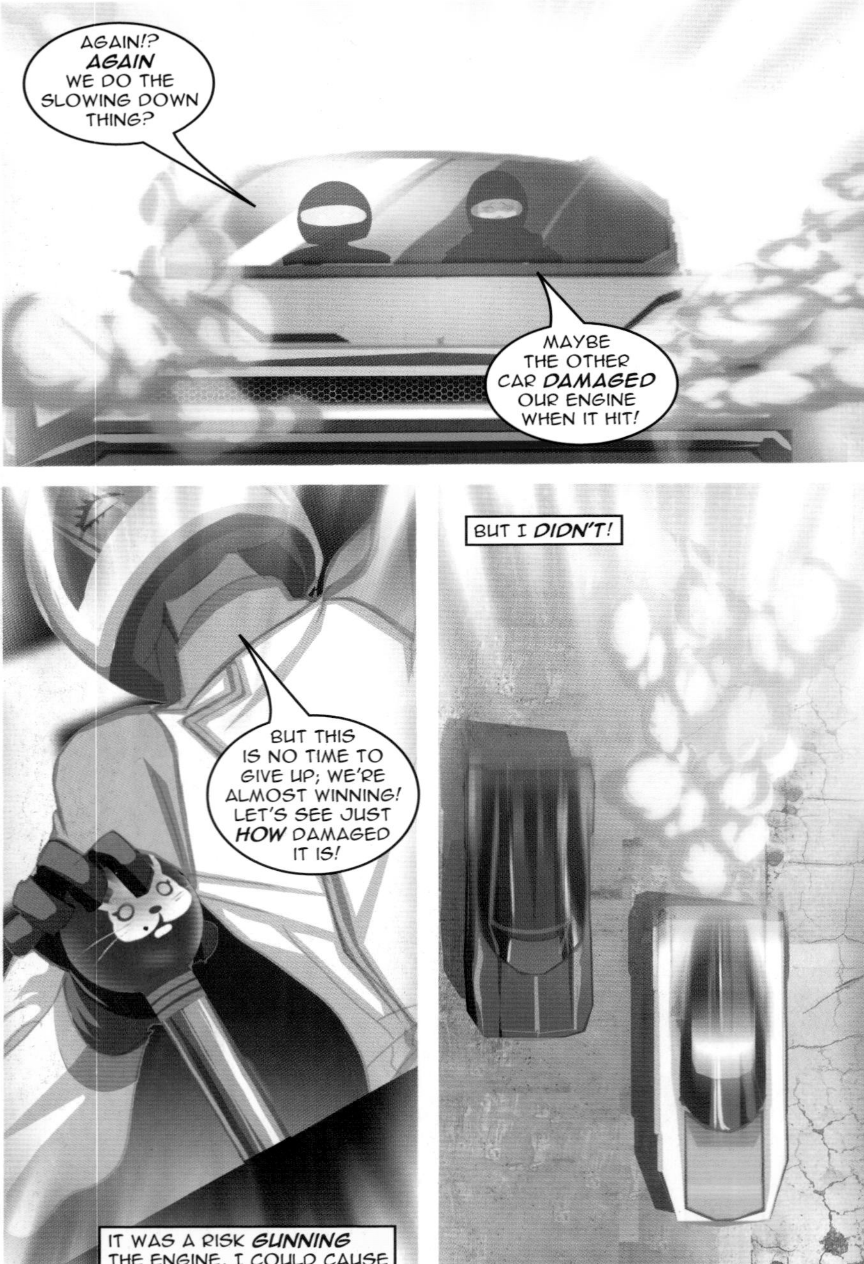
AGAIN!? AGAIN WE DO THE SLOWING DOWN THING?
MAYBE THE OTHER CAR DAMAGED OUR ENGINE WHEN IT HIT!
BUT THIS IS NO TIME TO GIVE UP; WE'RE ALMOST WINNING! LET'S SEE JUST HOW DAMAGED IT IS!
IT WAS A RISK GUNNING THE ENGINE, I COULD CAUSE A BIGGER PROBLEM!
BUT I DIDN'T!

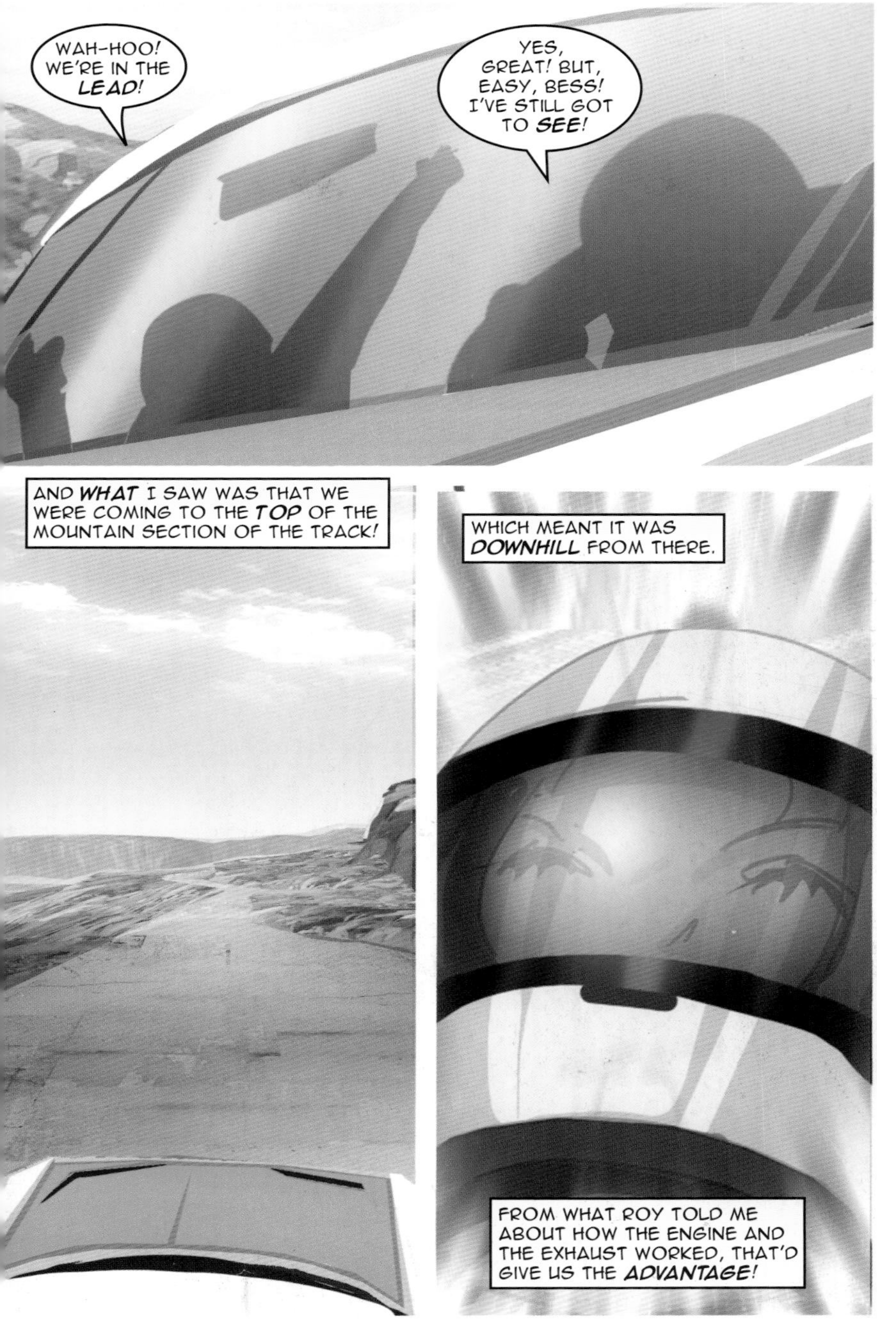
WAH-HOO! WE'RE IN THE LEAD!
YES, GREAT! BUT, EASY, BESS! I'VE STILL GOT TO SEE!
AND WHAT I SAW WAS THAT WE WERE COMING TO THE TOP OF THE MOUNTAIN SECTION OF THE TRACK!
WHICH MEANT IT WAS DOWNHILL FROM THERE.
FROM WHAT ROY TOLD ME ABOUT HOW THE ENGINE AND THE EXHAUST WORKED, THAT'D GIVE US THE ADVANTAGE!

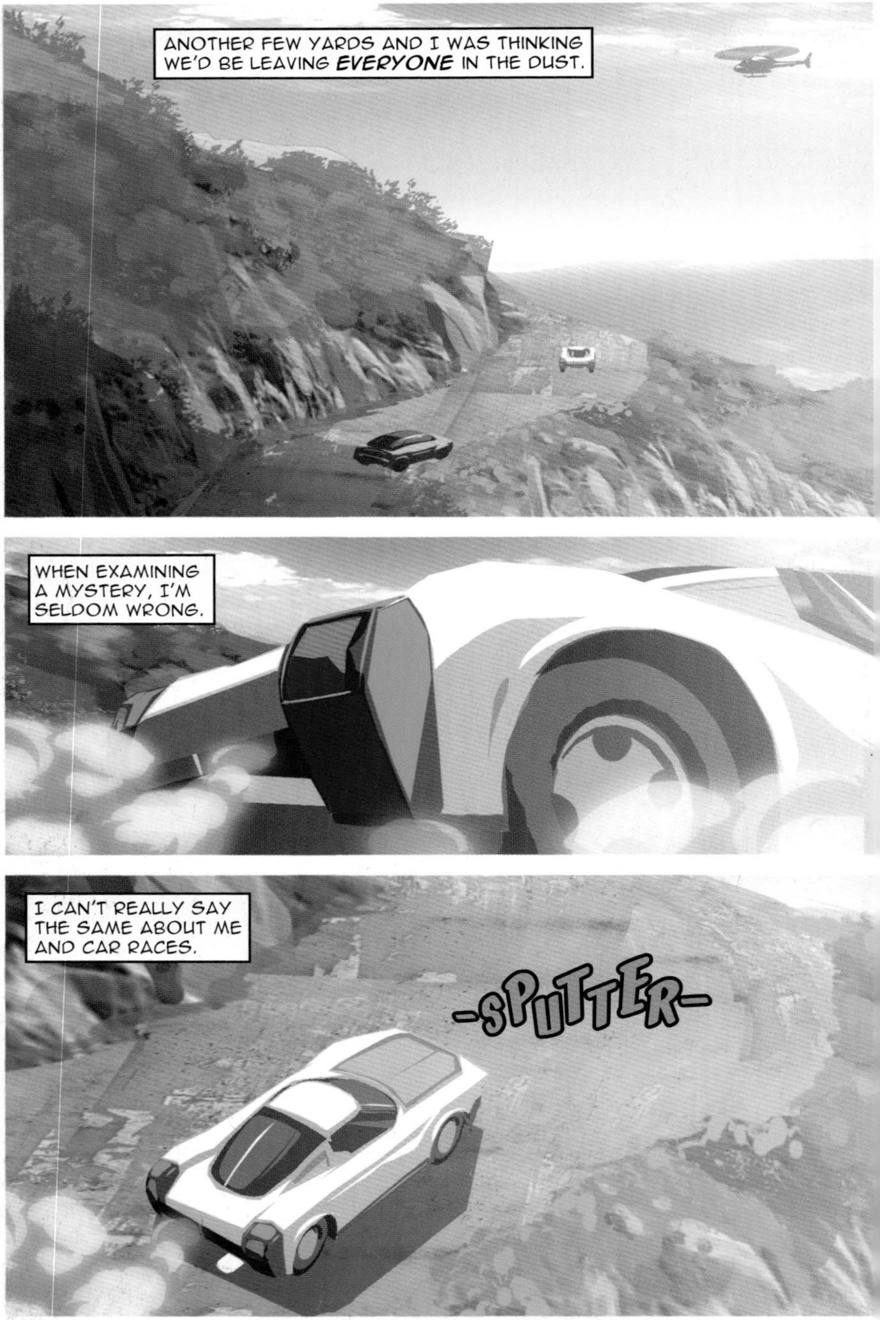
ANOTHER FEW YARDS AND I WAS THINKING WE'D BE LEAVING EVERYONE IN THE DUST.
WHEN EXAMINING A MYSTERY, I'M SELDOM WRONG.
I CAN'T REALLY SAY THE SAME ABOUT ME AND CAR RACES.
-SPUTTER-

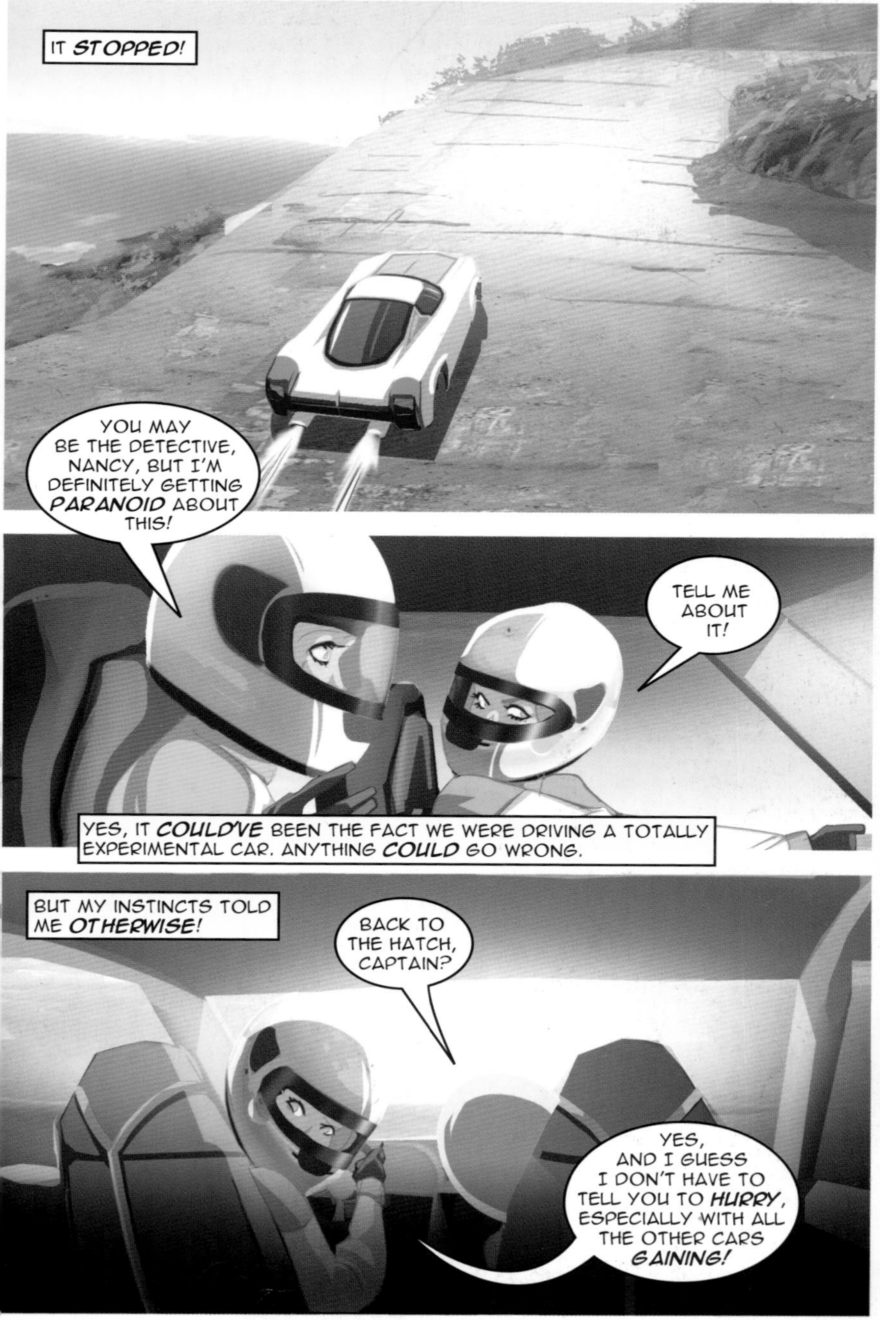
IT STOPPED!
YOU MAY BE THE DETECTIVE, NANCY, BUT I'M DEFINITELY GETTING PARANOID ABOUT THIS!
TELL ME ABOUT IT!
YES, IT COULD'VE BEEN THE FACT WE WERE DRIVING A TOTALLY EXPERIMENTAL CAR. ANYTHING COULD GO WRONG.
BUT MY INSTINCTS TOLD ME OTHERWISE!
BACK TO THE HATCH, CAPTAIN?
YES, AND I GUESS I DON'T HAVE TO TELL YOU TO HURRY, ESPECIALLY WITH ALL THE OTHER CARS GAINING!

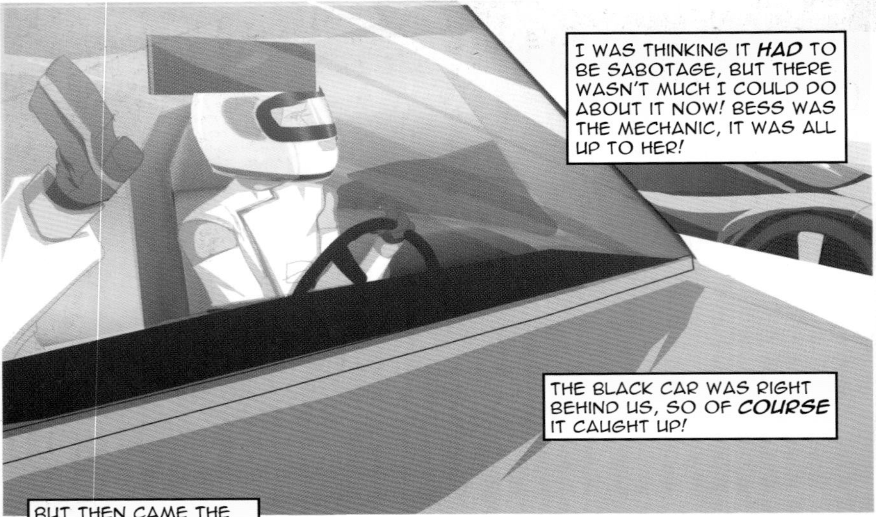
I WAS THINKING IT **HAD** TO BE SABOTAGE, BUT THERE WASN'T MUCH I COULD DO ABOUT IT NOW! BESS WAS THE MECHANIC, IT WAS ALL UP TO HER!
THE BLACK CAR WAS RIGHT BEHIND US, SO OF **COURSE** IT CAUGHT UP!

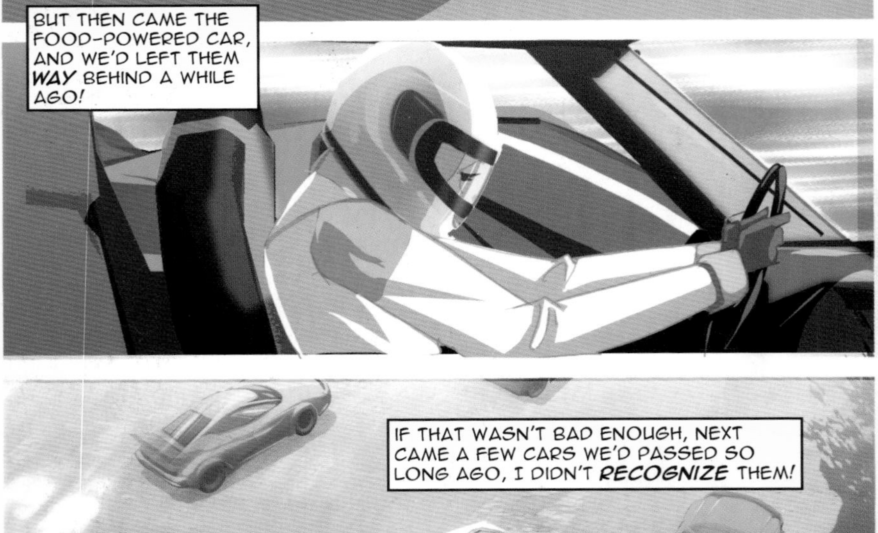
BUT THEN CAME THE FOOD-POWERED CAR, AND WE'D LEFT THEM **WAY** BEHIND A WHILE AGO!

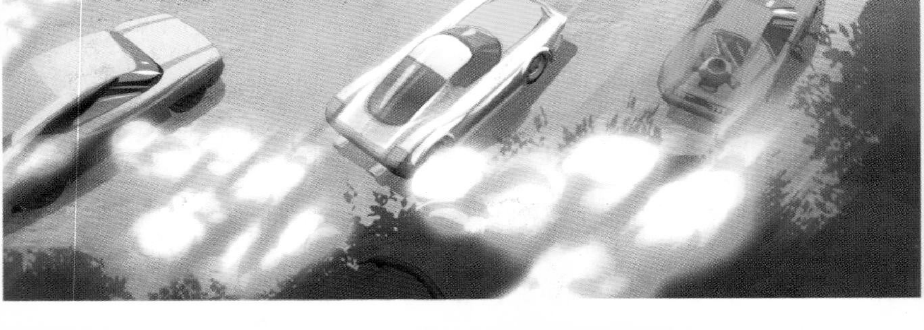
IF THAT WASN'T BAD ENOUGH, NEXT CAME A FEW CARS WE'D PASSED SO LONG AGO, I DIDN'T **RECOGNIZE** THEM!

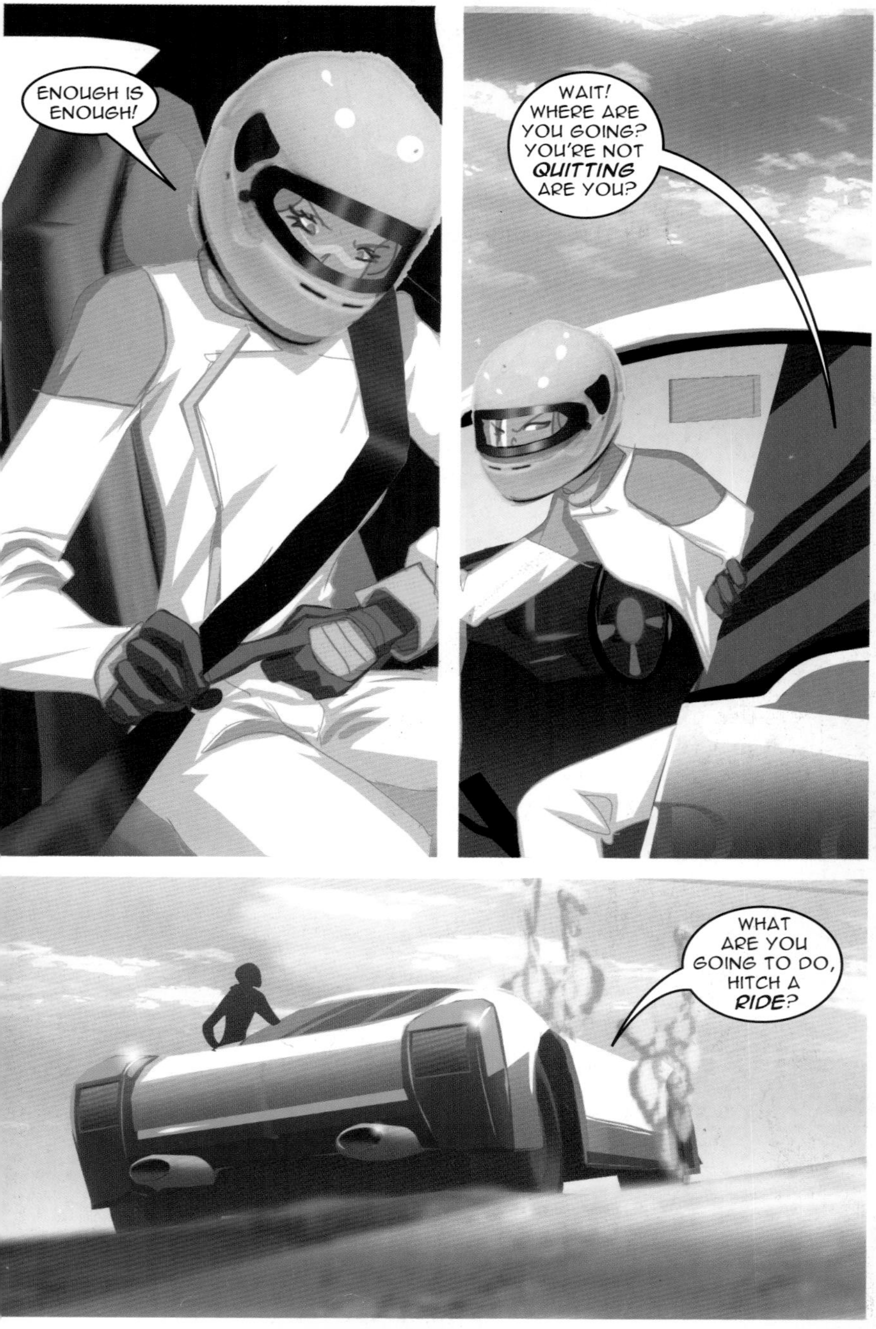
ENOUGH IS ENOUGH!
WAIT! WHERE ARE YOU GOING? YOU'RE NOT *QUITTING* ARE YOU?
WHAT ARE YOU GOING TO DO, HITCH A *RIDE*?

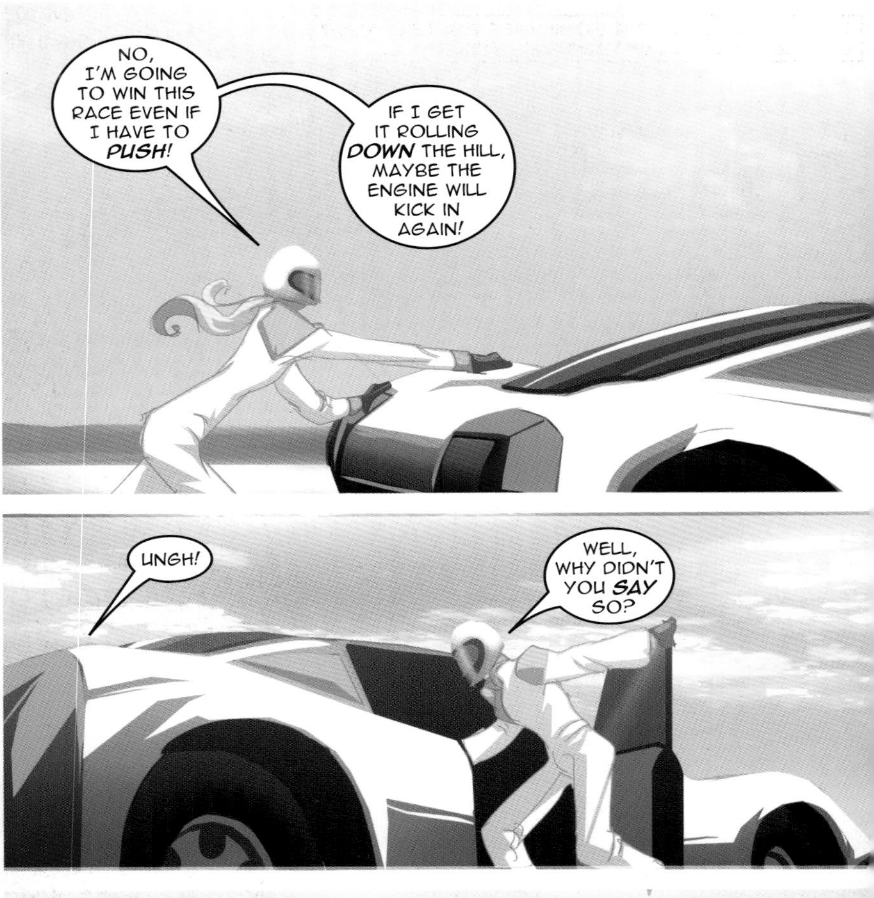
NO, I'M GOING TO WIN THIS RACE EVEN IF I HAVE TO PUSH!
IF I GET IT ROLLING DOWN THE HILL, MAYBE THE ENGINE WILL KICK IN AGAIN!
UNGH!
WELL, WHY DIDN'T YOU SAY SO?
URGH!
UNGH!

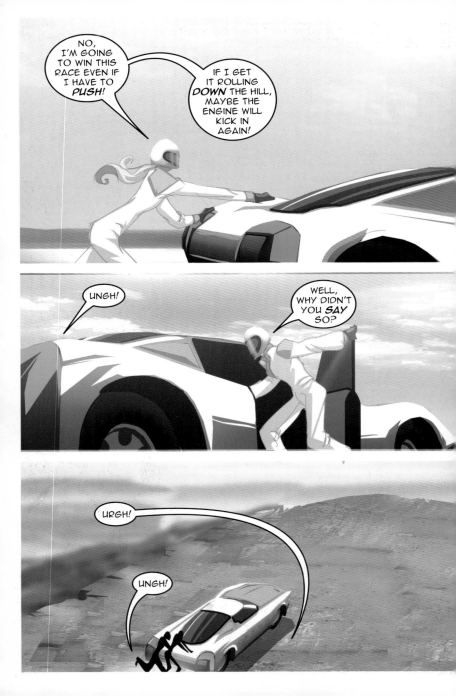

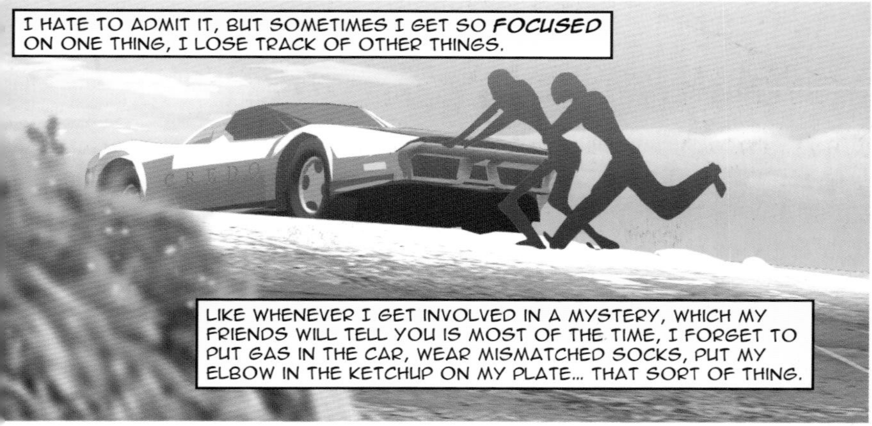
I HATE TO ADMIT IT, BUT SOMETIMES I GET SO *FOCUSED* ON ONE THING, I LOSE TRACK OF OTHER THINGS.
LIKE WHENEVER I GET INVOLVED IN A MYSTERY, WHICH MY FRIENDS WILL TELL YOU IS MOST OF THE TIME, I FORGET TO PUT GAS IN THE CAR, WEAR MISMATCHED SOCKS, PUT MY ELBOW IN THE KETCHUP ON MY PLATE... THAT SORT OF THING.

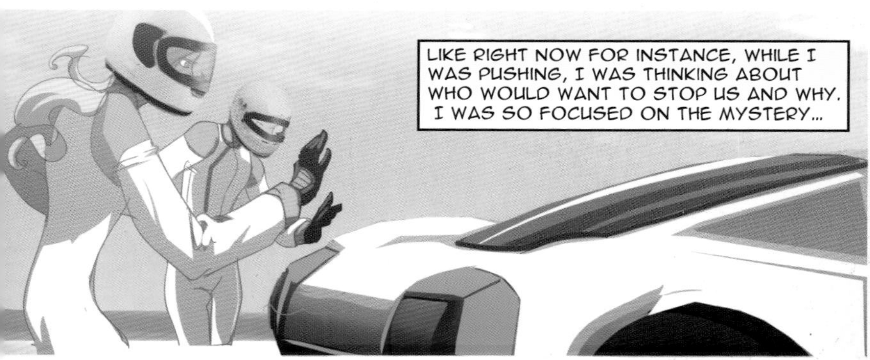
LIKE RIGHT NOW FOR INSTANCE, WHILE I WAS PUSHING, I WAS THINKING ABOUT WHO WOULD WANT TO STOP US AND WHY. I WAS SO FOCUSED ON THE MYSTERY...

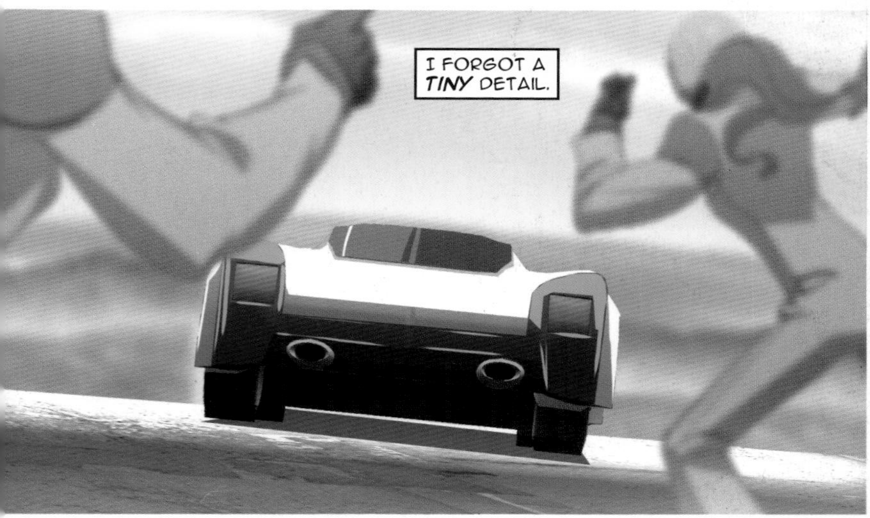
I FORGOT A *TINY* DETAIL.

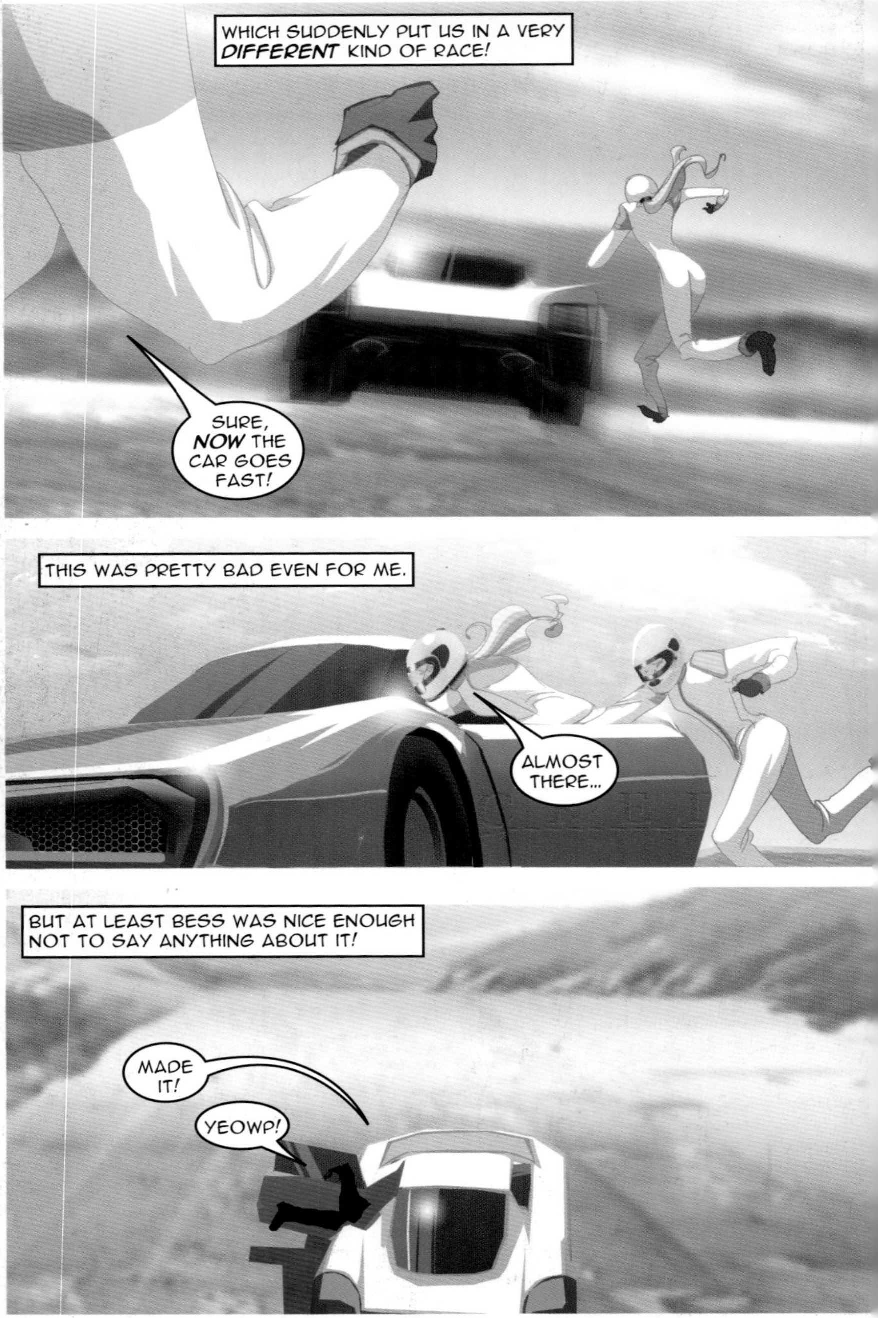
WHICH SUDDENLY PUT US IN A VERY DIFFERENT KIND OF RACE!
SURE, NOW THE CAR GOES FAST!
THIS WAS PRETTY BAD EVEN FOR ME.
ALMOST THERE...
BUT AT LEAST BESS WAS NICE ENOUGH NOT TO SAY ANYTHING ABOUT IT!
MADE IT!
YEOWP!

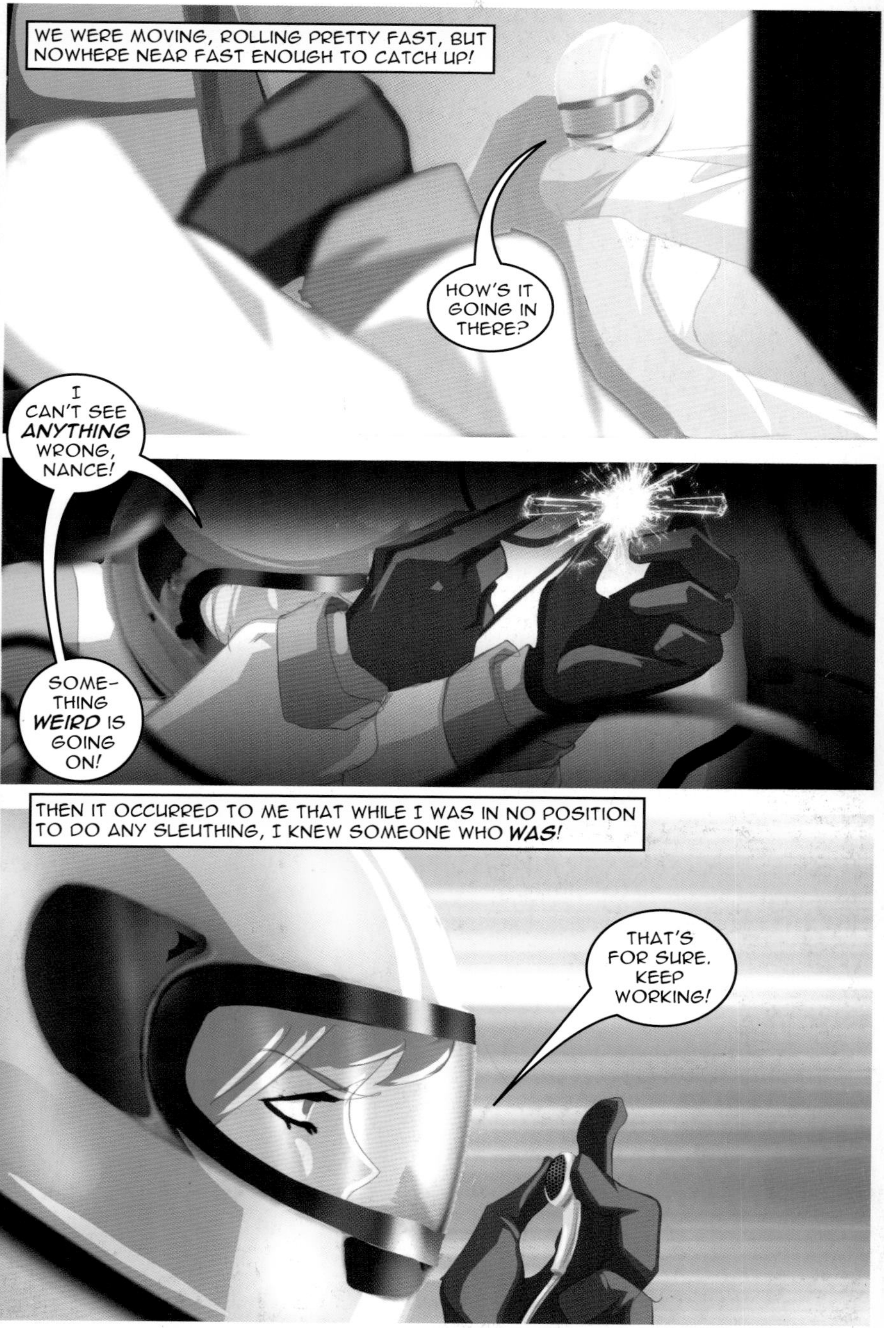
WE WERE MOVING, ROLLING PRETTY FAST, BUT NOWHERE NEAR FAST ENOUGH TO CATCH UP!
HOW'S IT GOING IN THERE?
I CAN'T SEE ANYTHING WRONG, NANCE!
SOME-THING WEIRD IS GOING ON!
THEN IT OCCURRED TO ME THAT WHILE I WAS IN NO POSITION TO DO ANY SLEUTHING, I KNEW SOMEONE WHO WAS!
THAT'S FOR SURE. KEEP WORKING!

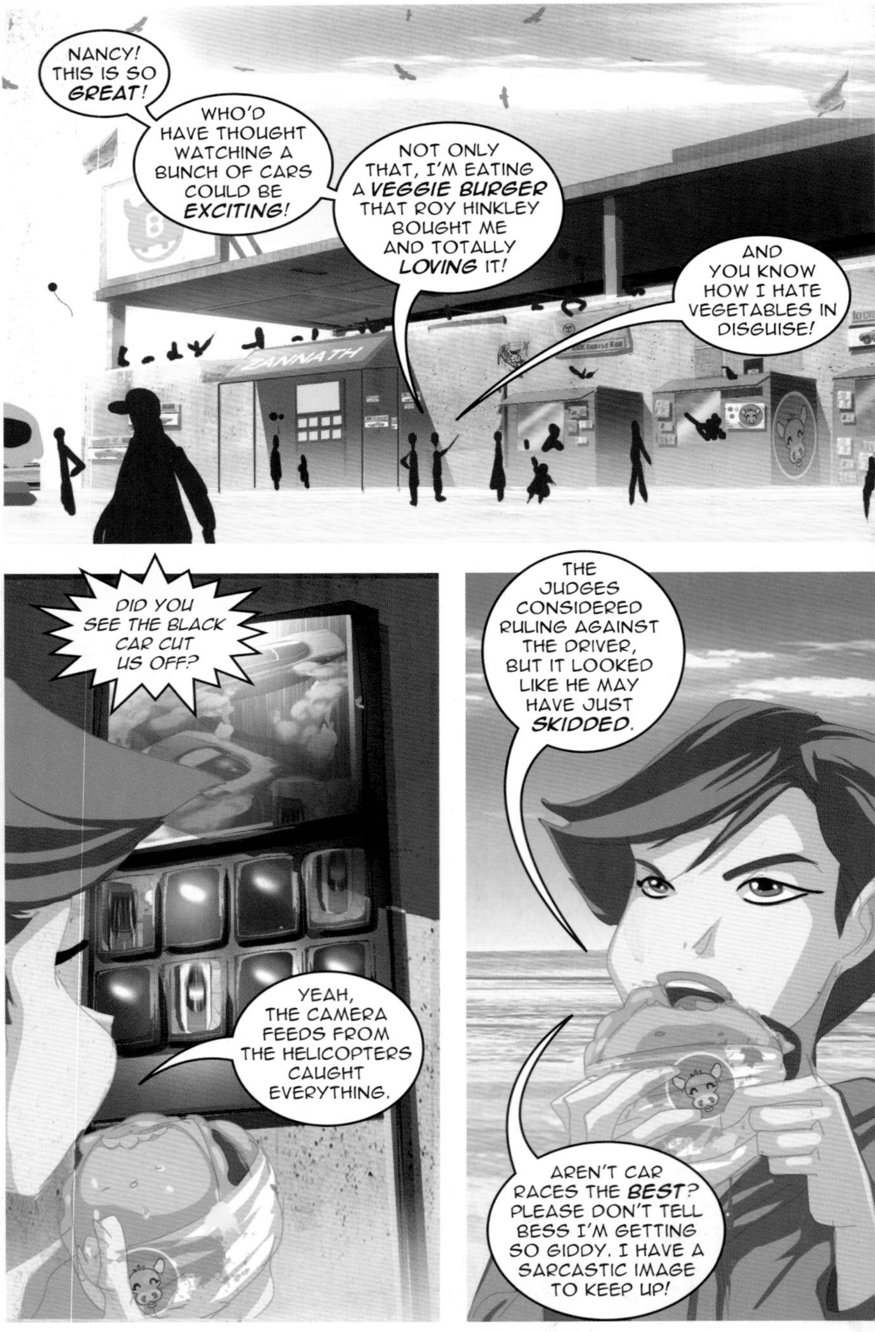
NANCY! THIS IS SO *GREAT*!
WHO'D HAVE THOUGHT WATCHING A BUNCH OF CARS COULD BE *EXCITING*!
NOT ONLY THAT, I'M EATING A *VEGGIE BURGER* THAT ROY HINKLEY BOUGHT ME AND TOTALLY *LOVING* IT!
AND YOU KNOW HOW I HATE VEGETABLES IN DISGUISE!
ZANNATH
DID YOU SEE THE BLACK CAR CUT US OFF?
YEAH, THE CAMERA FEEDS FROM THE HELICOPTERS CAUGHT EVERYTHING.
THE JUDGES CONSIDERED RULING AGAINST THE DRIVER, BUT IT LOOKED LIKE HE MAY HAVE JUST *SKIDDED*.
AREN'T CAR RACES THE *BEST*? PLEASE DON'T TELL BESS I'M GETTING SO GIDDY. I HAVE A SARCASTIC IMAGE TO KEEP UP!

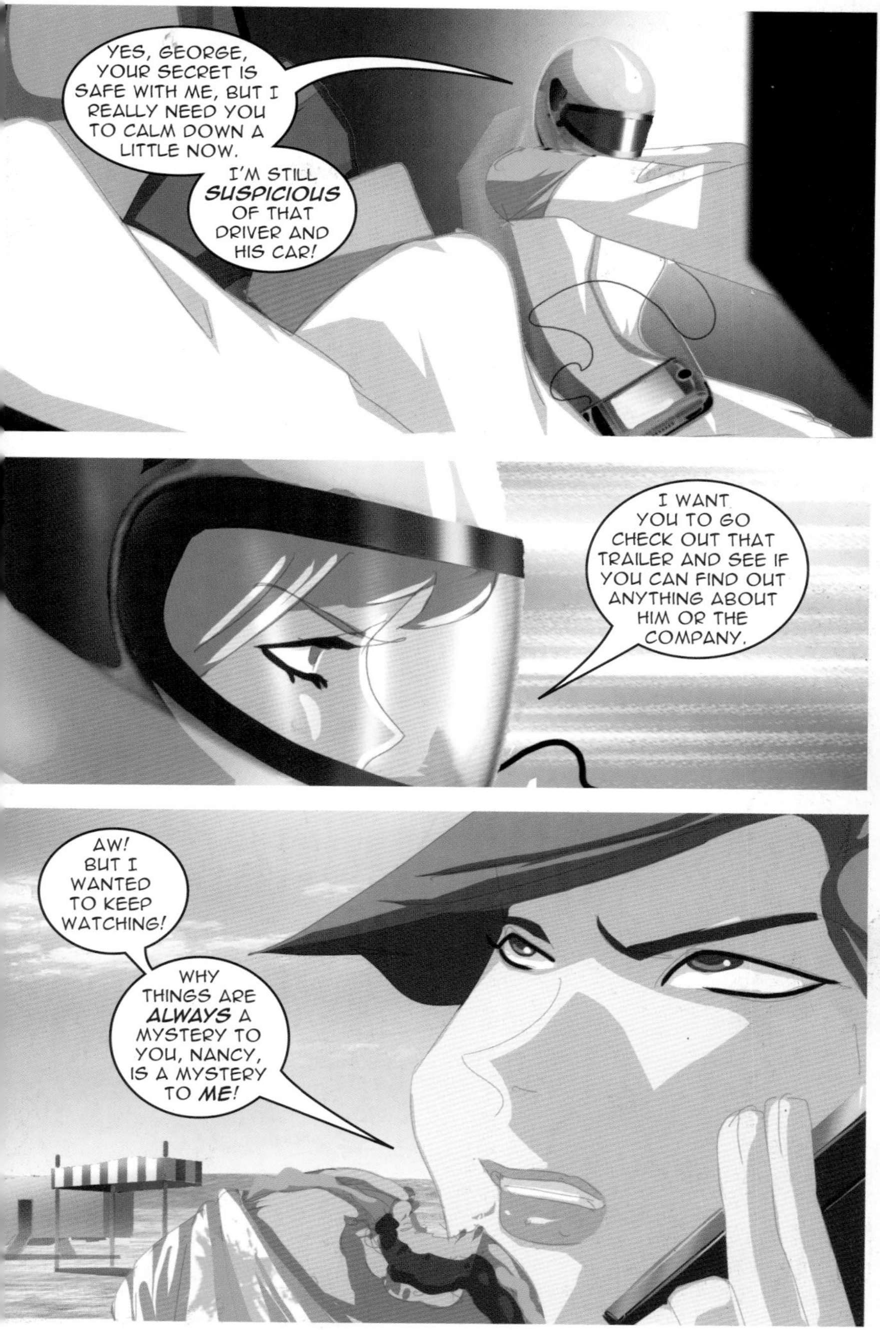
YES, GEORGE, YOUR SECRET IS SAFE WITH ME, BUT I REALLY NEED YOU TO CALM DOWN A LITTLE NOW.
I'M STILL **SUSPICIOUS** OF THAT DRIVER AND HIS CAR!
I WANT YOU TO GO CHECK OUT THAT TRAILER AND SEE IF YOU CAN FIND OUT ANYTHING ABOUT HIM OR THE COMPANY.
AW! BUT I WANTED TO KEEP WATCHING!
WHY THINGS ARE **ALWAYS** A MYSTERY TO YOU, NANCY, IS A MYSTERY TO **ME**!

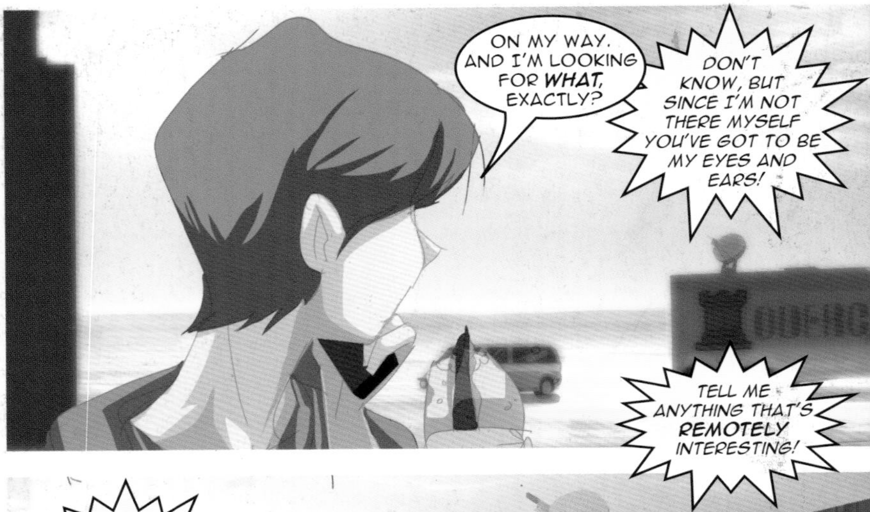
ON MY WAY. AND I'M LOOKING FOR **WHAT,** EXACTLY?
DON'T KNOW, BUT SINCE I'M NOT THERE MYSELF YOU'VE GOT TO BE MY EYES AND EARS!
TELL ME ANYTHING THAT'S **REMOTELY** INTERESTING!

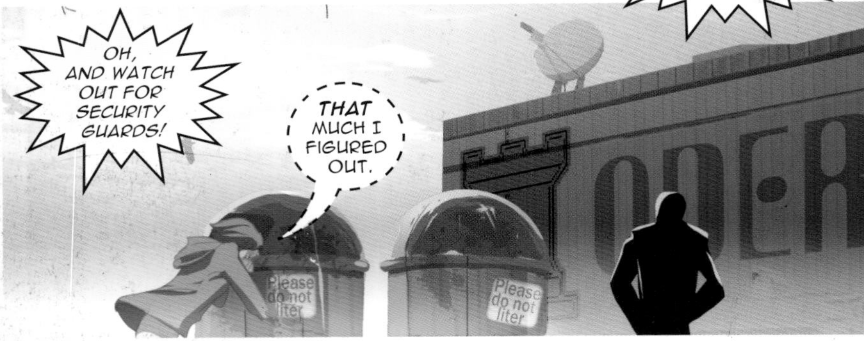
OH, AND WATCH OUT FOR SECURITY GUARDS!
THAT MUCH I FIGURED OUT.
Please do not liter
Please do not liter

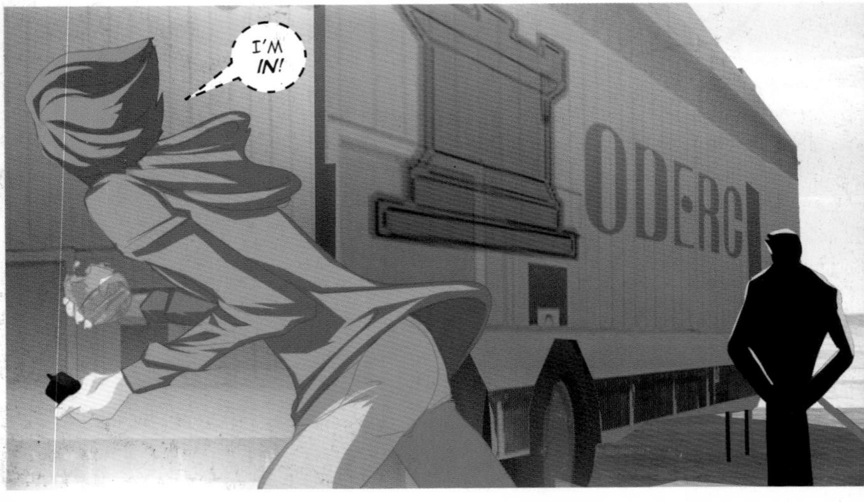
I'M **IN**!
ODERC

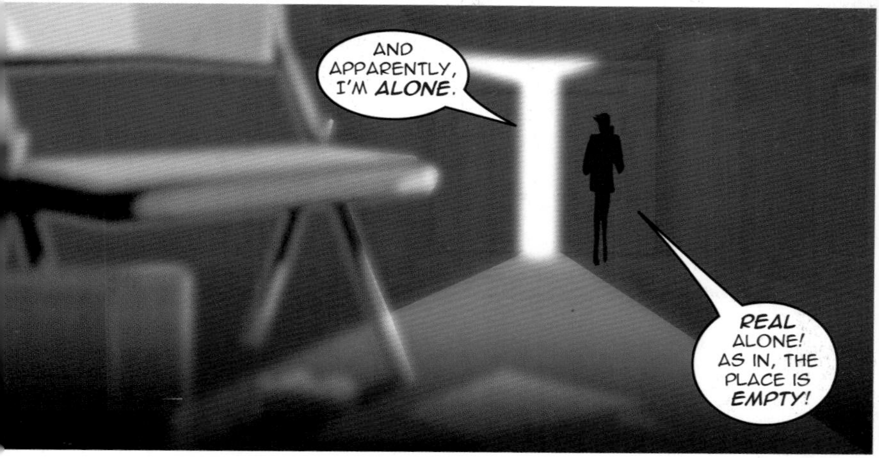
AND APPARENTLY, I'M ALONE.
REAL ALONE! AS IN, THE PLACE IS EMPTY!

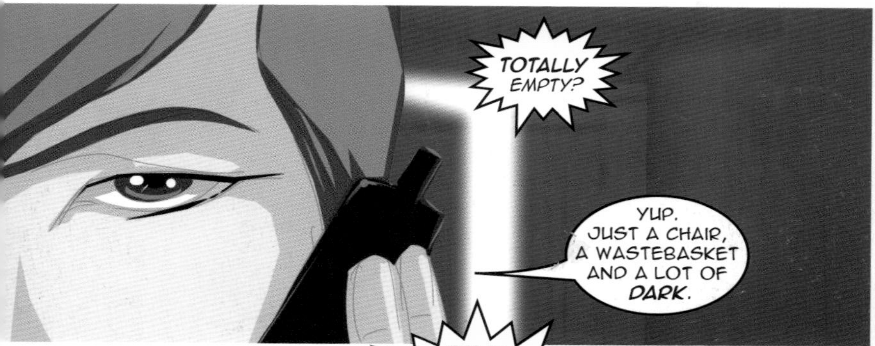
TOTALLY EMPTY?
YUP. JUST A CHAIR, A WASTEBASKET AND A LOT OF DARK.

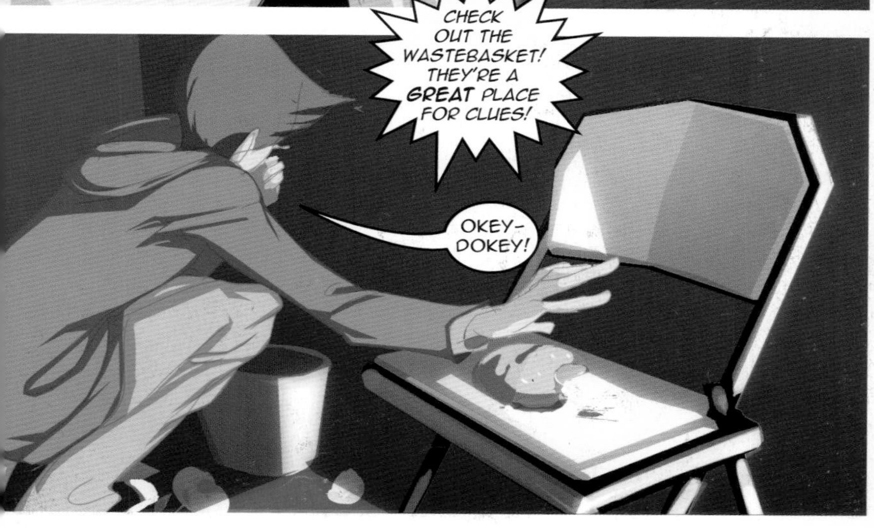
CHECK OUT THE WASTEBASKET! THEY'RE A GREAT PLACE FOR CLUES!
OKEY-DOKEY!

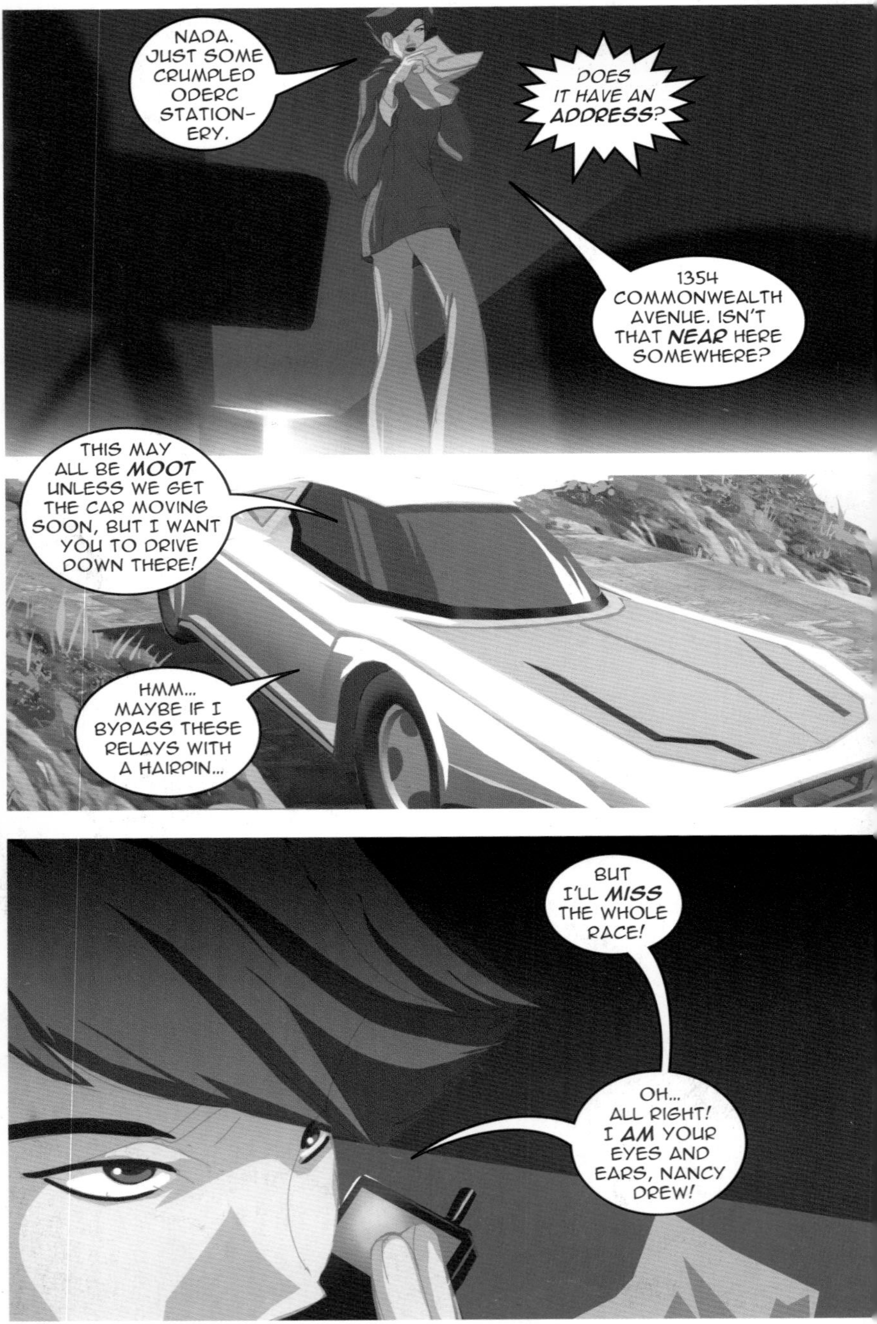
NADA. JUST SOME CRUMPLED ODERC STATION-ERY.
DOES IT HAVE AN ADDRESS?
1354 COMMONWEALTH AVENUE. ISN'T THAT NEAR HERE SOMEWHERE?
THIS MAY ALL BE MOOT UNLESS WE GET THE CAR MOVING SOON, BUT I WANT YOU TO DRIVE DOWN THERE!
HMM... MAYBE IF I BYPASS THESE RELAYS WITH A HAIRPIN...
BUT I'LL MISS THE WHOLE RACE!
OH... ALL RIGHT! I AM YOUR EYES AND EARS, NANCY DREW!

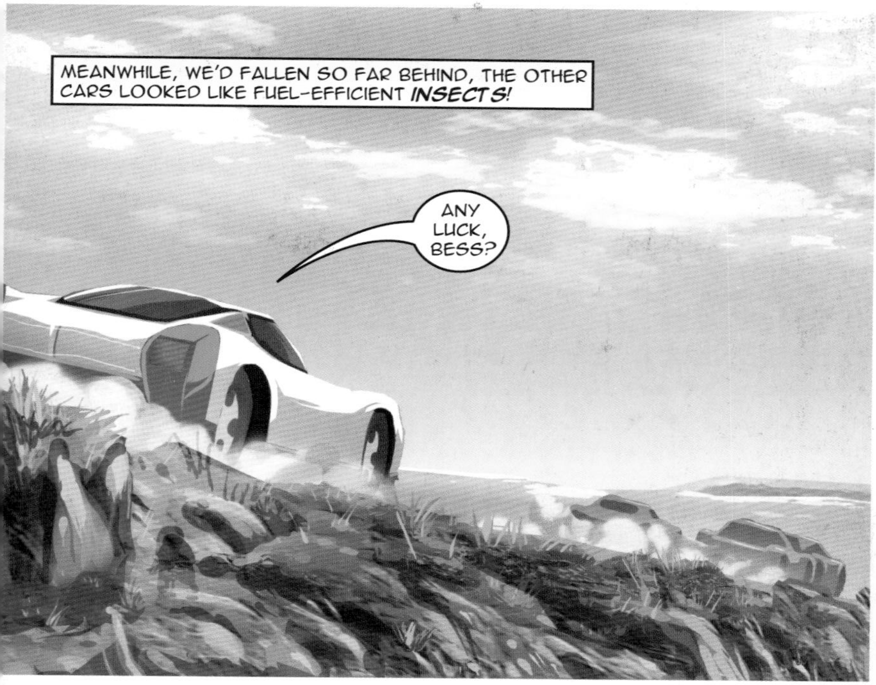
MEANWHILE, WE'D FALLEN SO FAR BEHIND, THE OTHER CARS LOOKED LIKE FUEL-EFFICIENT *INSECTS!*
ANY LUCK, BESS?

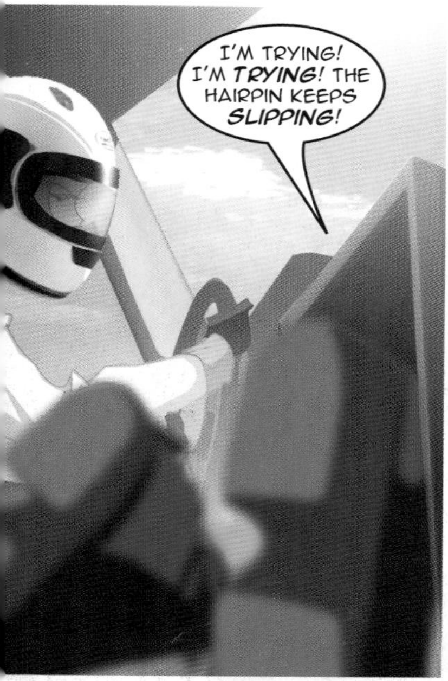
I'M TRYING! I'M *TRYING!* THE HAIRPIN KEEPS *SLIPPING!*

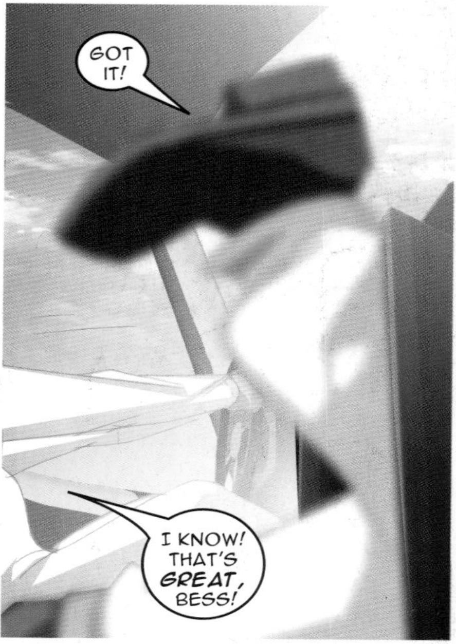
GOT IT!
I KNOW! THAT'S *GREAT*, BESS!

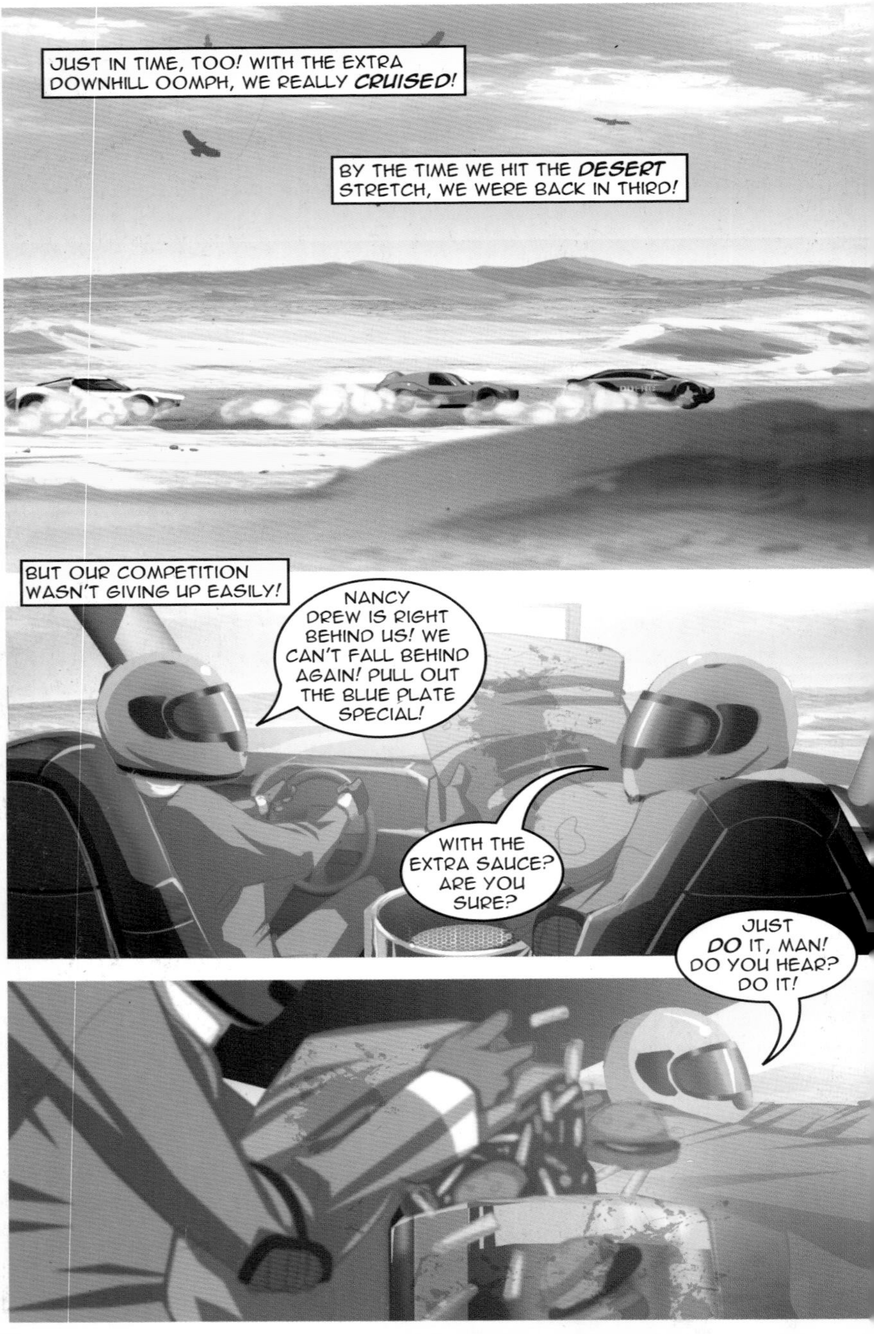
JUST IN TIME, TOO! WITH THE EXTRA DOWNHILL OOMPH, WE REALLY *CRUISED*!
BY THE TIME WE HIT THE *DESERT* STRETCH, WE WERE BACK IN THIRD!
BUT OUR COMPETITION WASN'T GIVING UP EASILY!
NANCY DREW IS RIGHT BEHIND US! WE CAN'T FALL BEHIND AGAIN! PULL OUT THE BLUE PLATE SPECIAL!
WITH THE EXTRA SAUCE? ARE YOU SURE?
JUST *DO* IT, MAN! DO YOU HEAR? DO IT!

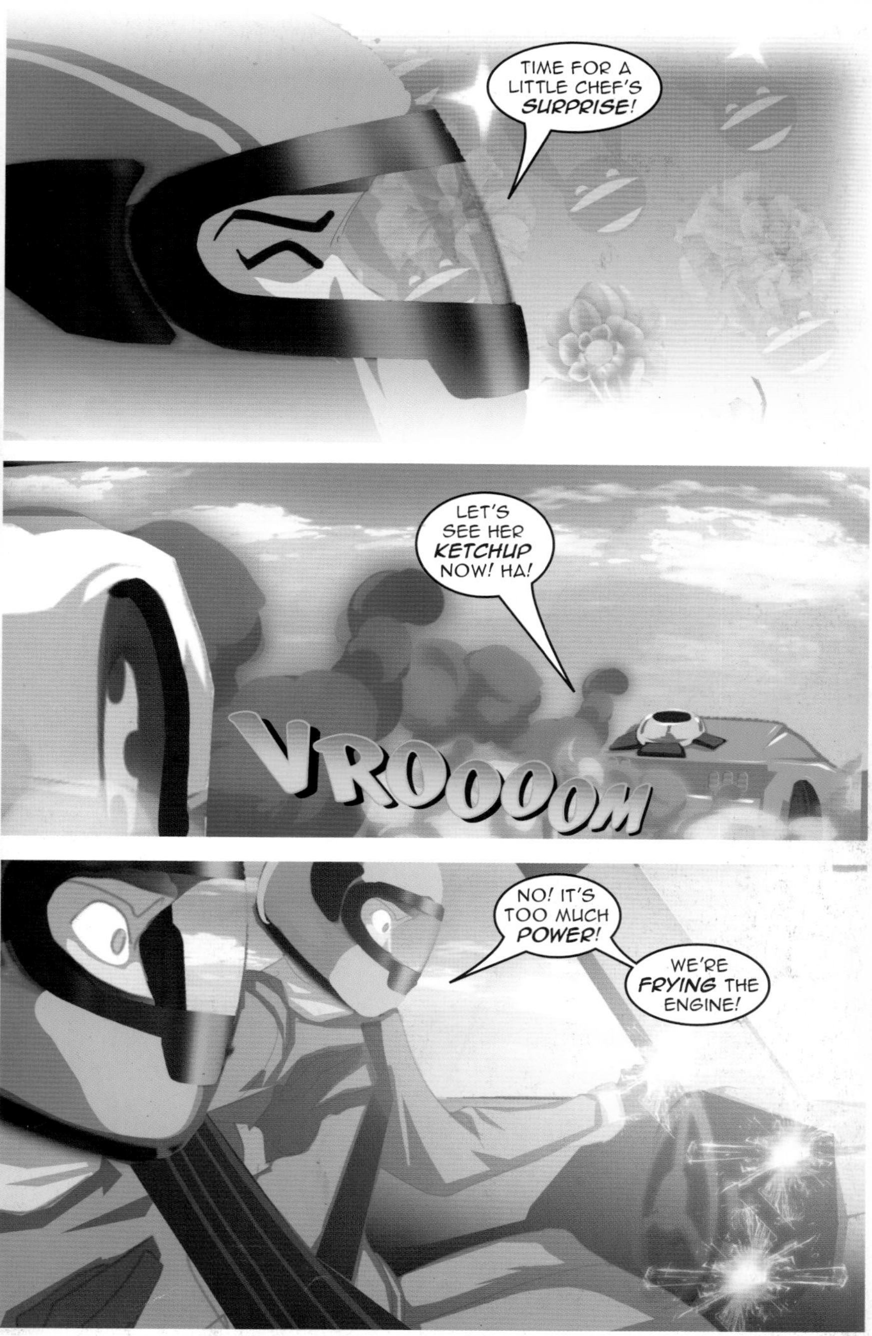
TIME FOR A LITTLE CHEF'S SURPRISE!
LET'S SEE HER KETCHUP NOW! HA!
VROOOOM
NO! IT'S TOO MUCH POWER!
WE'RE FRYING THE ENGINE!

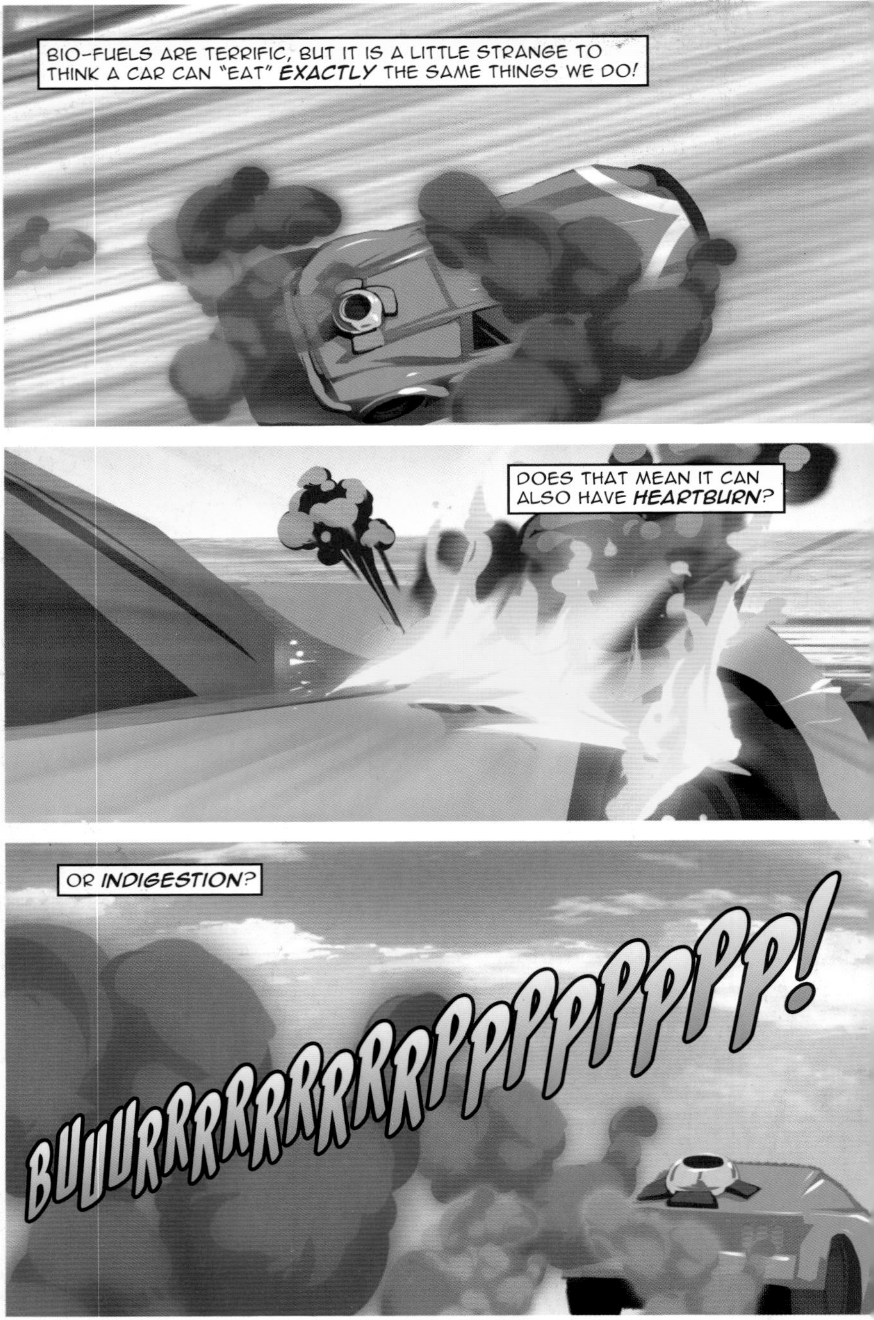
BIO-FUELS ARE TERRIFIC, BUT IT IS A LITTLE STRANGE TO THINK A CAR CAN "EAT" EXACTLY THE SAME THINGS WE DO!
DOES THAT MEAN IT CAN ALSO HAVE HEARTBURN?
OR INDIGESTION?
BUURRRRRRRRRPPPPPPPPP!

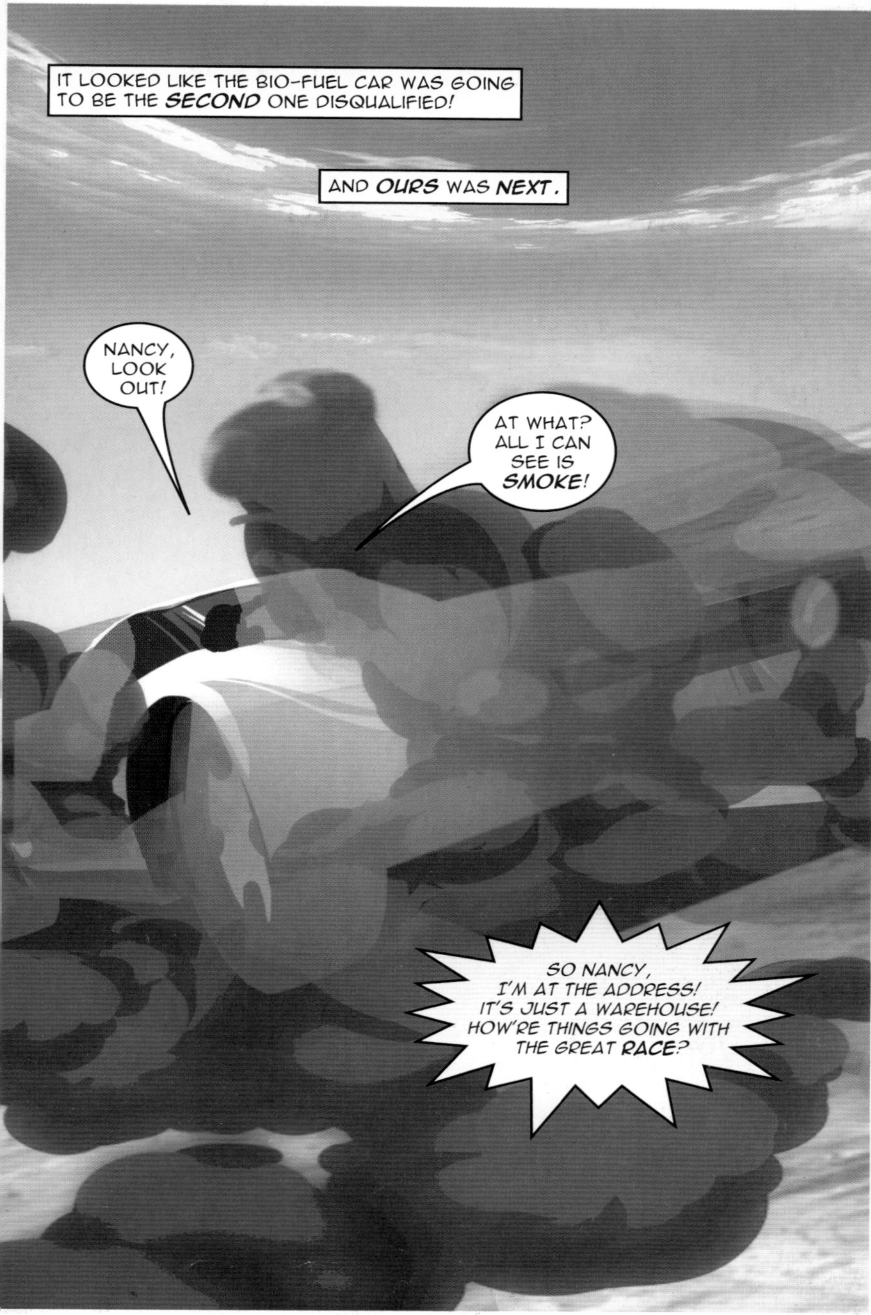
IT LOOKED LIKE THE BIO-FUEL CAR WAS GOING TO BE THE **SECOND** ONE DISQUALIFIED!
AND **OURS** WAS **NEXT**.
NANCY, LOOK OUT!
AT WHAT? ALL I CAN SEE IS **SMOKE**!
SO NANCY, I'M AT THE ADDRESS! IT'S JUST A WAREHOUSE! HOW'RE THINGS GOING WITH THE GREAT **RACE**?

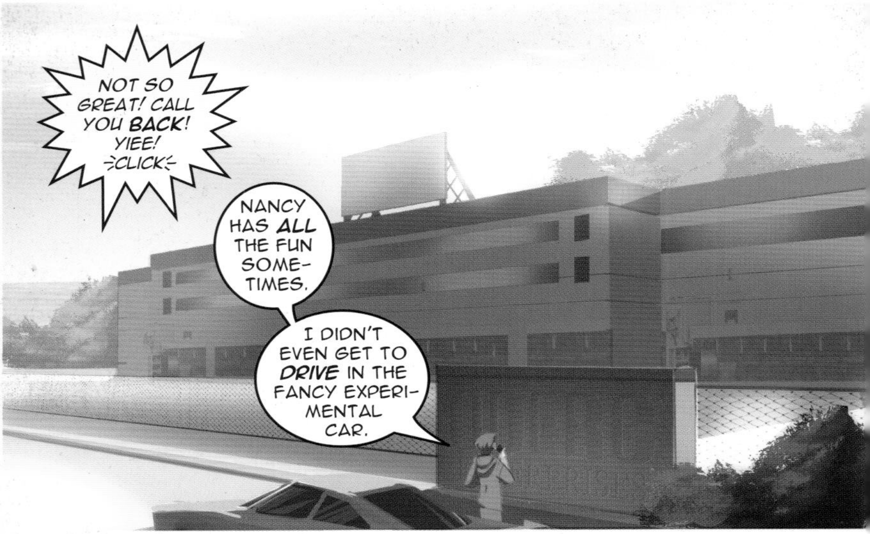
NOT SO GREAT! CALL YOU BACK! YIEE! ≡CLICK≡
NANCY HAS ALL THE FUN SOME-TIMES.
I DIDN'T EVEN GET TO DRIVE IN THE FANCY EXPERI-MENTAL CAR.

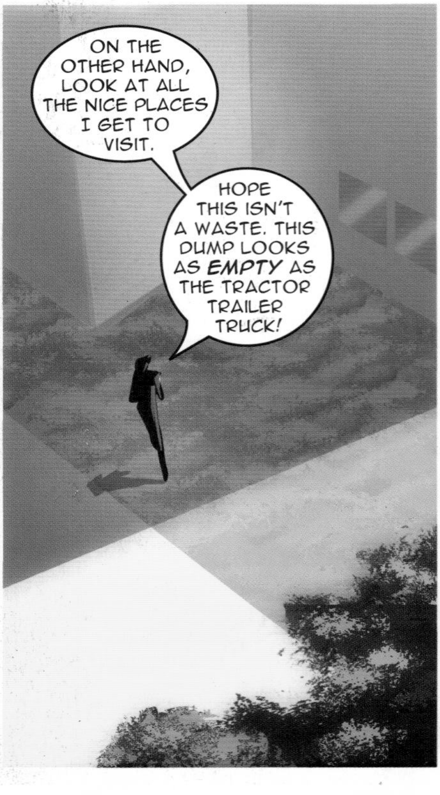
ON THE OTHER HAND, LOOK AT ALL THE NICE PLACES I GET TO VISIT.
HOPE THIS ISN'T A WASTE. THIS DUMP LOOKS AS EMPTY AS THE TRACTOR TRAILER TRUCK!

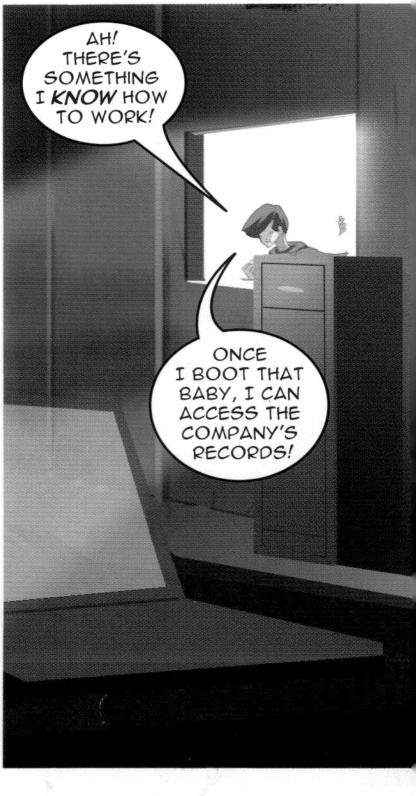
AH! THERE'S SOMETHING I KNOW HOW TO WORK!
ONCE I BOOT THAT BABY, I CAN ACCESS THE COMPANY'S RECORDS!

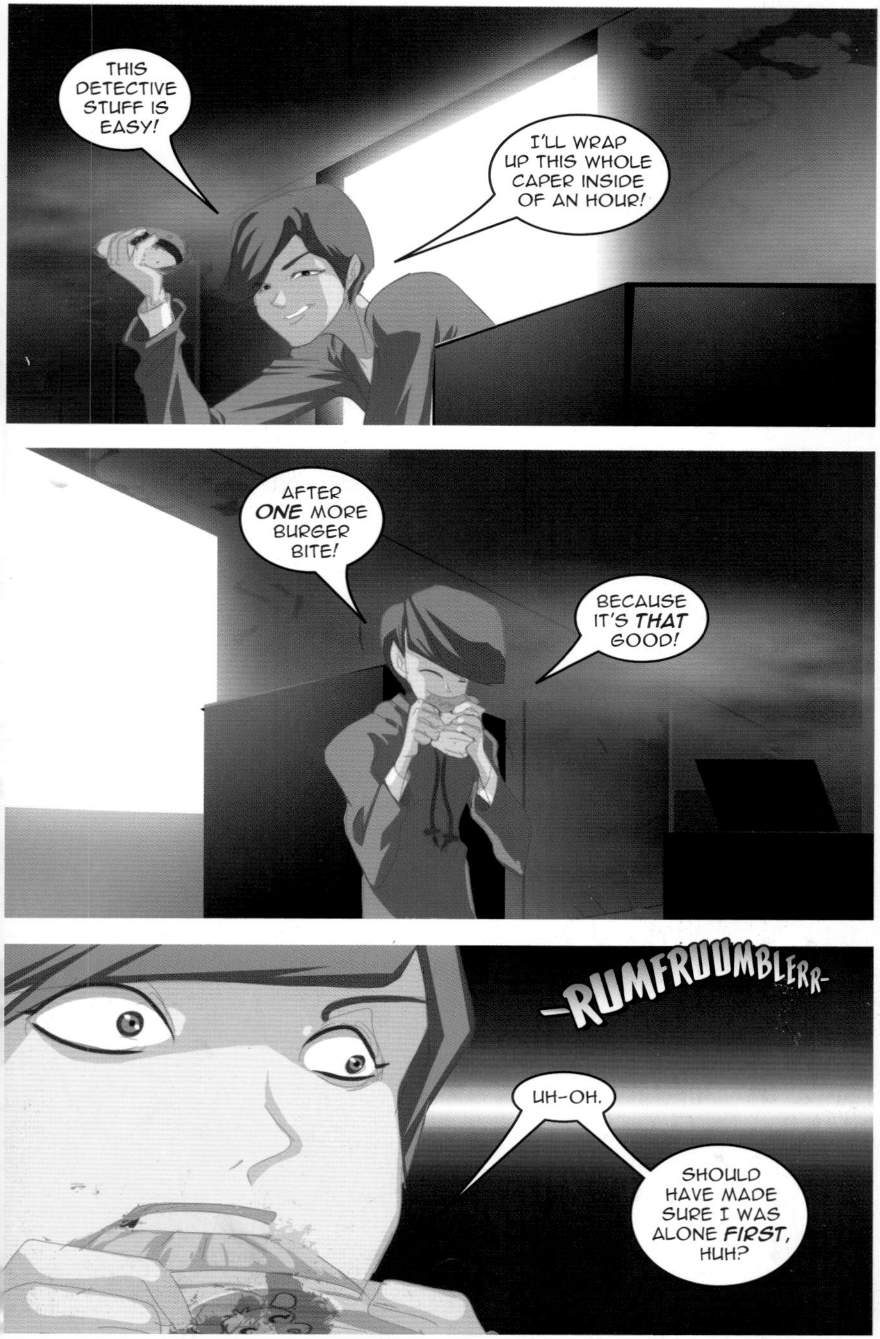
THIS DETECTIVE STUFF IS EASY!
I'LL WRAP UP THIS WHOLE CAPER INSIDE OF AN HOUR!
AFTER *ONE* MORE BURGER BITE!
BECAUSE IT'S *THAT* GOOD!
-RUMFRUUMBLERR-
UH-OH.
SHOULD HAVE MADE SURE I WAS ALONE *FIRST*, HUH?

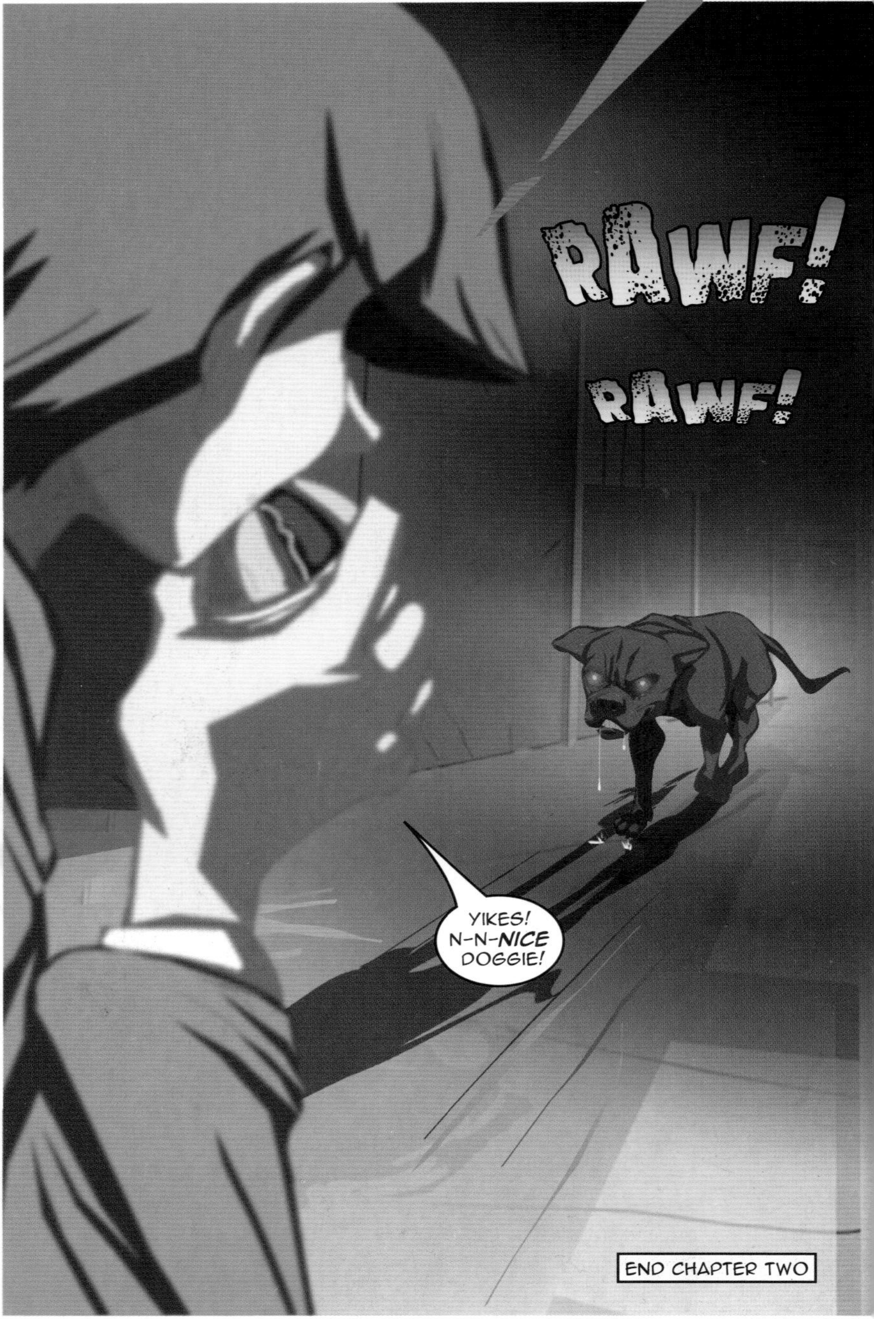
RAWF!
RAWF!
YIKES! N-N-NICE DOGGIE!
END CHAPTER TWO

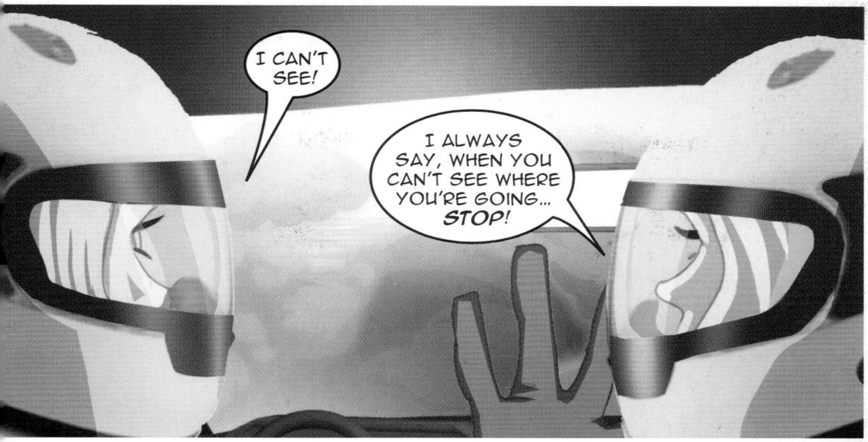
I CAN'T SEE!
I ALWAYS SAY, WHEN YOU CAN'T SEE WHERE YOU'RE GOING... STOP!

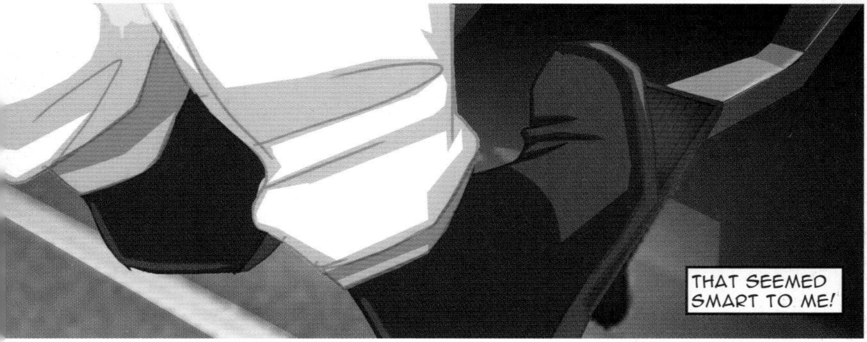
THAT SEEMED SMART TO ME!

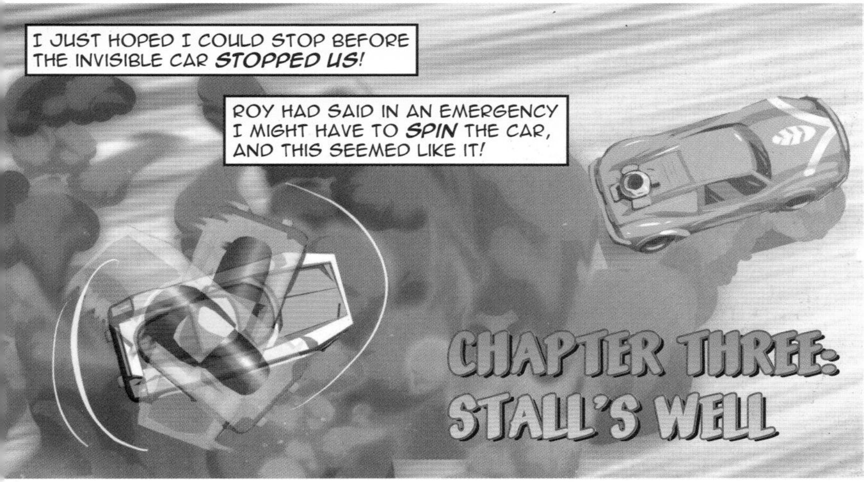
I JUST HOPED I COULD STOP BEFORE THE INVISIBLE CAR STOPPED US!
ROY HAD SAID IN AN EMERGENCY I MIGHT HAVE TO SPIN THE CAR, AND THIS SEEMED LIKE IT!
CHAPTER THREE: STALL'S WELL

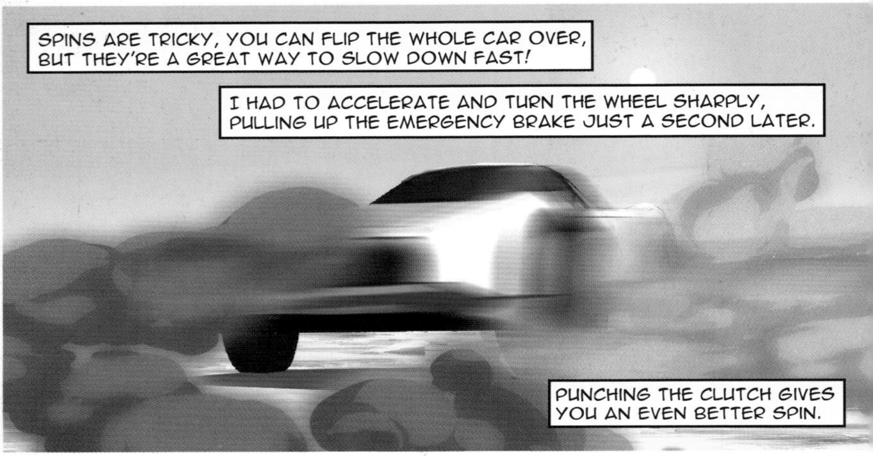
SPINS ARE TRICKY, YOU CAN FLIP THE WHOLE CAR OVER, BUT THEY'RE A GREAT WAY TO SLOW DOWN FAST!
I HAD TO ACCELERATE AND TURN THE WHEEL SHARPLY, PULLING UP THE EMERGENCY BRAKE JUST A SECOND LATER.
PUNCHING THE CLUTCH GIVES YOU AN EVEN BETTER SPIN.

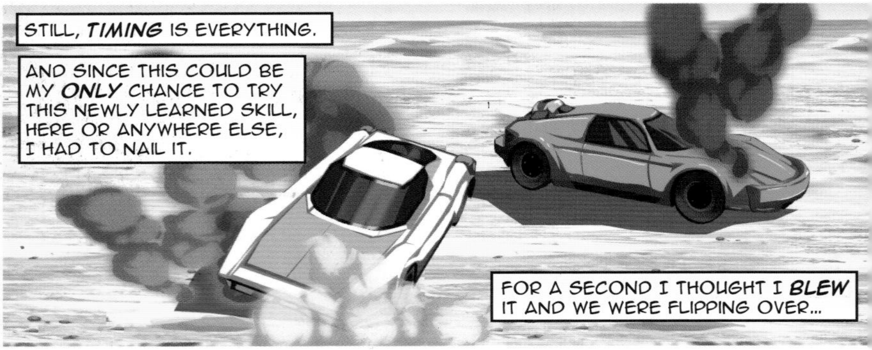
STILL, *TIMING* IS EVERYTHING.
AND SINCE THIS COULD BE MY *ONLY* CHANCE TO TRY THIS NEWLY LEARNED SKILL, HERE OR ANYWHERE ELSE, I HAD TO NAIL IT.
FOR A SECOND I THOUGHT I *BLEW* IT AND WE WERE FLIPPING OVER...

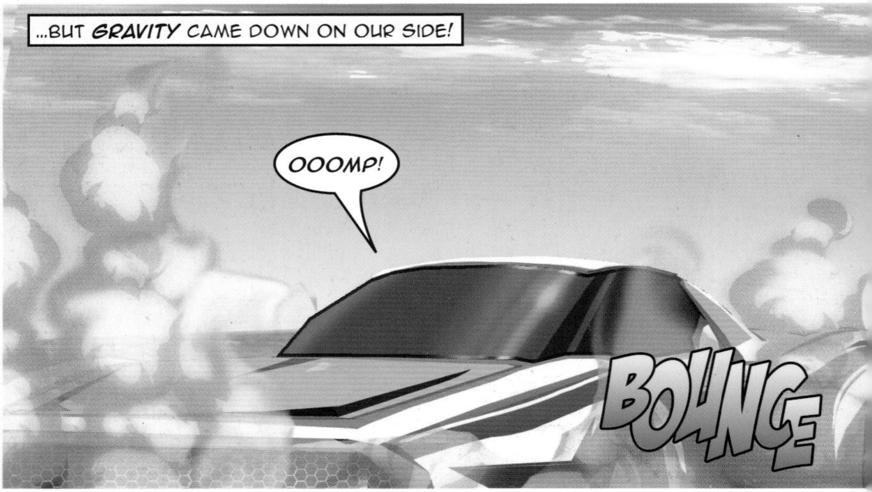
...BUT *GRAVITY* CAME DOWN ON OUR SIDE!
OOOMP!
BOUNCE

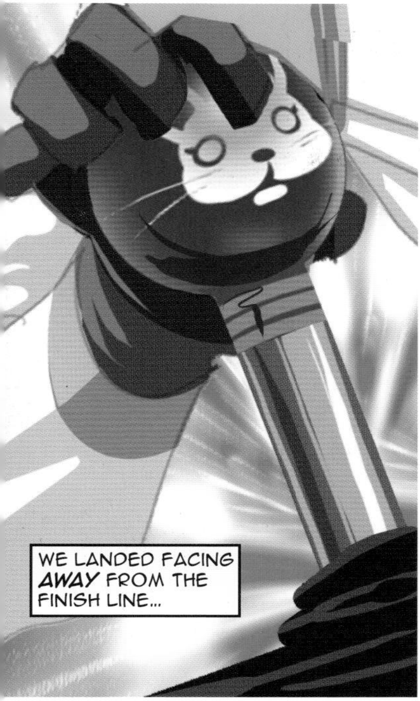
WE LANDED FACING *AWAY* FROM THE FINISH LINE...

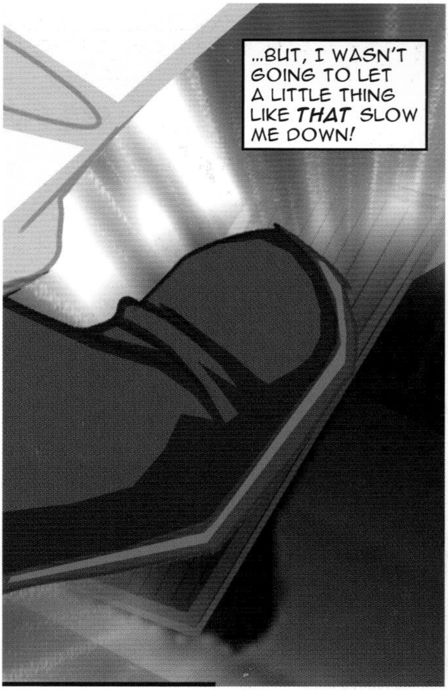
...BUT, I WASN'T GOING TO LET A LITTLE THING LIKE *THAT* SLOW ME DOWN!

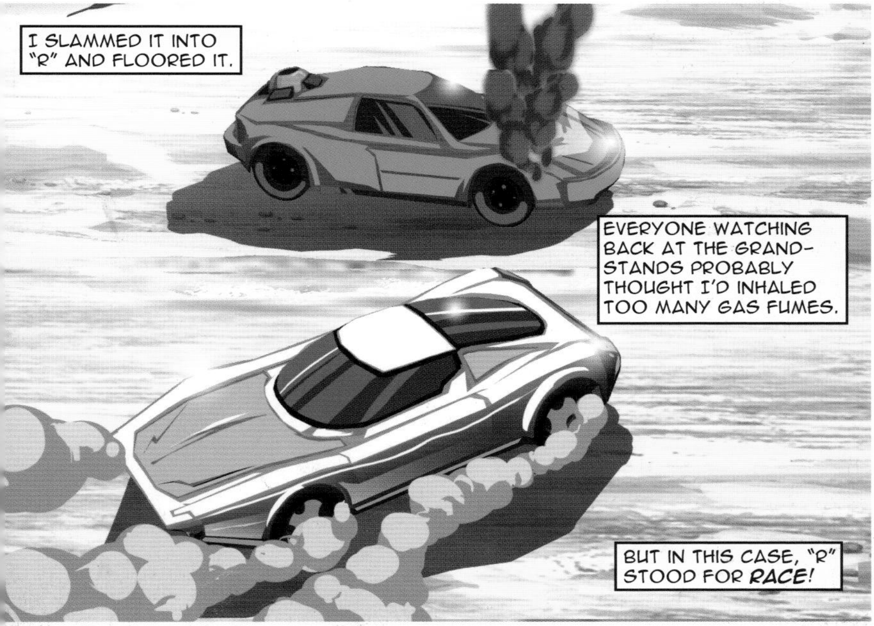
I SLAMMED IT INTO "R" AND FLOORED IT.
EVERYONE WATCHING BACK AT THE GRAND-STANDS PROBABLY THOUGHT I'D INHALED TOO MANY GAS FUMES.
BUT IN THIS CASE, "R" STOOD FOR *RACE*!

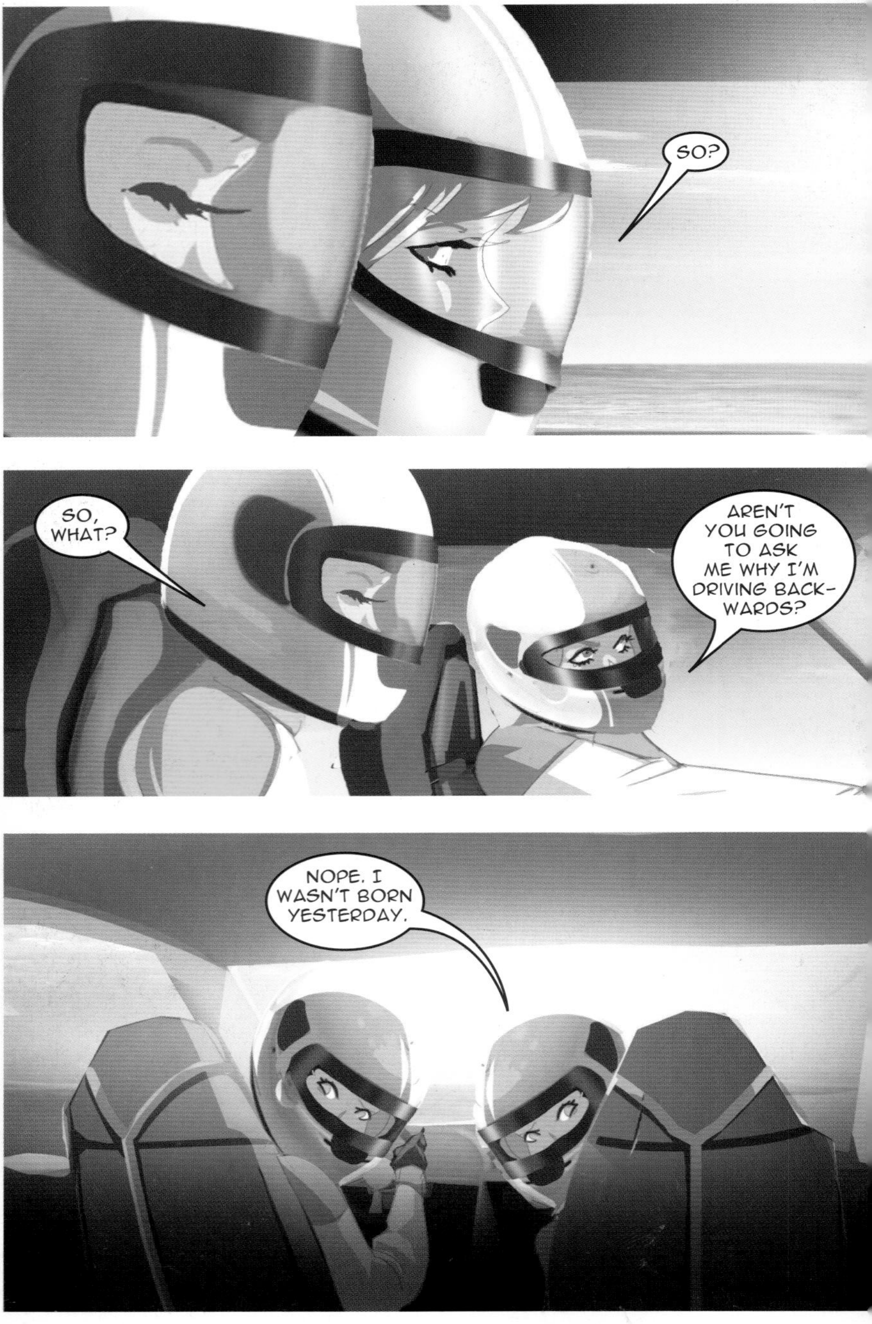
SO?
SO, WHAT?
AREN'T YOU GOING TO ASK ME WHY I'M DRIVING BACK-WARDS?
NOPE. I WASN'T BORN YESTERDAY.

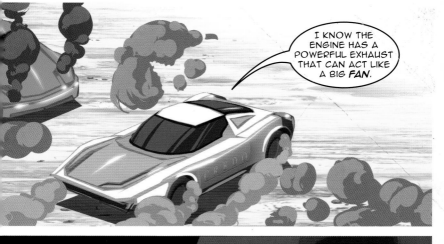

I KNOW THE ENGINE HAS A POWERFUL EXHAUST THAT CAN ACT LIKE A BIG *FAN*.

BESS AND I WERE LIKE A WELL-OILED MACHINE.

AND, SINCE WE WERE *DRIVING* A WELL-OILED MACHINE.

WE WERE BOUND TO *WIN*!

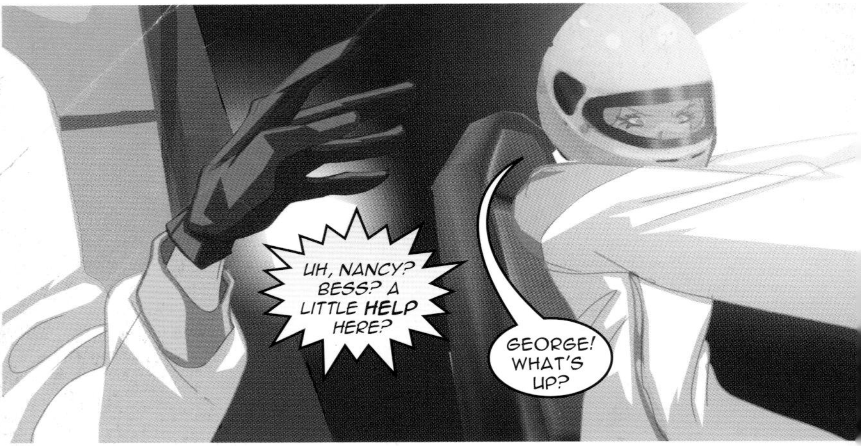
UH, NANCY? BESS? A LITTLE HELP HERE?
GEORGE! WHAT'S UP?

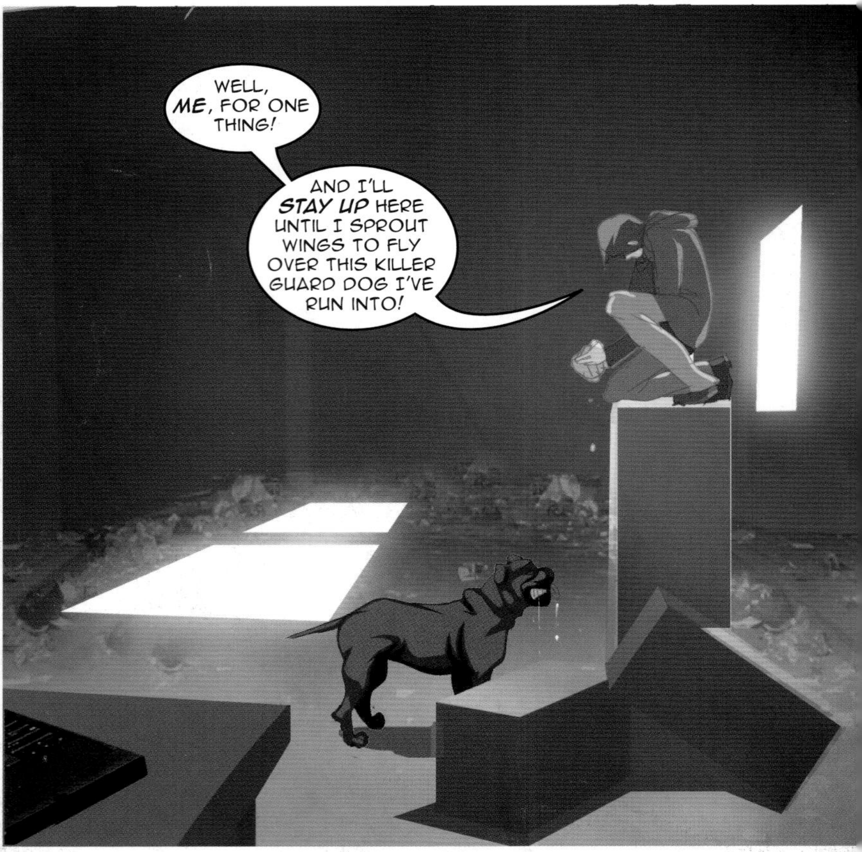
WELL, ME, FOR ONE THING!
AND I'LL STAY UP HERE UNTIL I SPROUT WINGS TO FLY OVER THIS KILLER GUARD DOG I'VE RUN INTO!

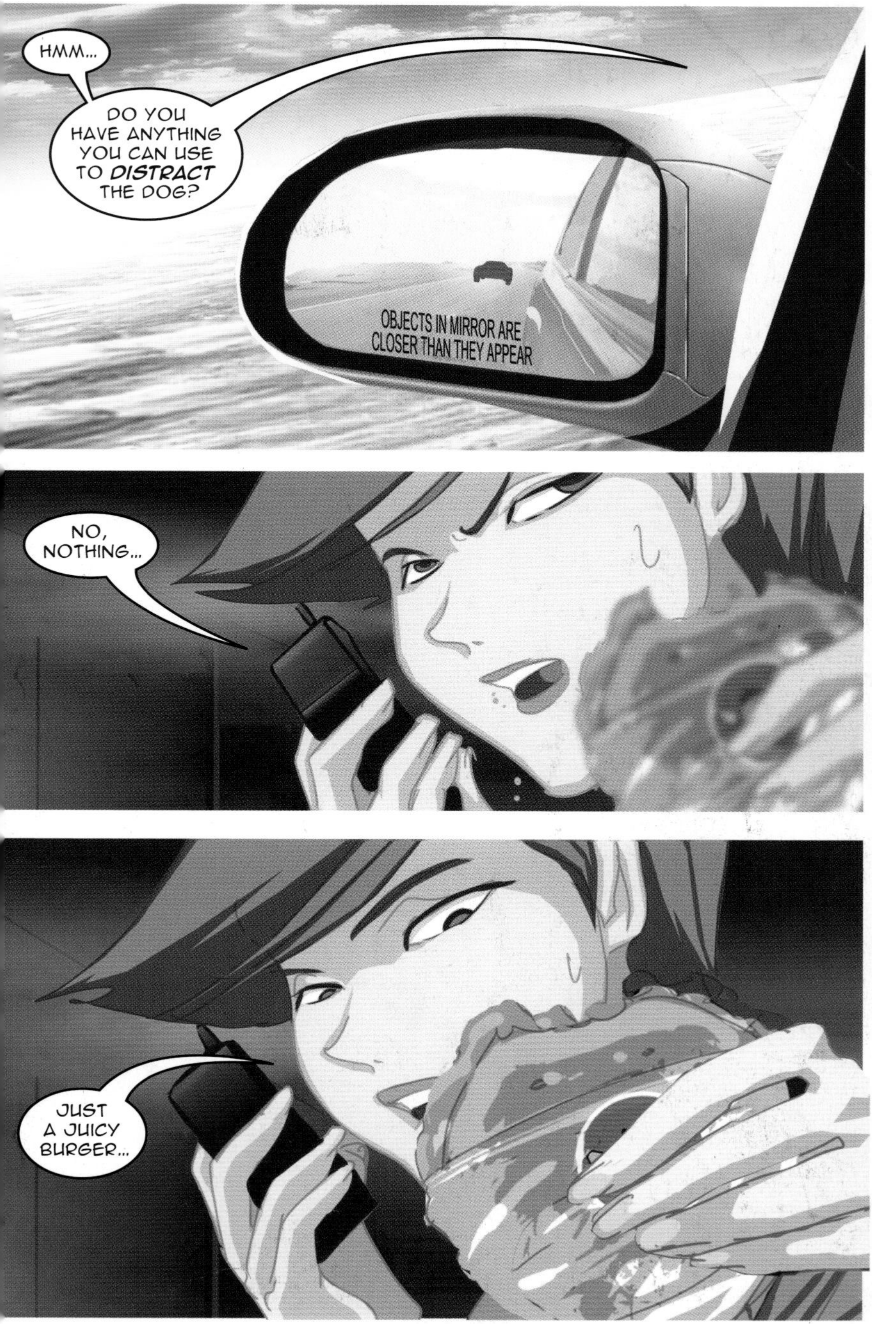
HMM...
DO YOU HAVE ANYTHING YOU CAN USE TO DISTRACT THE DOG?
OBJECTS IN MIRROR ARE CLOSER THAN THEY APPEAR
NO, NOTHING...
JUST A JUICY BURGER...

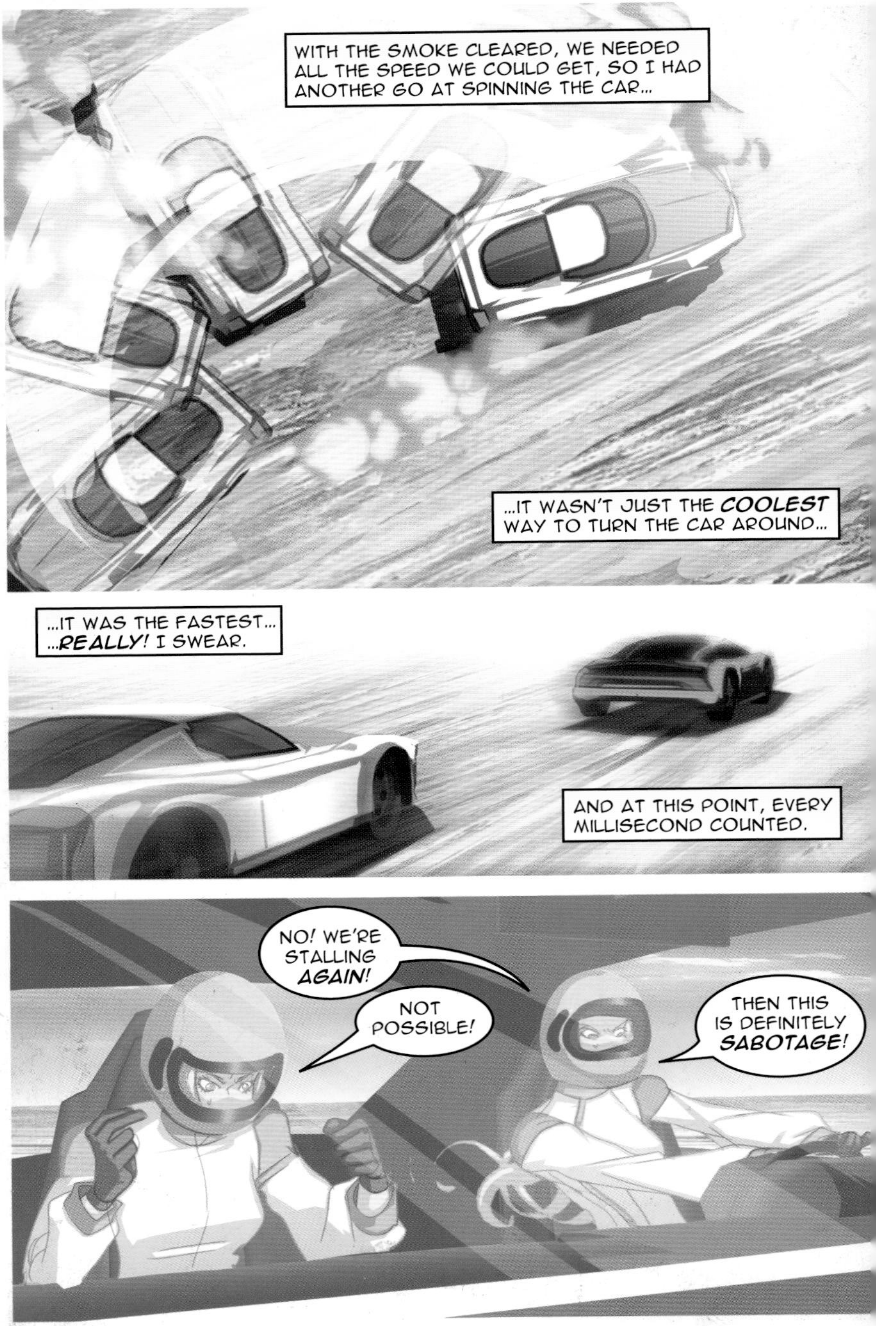
WITH THE SMOKE CLEARED, WE NEEDED ALL THE SPEED WE COULD GET, SO I HAD ANOTHER GO AT SPINNING THE CAR...
...IT WASN'T JUST THE COOLEST WAY TO TURN THE CAR AROUND...
...IT WAS THE FASTEST... ...REALLY! I SWEAR.
AND AT THIS POINT, EVERY MILLISECOND COUNTED.
NO! WE'RE STALLING AGAIN!
NOT POSSIBLE!
THEN THIS IS DEFINITELY SABOTAGE!

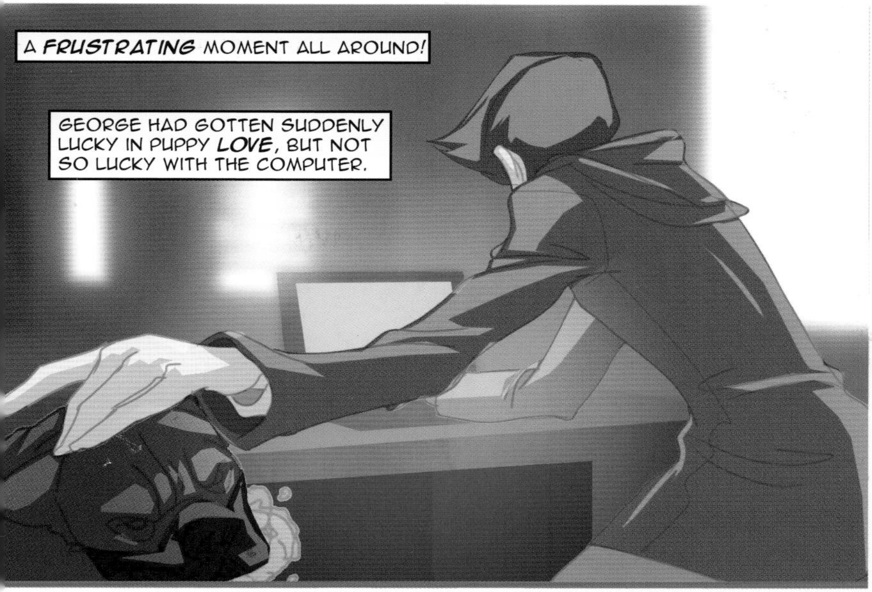
A FRUSTRATING MOMENT ALL AROUND!
GEORGE HAD GOTTEN SUDDENLY LUCKY IN PUPPY LOVE, BUT NOT SO LUCKY WITH THE COMPUTER.

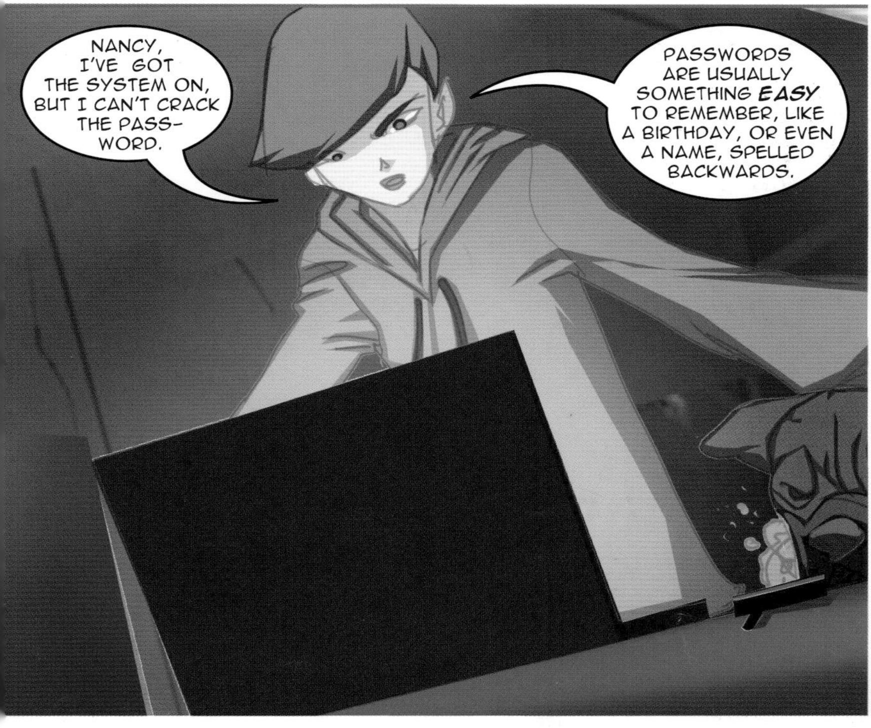
NANCY, I'VE GOT THE SYSTEM ON, BUT I CAN'T CRACK THE PASS-WORD.
PASSWORDS ARE USUALLY SOMETHING EASY TO REMEMBER, LIKE A BIRTHDAY, OR EVEN A NAME, SPELLED BACKWARDS.

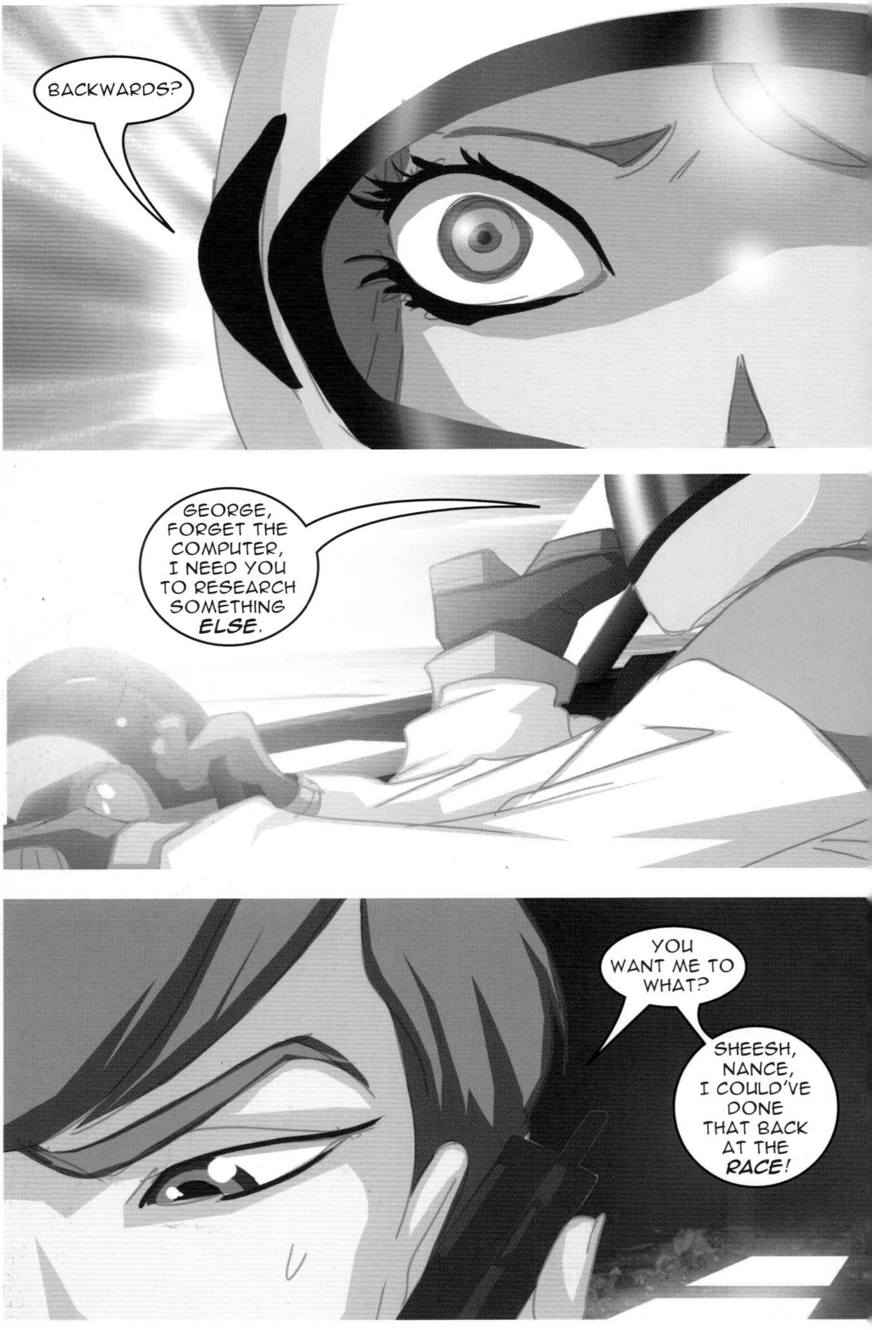
BACKWARDS?
GEORGE, FORGET THE COMPUTER, I NEED YOU TO RESEARCH SOMETHING ELSE.
YOU WANT ME TO WHAT?
SHEESH, NANCE, I COULD'VE DONE THAT BACK AT THE RACE!

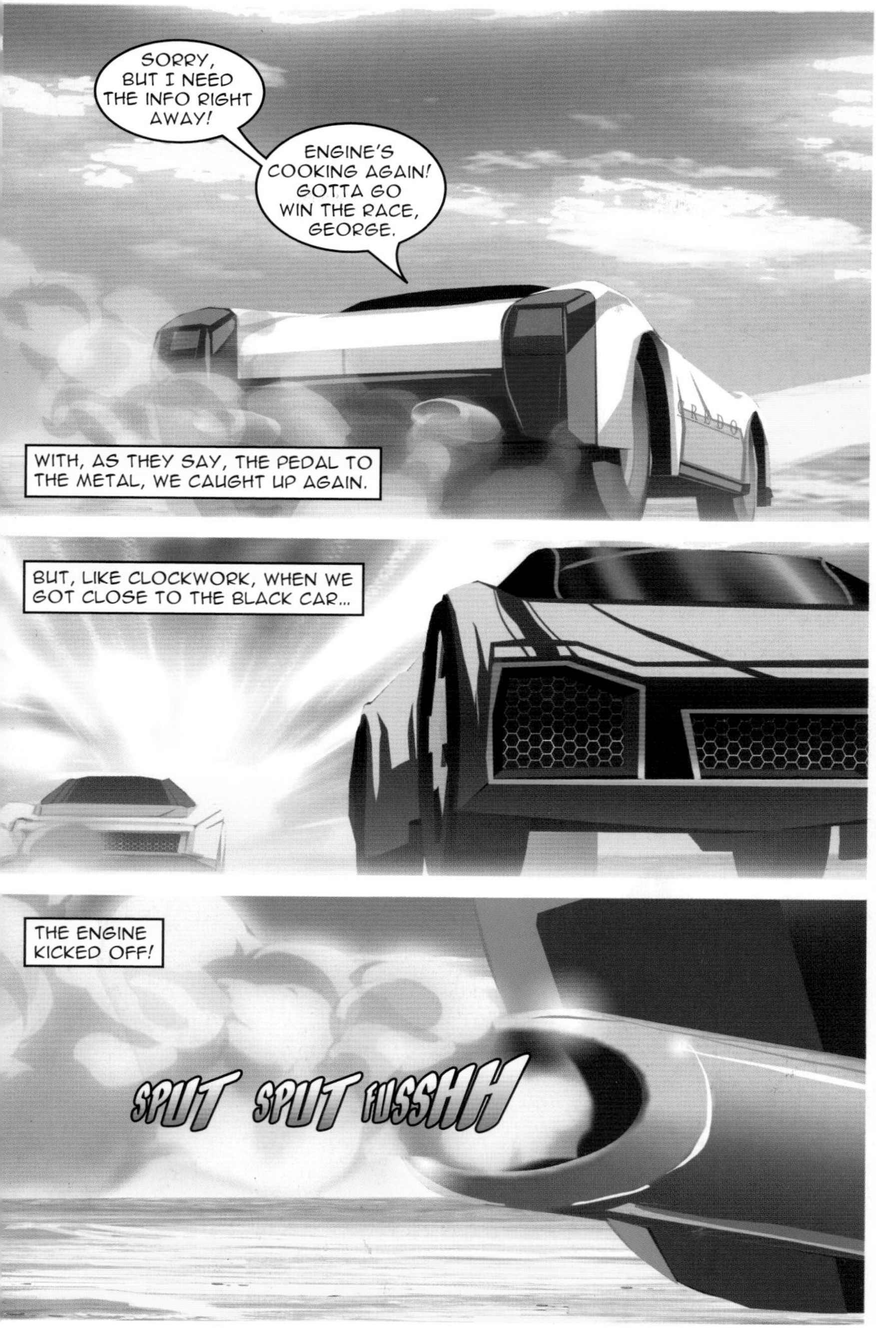
SORRY, BUT I NEED THE INFO RIGHT AWAY!
ENGINE'S COOKING AGAIN! GOTTA GO WIN THE RACE, GEORGE.
WITH, AS THEY SAY, THE PEDAL TO THE METAL, WE CAUGHT UP AGAIN.
BUT, LIKE CLOCKWORK, WHEN WE GOT CLOSE TO THE BLACK CAR...
THE ENGINE KICKED OFF!
SPUT SPUT FUSSHH

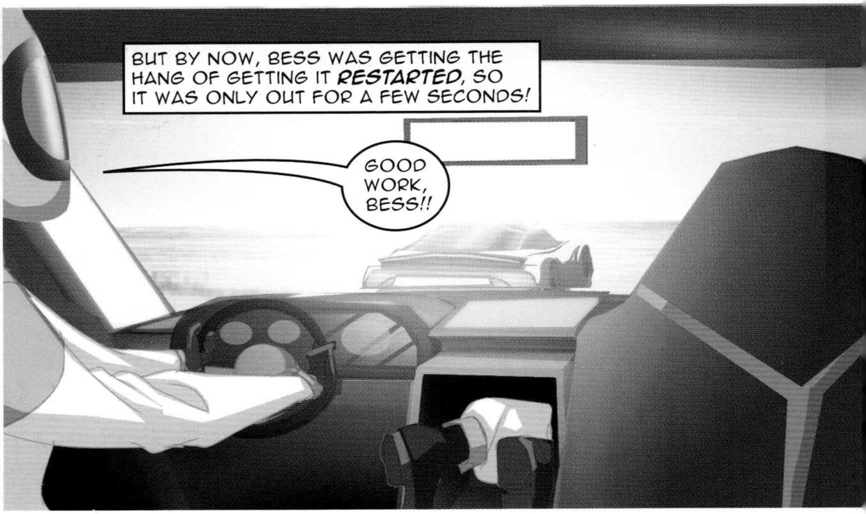
BUT BY NOW, BESS WAS GETTING THE HANG OF GETTING IT **RESTARTED**, SO IT WAS ONLY OUT FOR A FEW SECONDS!
GOOD WORK, BESS!!

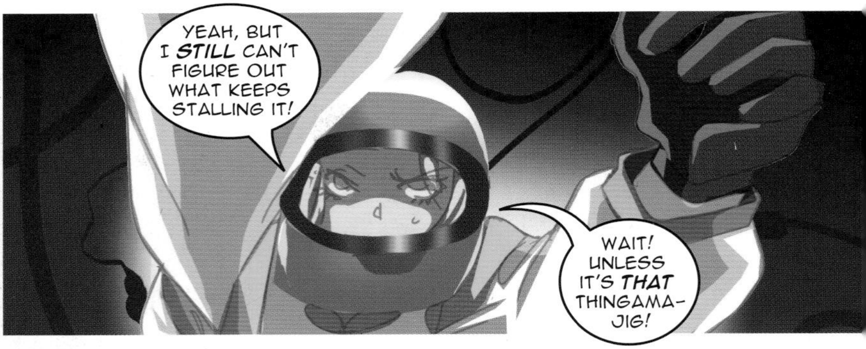
YEAH, BUT I **STILL** CAN'T FIGURE OUT WHAT KEEPS STALLING IT!
WAIT! UNLESS IT'S **THAT** THINGAMA-JIG!

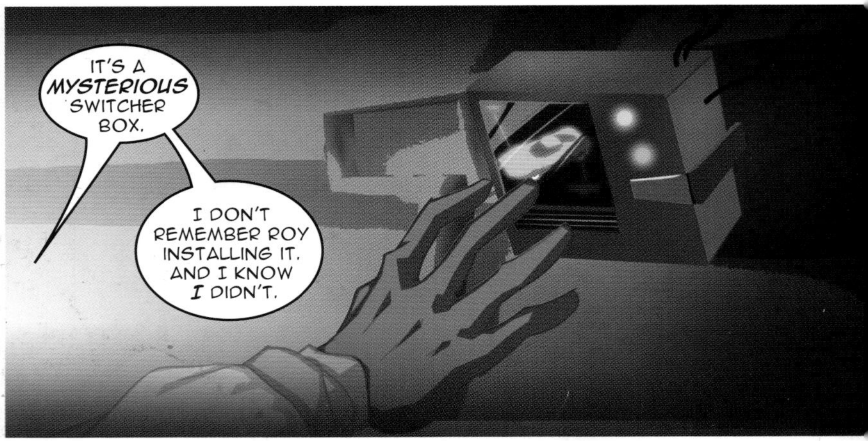
IT'S A **MYSTERIOUS** SWITCHER BOX.
I DON'T REMEMBER ROY INSTALLING IT. AND I KNOW **I** DIDN'T.

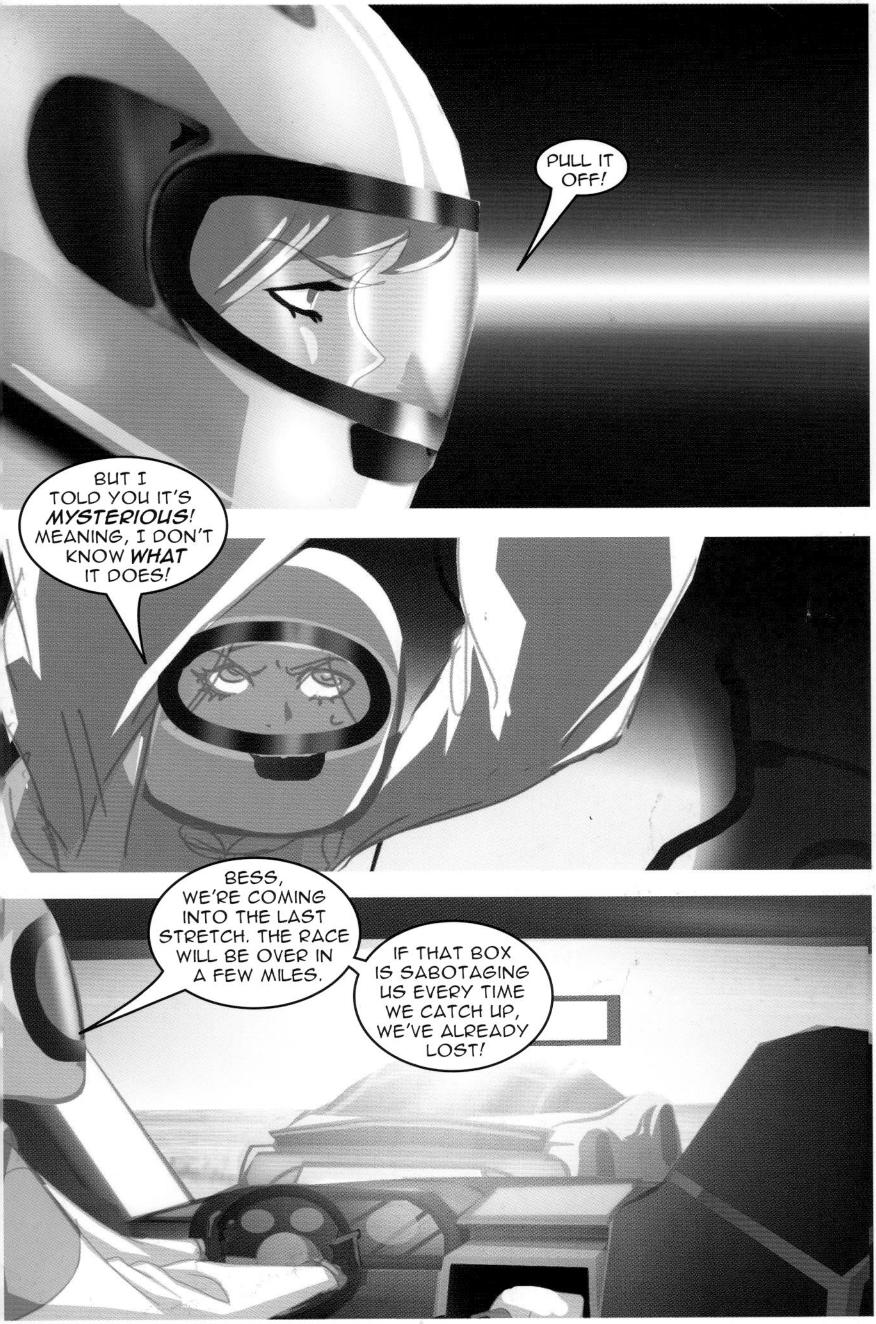
PULL IT OFF!
BUT I TOLD YOU IT'S *MYSTERIOUS*! MEANING, I DON'T KNOW *WHAT* IT DOES!
BESS, WE'RE COMING INTO THE LAST STRETCH. THE RACE WILL BE OVER IN A FEW MILES.
IF THAT BOX IS SABOTAGING US EVERY TIME WE CATCH UP, WE'VE ALREADY LOST!

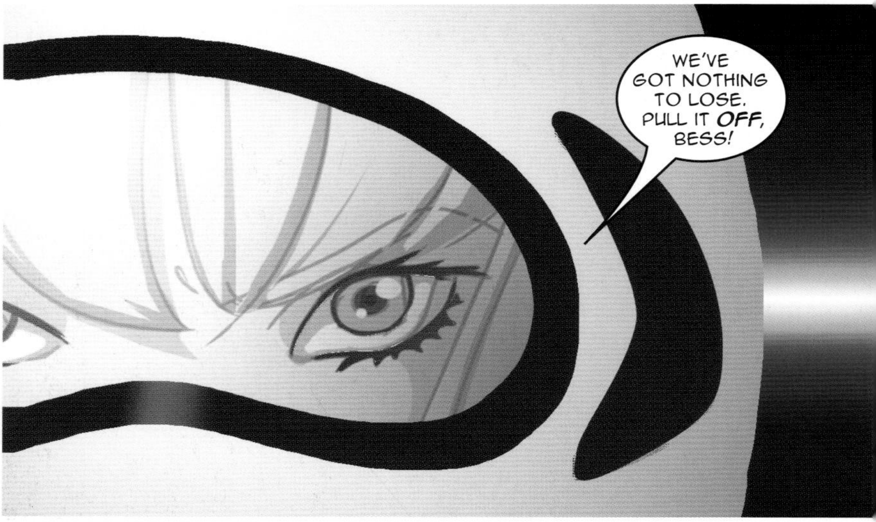
WE'VE GOT NOTHING TO LOSE. PULL IT OFF, BESS!

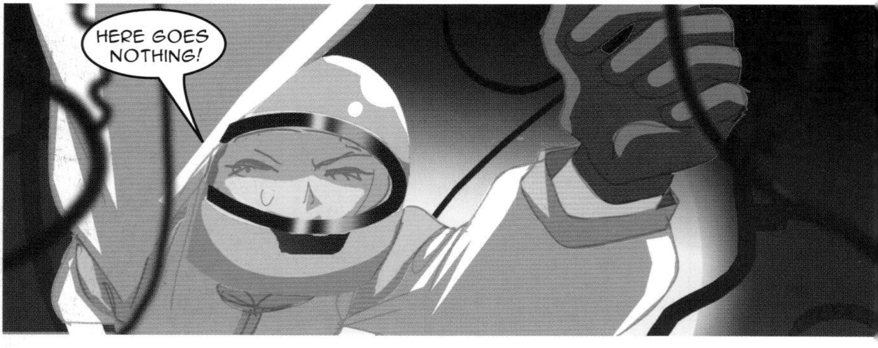
HERE GOES NOTHING!

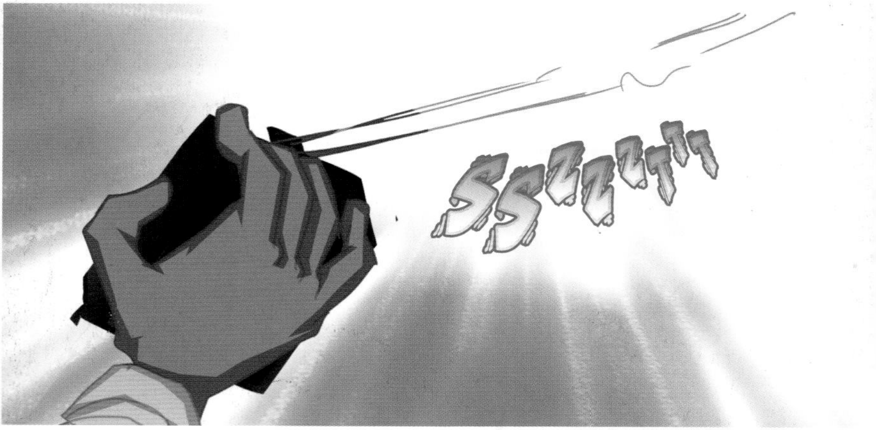
SSZZZTTT

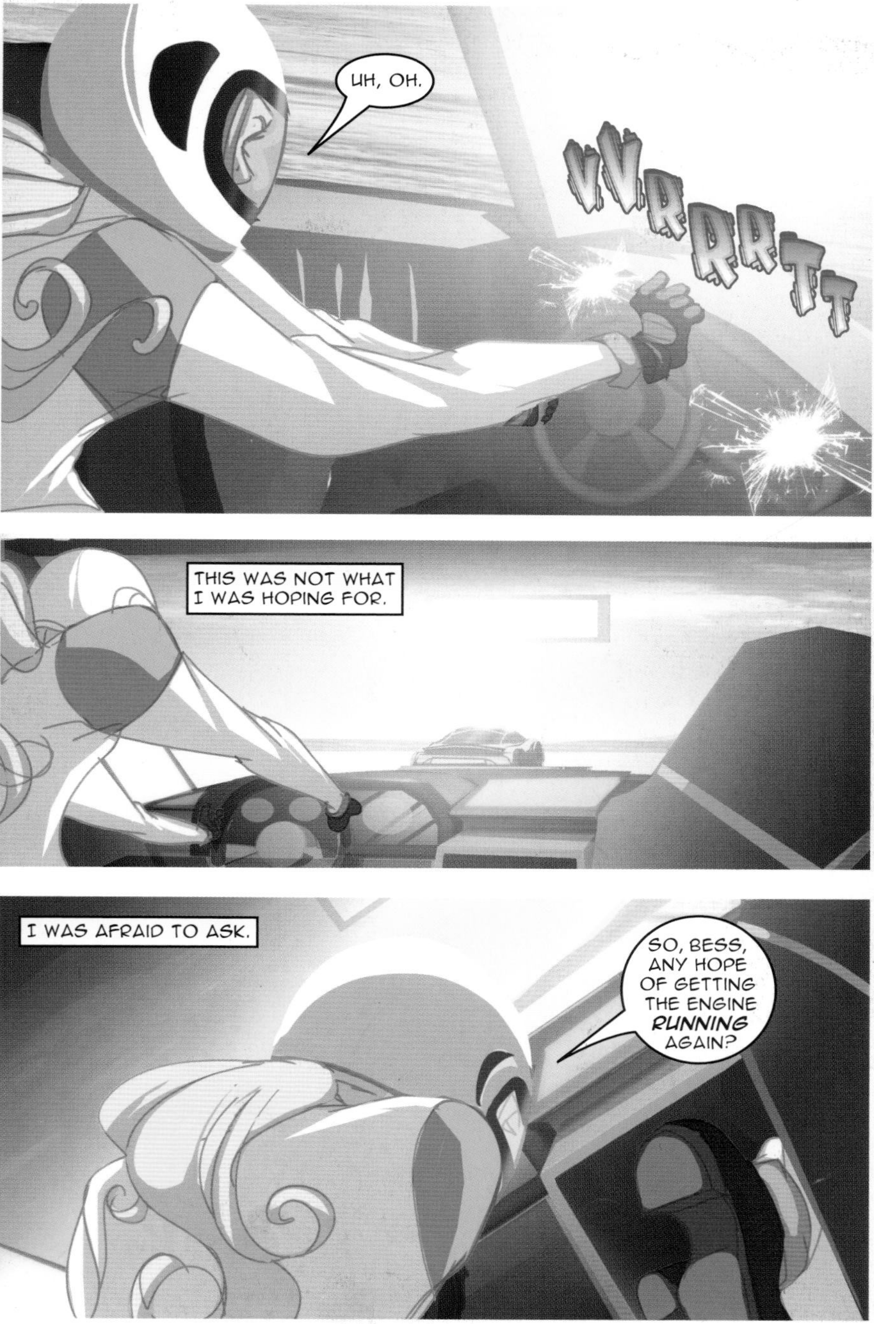
UH, OH.
VVRRRTTT
THIS WAS NOT WHAT I WAS HOPING FOR.
I WAS AFRAID TO ASK.
SO, BESS, ANY HOPE OF GETTING THE ENGINE *RUNNING* AGAIN?

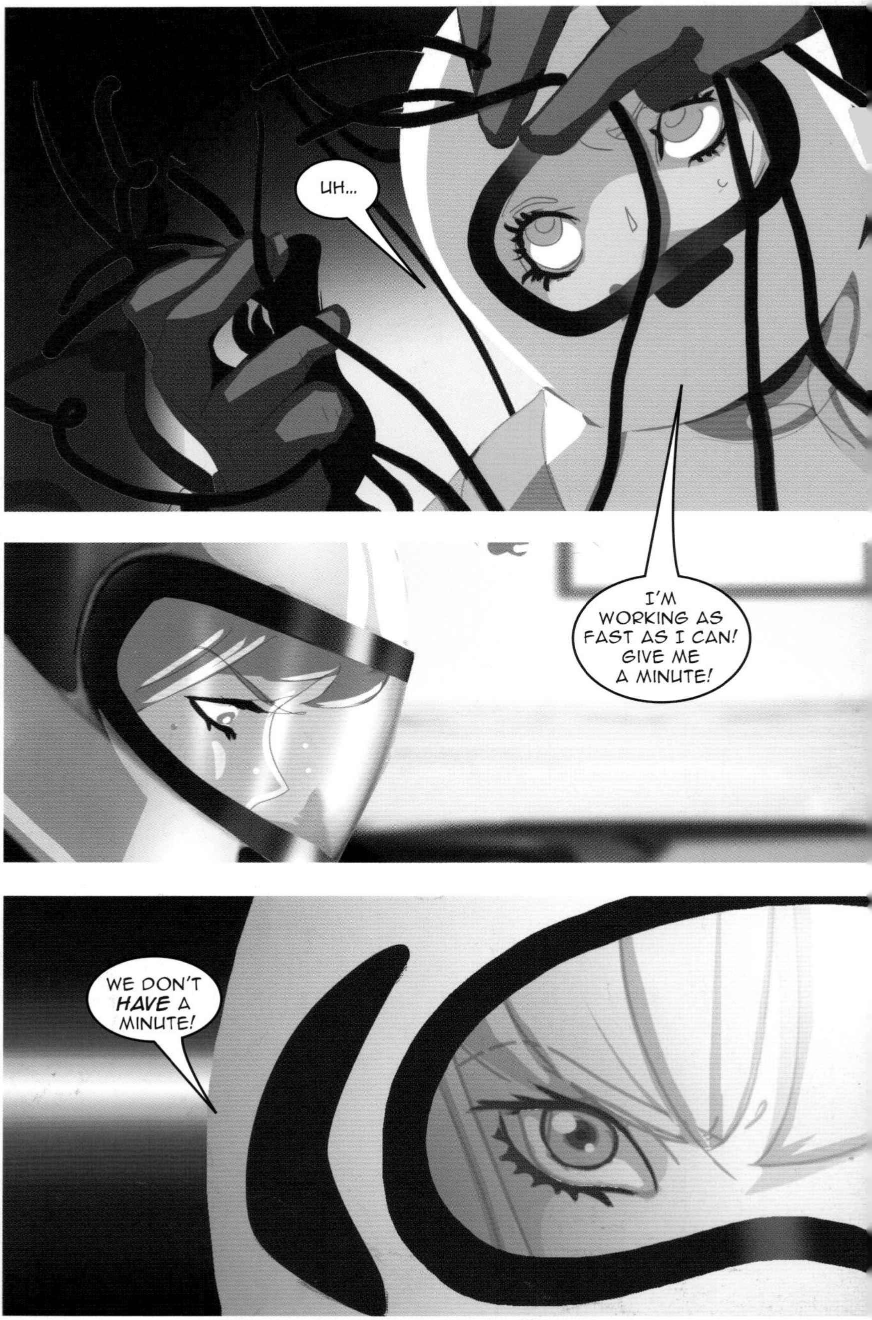
UH...
I'M WORKING AS FAST AS I CAN! GIVE ME A MINUTE!
WE DON'T *HAVE* A MINUTE!

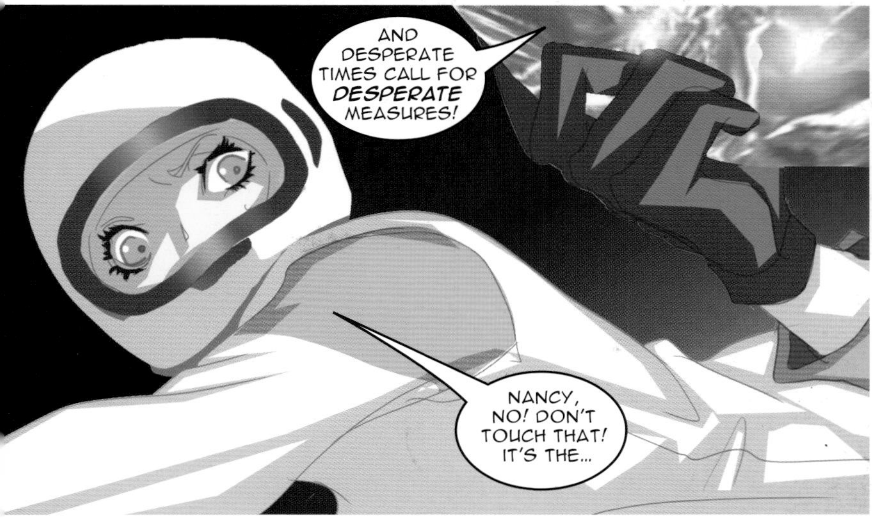
AND DESPERATE TIMES CALL FOR DESPERATE MEASURES!
NANCY, NO! DON'T TOUCH THAT! IT'S THE...

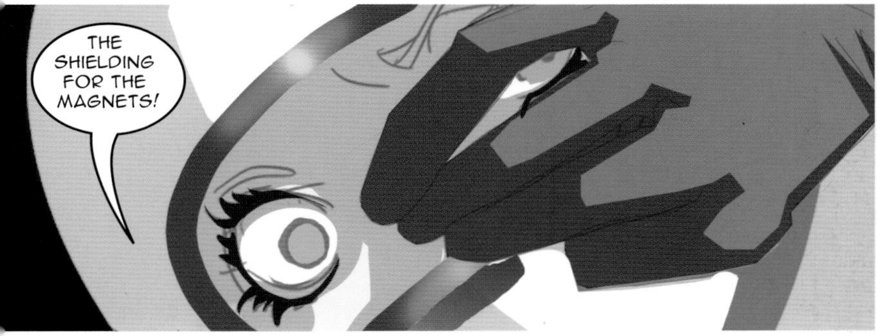
THE SHIELDING FOR THE MAGNETS!

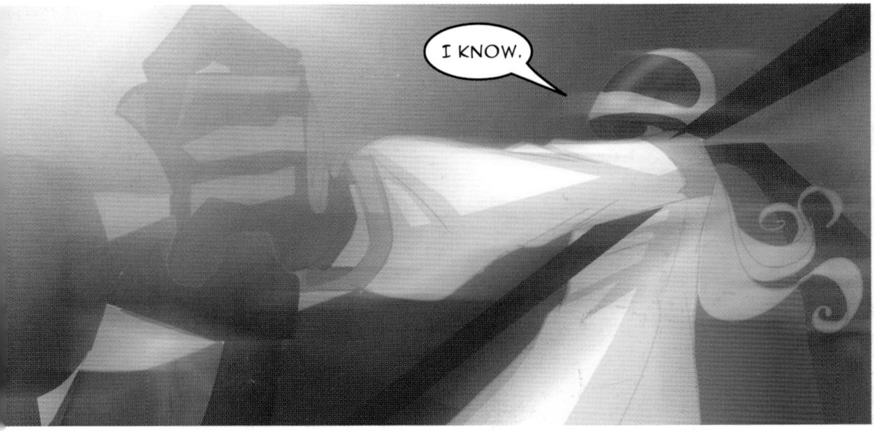
I KNOW.

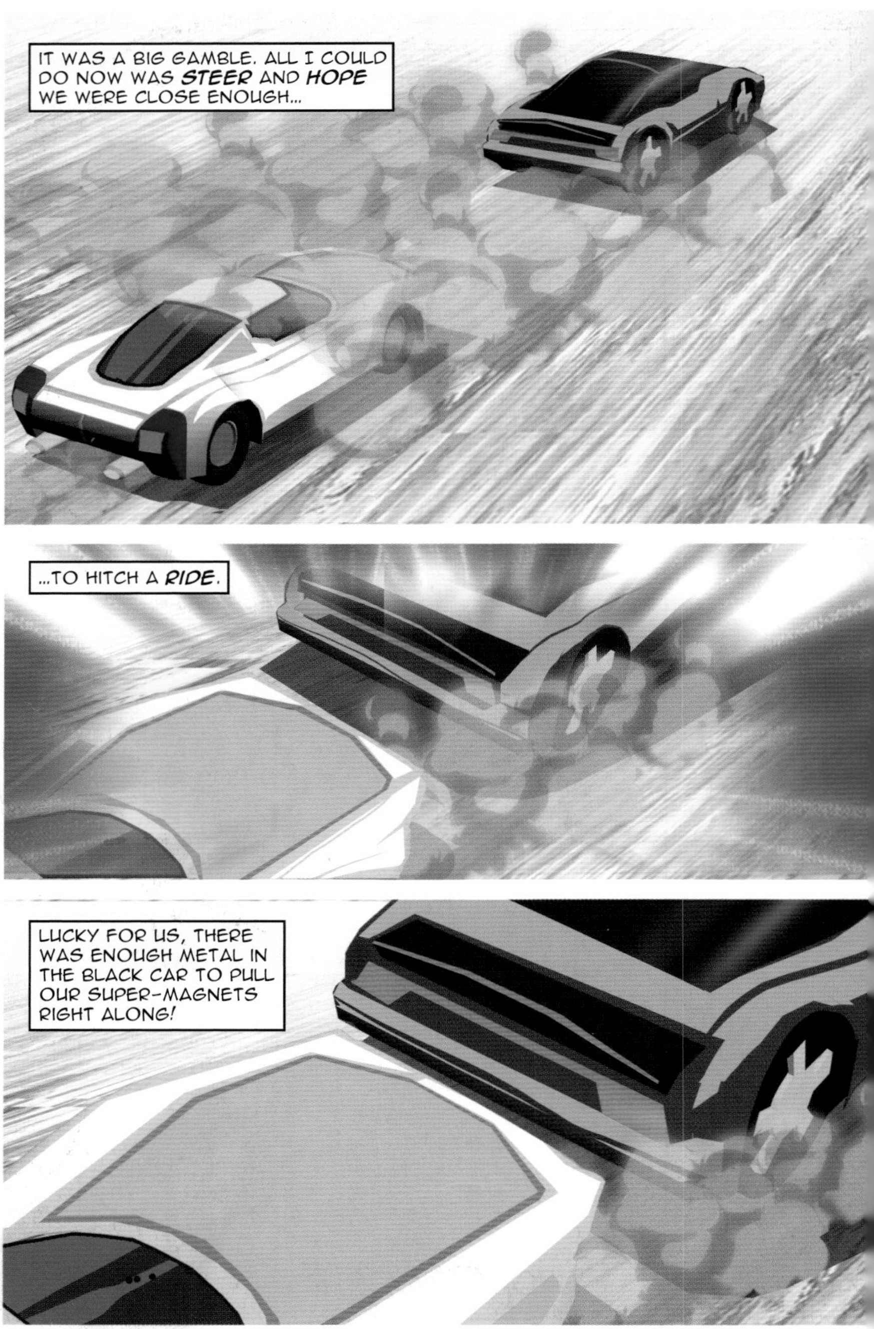
IT WAS A BIG GAMBLE. ALL I COULD DO NOW WAS STEER AND HOPE WE WERE CLOSE ENOUGH...
...TO HITCH A RIDE.
LUCKY FOR US, THERE WAS ENOUGH METAL IN THE BLACK CAR TO PULL OUR SUPER-MAGNETS RIGHT ALONG!

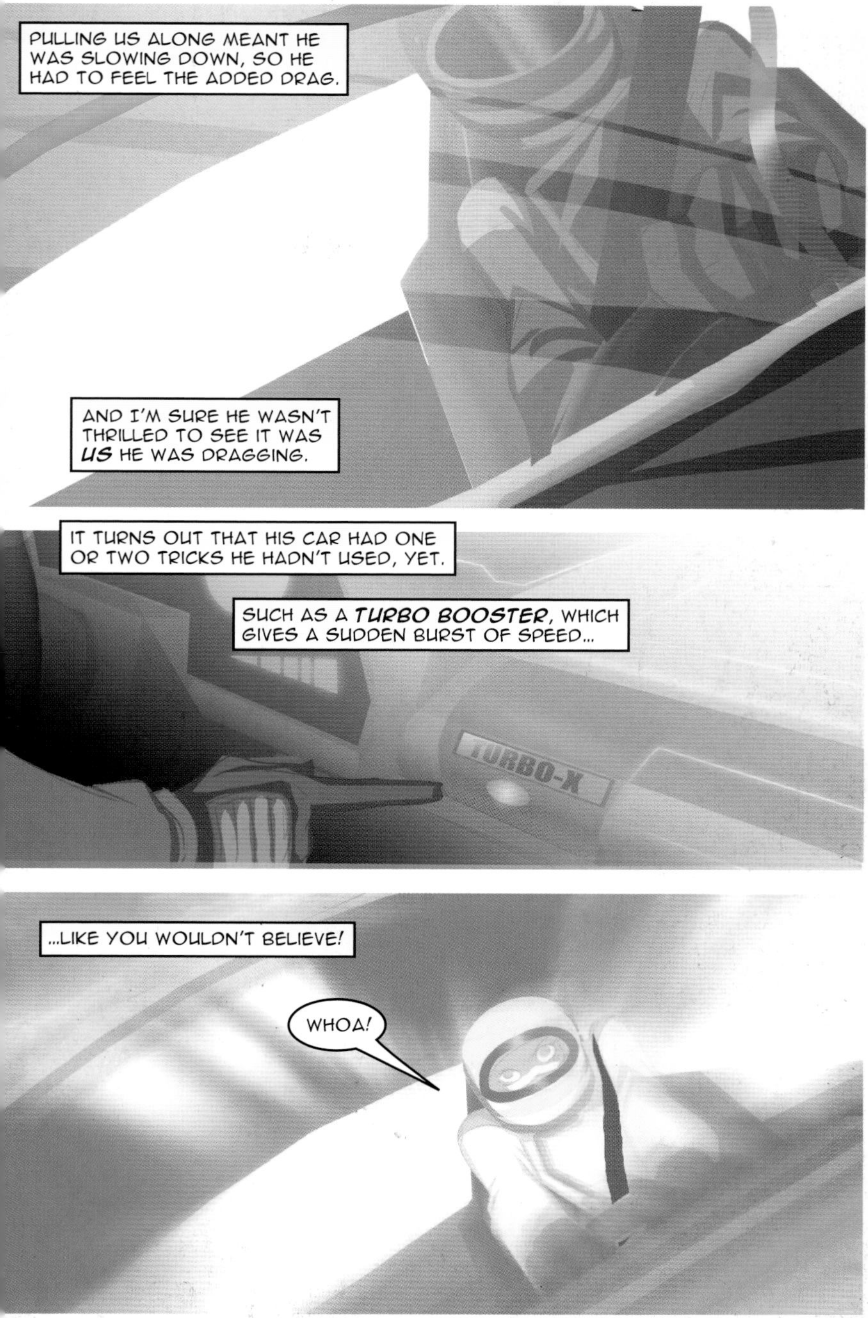
PULLING US ALONG MEANT HE WAS SLOWING DOWN, SO HE HAD TO FEEL THE ADDED DRAG.
AND I'M SURE HE WASN'T THRILLED TO SEE IT WAS ***US*** HE WAS DRAGGING.
IT TURNS OUT THAT HIS CAR HAD ONE OR TWO TRICKS HE HADN'T USED, YET.
SUCH AS A ***TURBO BOOSTER***, WHICH GIVES A SUDDEN BURST OF SPEED...
TURBO-X
...LIKE YOU WOULDN'T BELIEVE!
WHOA!

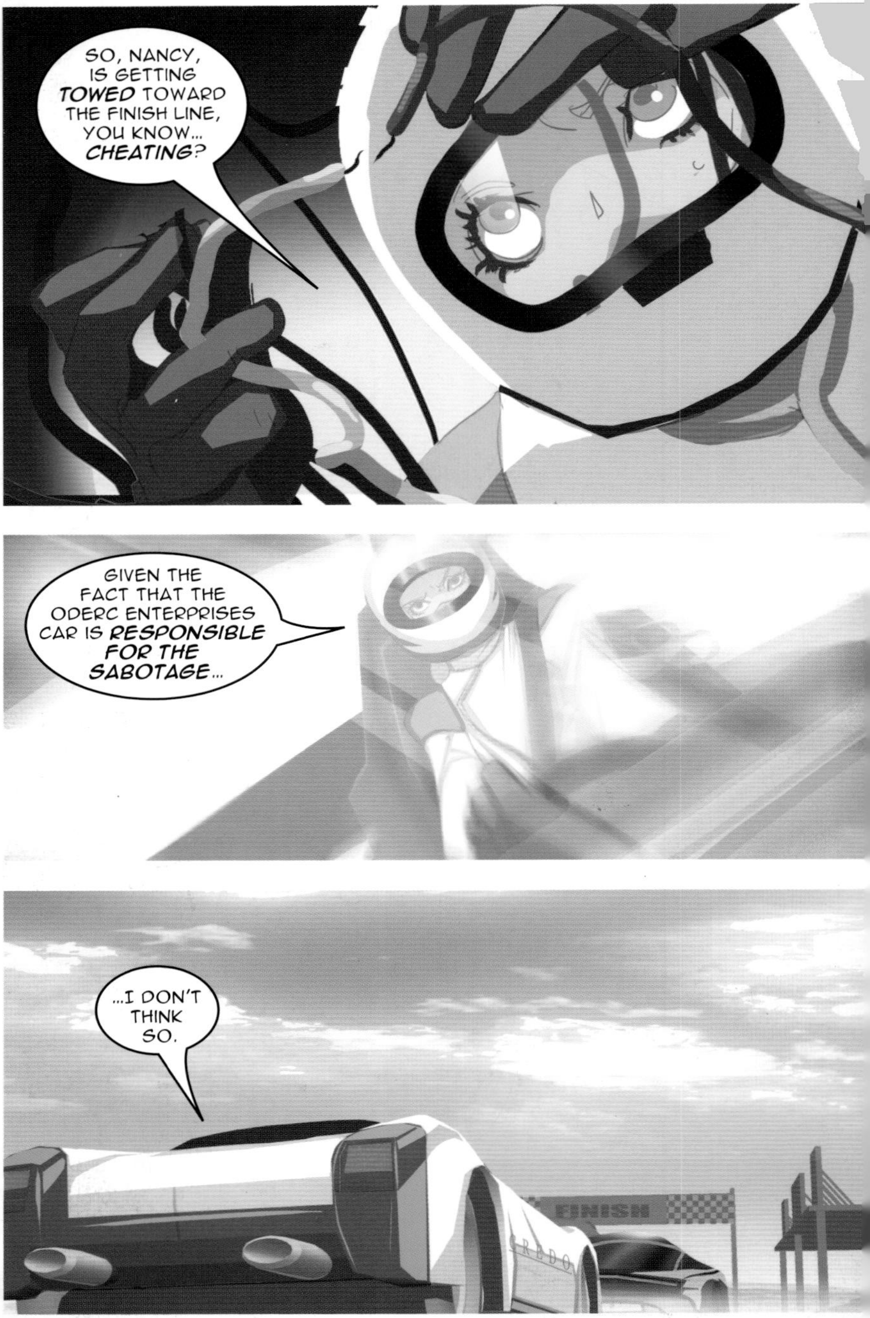
SO, NANCY, IS GETTING TOWED TOWARD THE FINISH LINE, YOU KNOW... CHEATING?
GIVEN THE FACT THAT THE ODERC ENTERPRISES CAR IS RESPONSIBLE FOR THE SABOTAGE...
...I DON'T THINK SO.
FINISH
CREDO

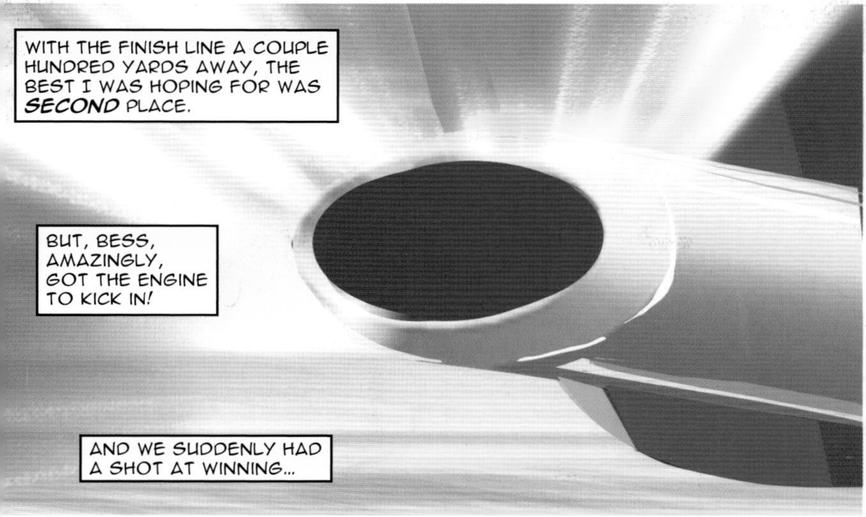
WITH THE FINISH LINE A COUPLE HUNDRED YARDS AWAY, THE BEST I WAS HOPING FOR WAS *SECOND* PLACE.
BUT, BESS, AMAZINGLY, GOT THE ENGINE TO KICK IN!
AND WE SUDDENLY HAD A SHOT AT WINNING...

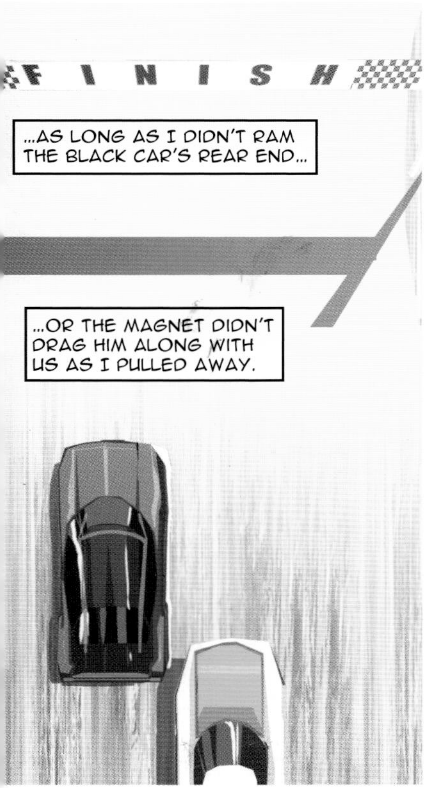
FINISH
...AS LONG AS I DIDN'T RAM THE BLACK CAR'S REAR END...
...OR THE MAGNET DIDN'T DRAG HIM ALONG WITH US AS I PULLED AWAY.

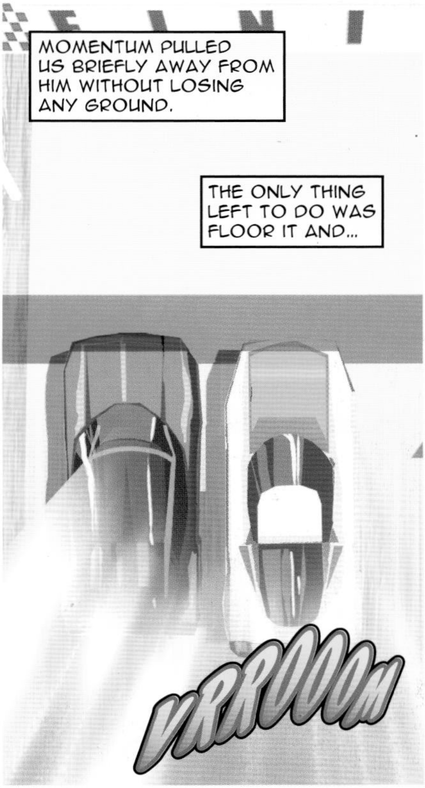
MOMENTUM PULLED US BRIEFLY AWAY FROM HIM WITHOUT LOSING ANY GROUND.
THE ONLY THING LEFT TO DO WAS FLOOR IT AND...
VRRROOOM

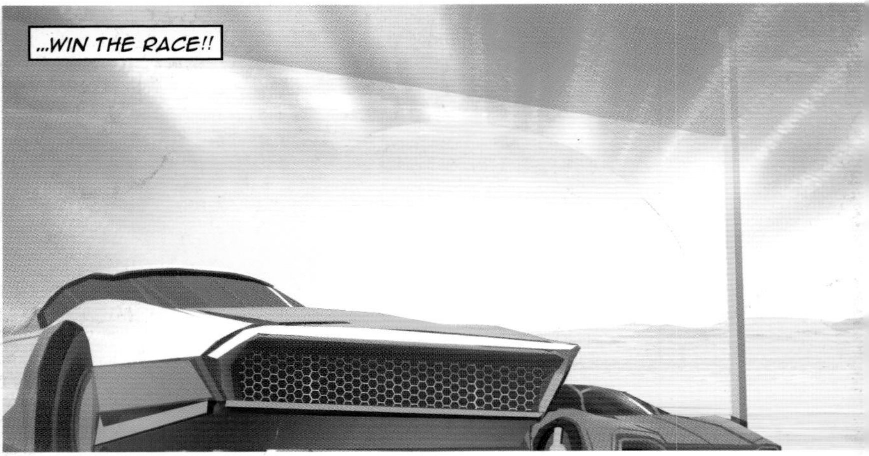
...WIN THE RACE!!

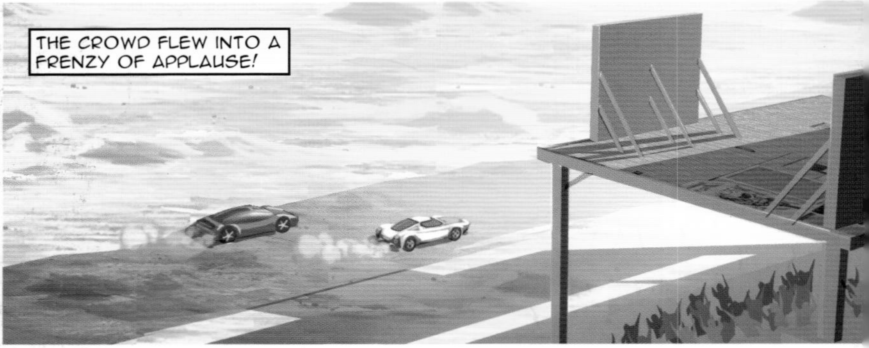
THE CROWD FLEW INTO A FRENZY OF APPLAUSE!

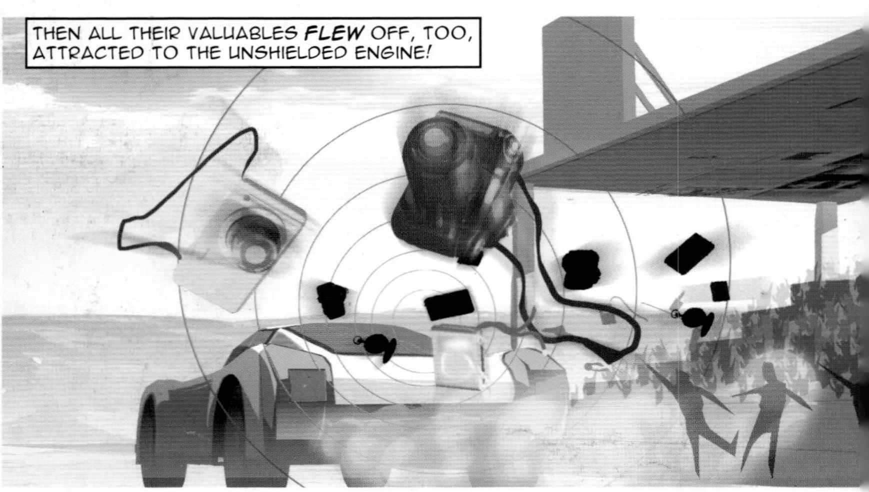
THEN ALL THEIR VALUABLES FLEW OFF, TOO, ATTRACTED TO THE UNSHIELDED ENGINE!

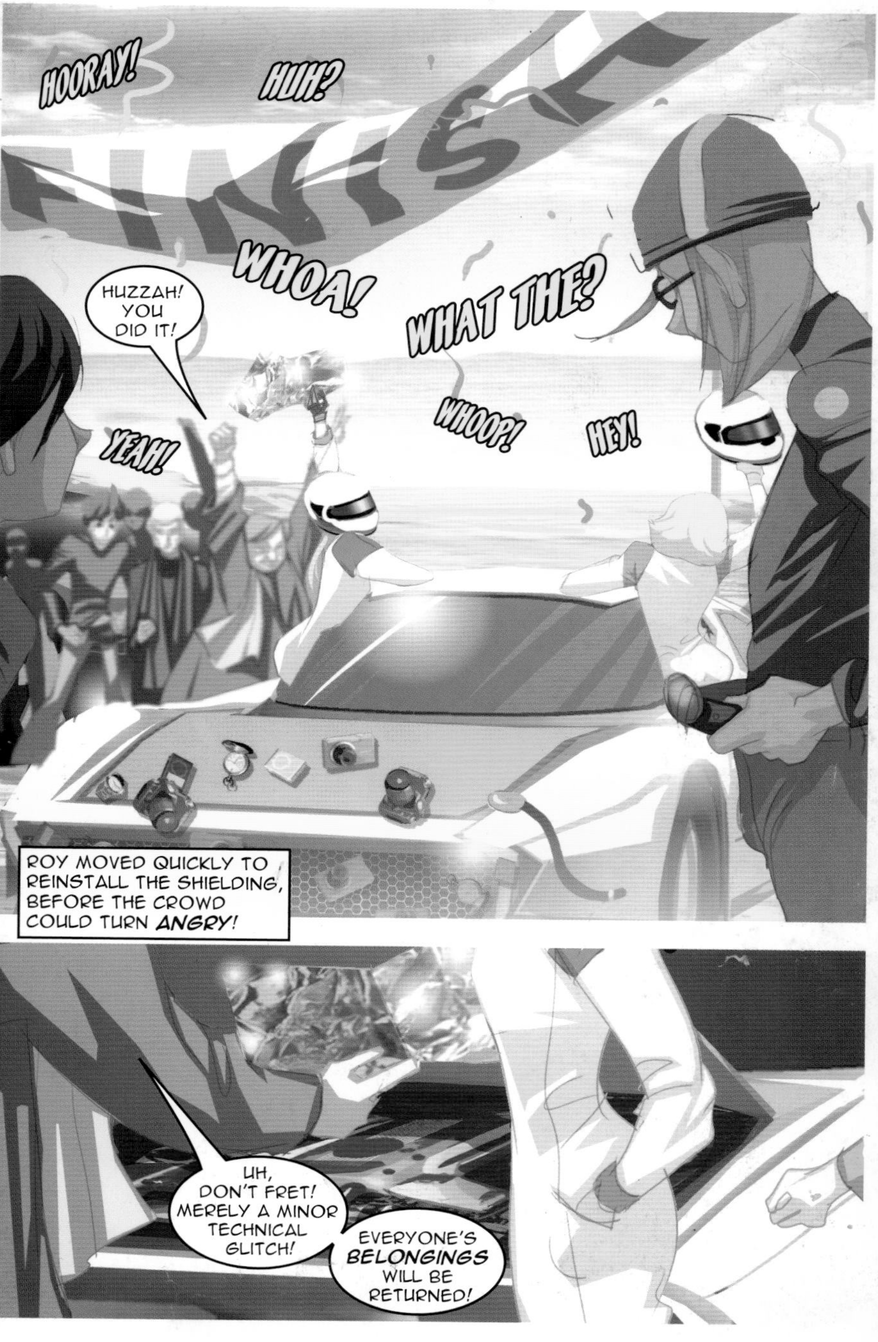
HOORAY!
HUH?
WHOA!
WHAT THE?
HUZZAH! YOU DID IT!
YEAH!
WHOOP!
HEY!
ROY MOVED QUICKLY TO REINSTALL THE SHIELDING, BEFORE THE CROWD COULD TURN ANGRY!
UH, DON'T FRET! MERELY A MINOR TECHNICAL GLITCH!
EVERYONE'S BELONGINGS WILL BE RETURNED!

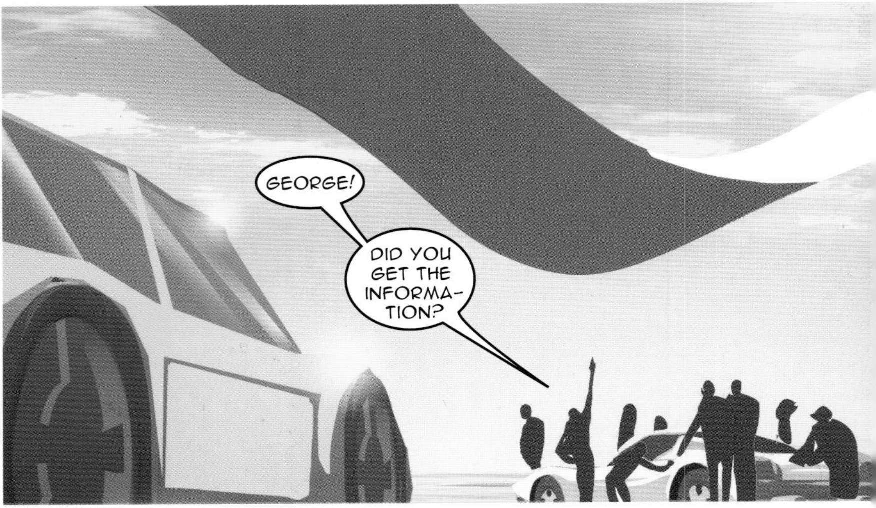
GEORGE!
DID YOU GET THE INFORMATION?

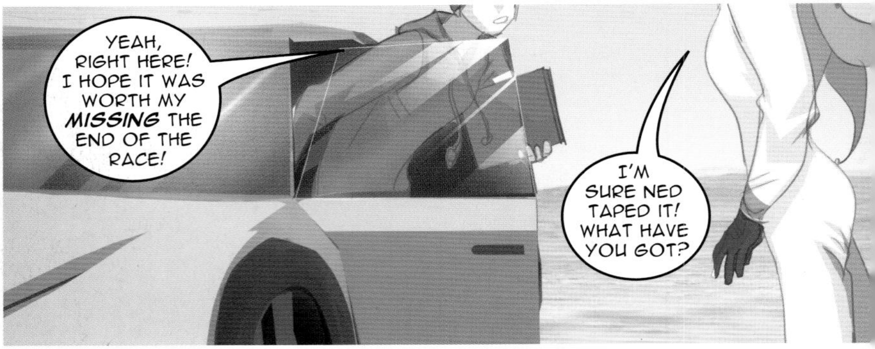
YEAH, RIGHT HERE! I HOPE IT WAS WORTH MY *MISSING* THE END OF THE RACE!
I'M SURE NED TAPED IT! WHAT HAVE YOU GOT?

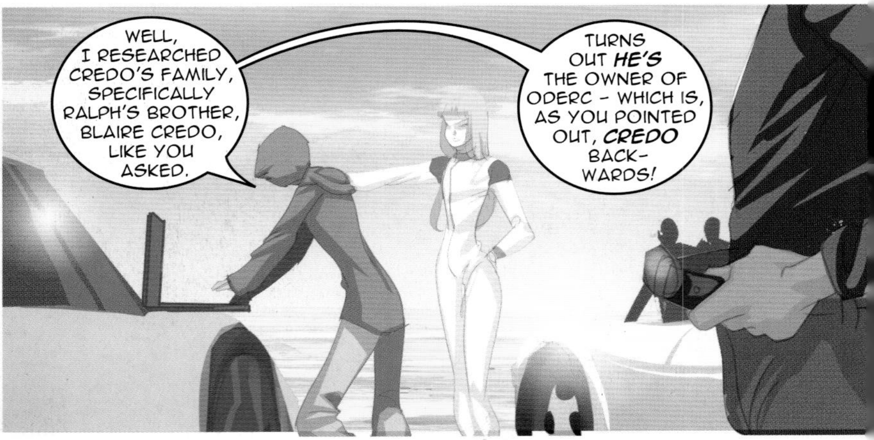
WELL, I RESEARCHED CREDO'S FAMILY, SPECIFICALLY RALPH'S BROTHER, BLAIRE CREDO, LIKE YOU ASKED.
TURNS OUT *HE'S* THE OWNER OF ODERC - WHICH IS, AS YOU POINTED OUT, *CREDO* BACK-WARDS!

HOW'S THAT FOR A KICK IN THE HEAD?!

OUR SABOTEUR WAS *CREDO*, HIMSELF, ALL ALONG!

OOP! FLYING LAPTOP...

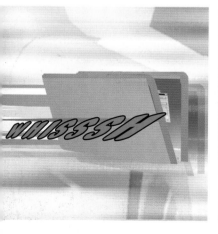

WHOOSSH

THIS OUGHT TO DO IT.

SLAMMM

EXCEPT MAYBE FOR *THAT*.

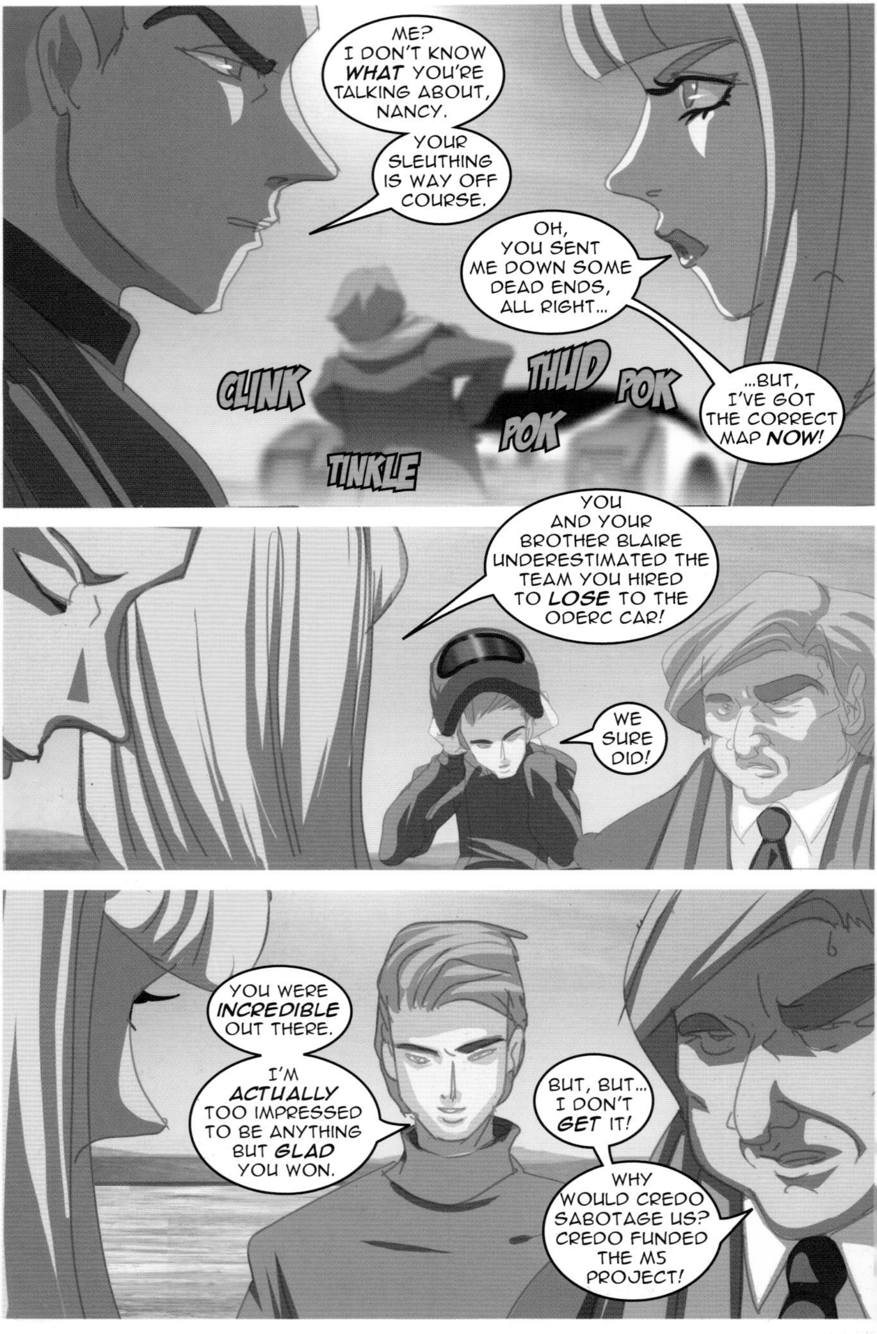
ME?
I DON'T KNOW WHAT YOU'RE TALKING ABOUT, NANCY.
YOUR SLEUTHING IS WAY OFF COURSE.
OH, YOU SENT ME DOWN SOME DEAD ENDS, ALL RIGHT...
CLINK
THUD
POK
POK
TINKLE
...BUT, I'VE GOT THE CORRECT MAP NOW!
YOU AND YOUR BROTHER BLAIRE UNDERESTIMATED THE TEAM YOU HIRED TO LOSE TO THE ODERC CAR!
WE SURE DID!
YOU WERE INCREDIBLE OUT THERE.
I'M ACTUALLY TOO IMPRESSED TO BE ANYTHING BUT GLAD YOU WON.
BUT, BUT... I DON'T GET IT!
WHY WOULD CREDO SABOTAGE US? CREDO FUNDED THE M5 PROJECT!

SEE NANCY DREW GRAPHIC NOVELS #9 AND #10.

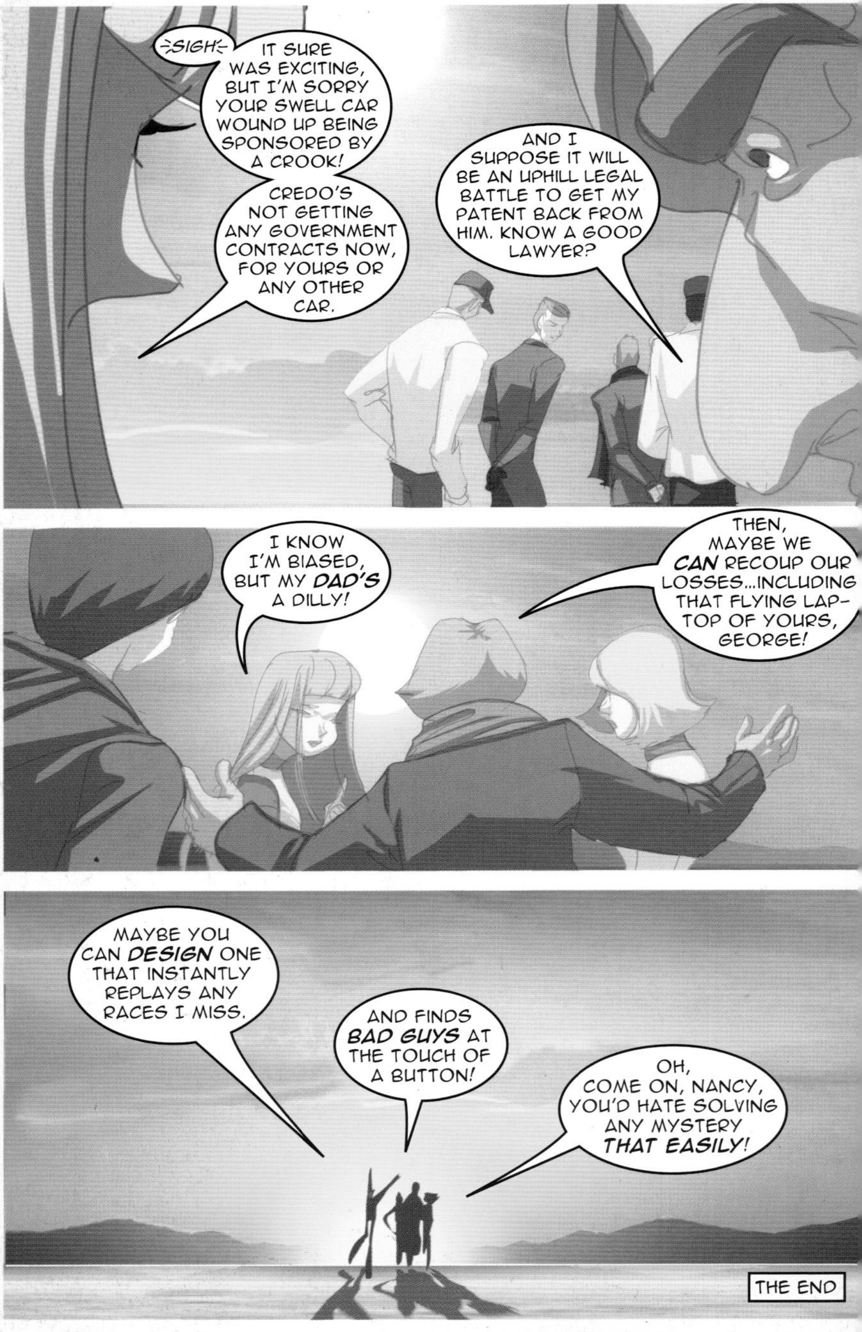
SIGH
IT SURE WAS EXCITING, BUT I'M SORRY YOUR SWELL CAR WOUND UP BEING SPONSORED BY A CROOK!
CREDO'S NOT GETTING ANY GOVERNMENT CONTRACTS NOW, FOR YOURS OR ANY OTHER CAR.
AND I SUPPOSE IT WILL BE AN UPHILL LEGAL BATTLE TO GET MY PATENT BACK FROM HIM. KNOW A GOOD LAWYER?
I KNOW I'M BIASED, BUT MY DAD'S A DILLY!
THEN, MAYBE WE CAN RECOUP OUR LOSSES...INCLUDING THAT FLYING LAP-TOP OF YOURS, GEORGE!
MAYBE YOU CAN DESIGN ONE THAT INSTANTLY REPLAYS ANY RACES I MISS.
AND FINDS BAD GUYS AT THE TOUCH OF A BUTTON!
OH, COME ON, NANCY, YOU'D HATE SOLVING ANY MYSTERY THAT EASILY!
THE END

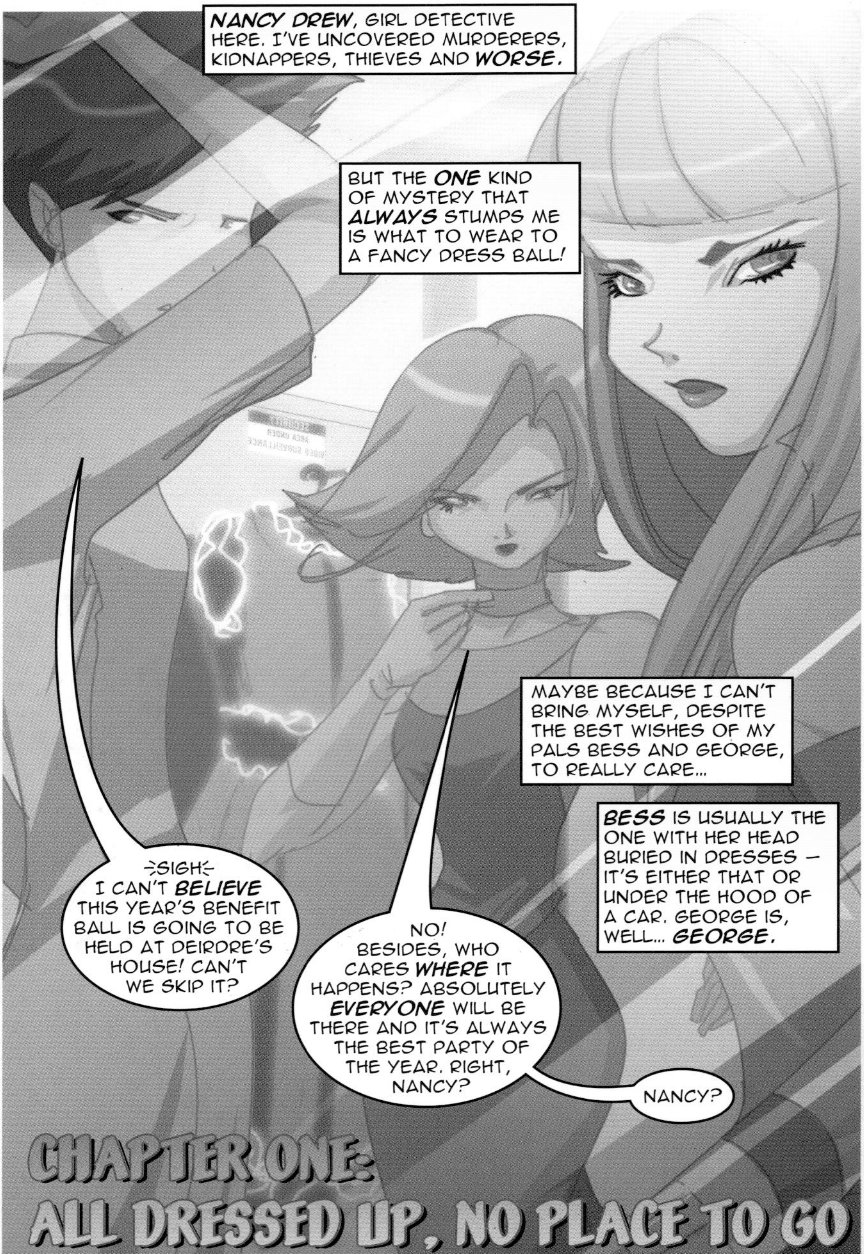
NANCY DREW, GIRL DETECTIVE HERE. I'VE UNCOVERED MURDERERS, KIDNAPPERS, THIEVES AND WORSE.
BUT THE ONE KIND OF MYSTERY THAT ALWAYS STUMPS ME IS WHAT TO WEAR TO A FANCY DRESS BALL!
SECURITY AREA UNDER VIDEO SURVEILLANCE
MAYBE BECAUSE I CAN'T BRING MYSELF, DESPITE THE BEST WISHES OF MY PALS BESS AND GEORGE, TO REALLY CARE...
BESS IS USUALLY THE ONE WITH HER HEAD BURIED IN DRESSES – IT'S EITHER THAT OR UNDER THE HOOD OF A CAR. GEORGE IS, WELL... GEORGE.
SIGH I CAN'T BELIEVE THIS YEAR'S BENEFIT BALL IS GOING TO BE HELD AT DEIRDRE'S HOUSE! CAN'T WE SKIP IT?
NO! BESIDES, WHO CARES WHERE IT HAPPENS? ABSOLUTELY EVERYONE WILL BE THERE AND IT'S ALWAYS THE BEST PARTY OF THE YEAR. RIGHT, NANCY?
NANCY?
CHAPTER ONE:
ALL DRESSED UP, NO PLACE TO GO

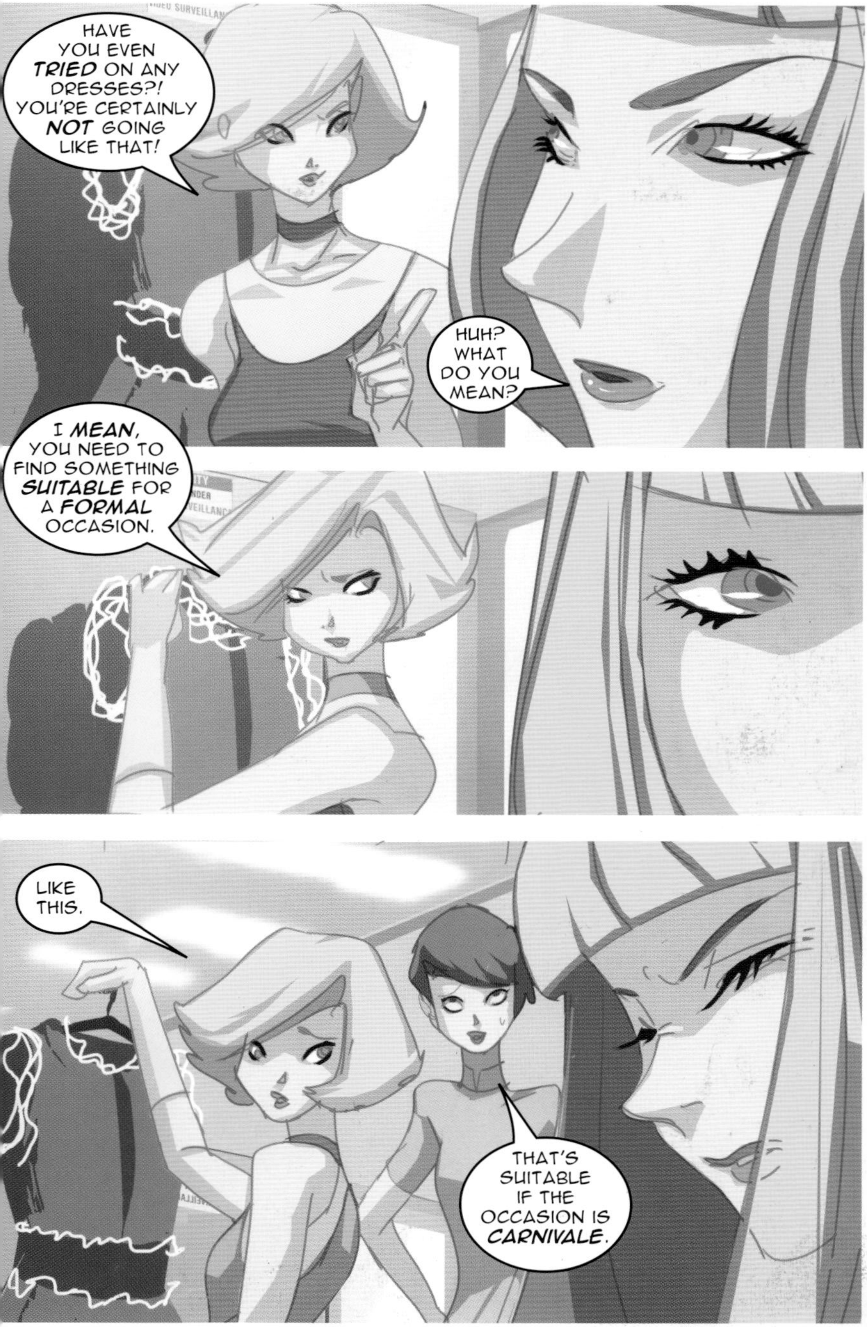
HAVE YOU EVEN TRIED ON ANY DRESSES?! YOU'RE CERTAINLY NOT GOING LIKE THAT!
HUH? WHAT DO YOU MEAN?
I MEAN, YOU NEED TO FIND SOMETHING SUITABLE FOR A FORMAL OCCASION.
LIKE THIS.
THAT'S SUITABLE IF THE OCCASION IS CARNIVALE.

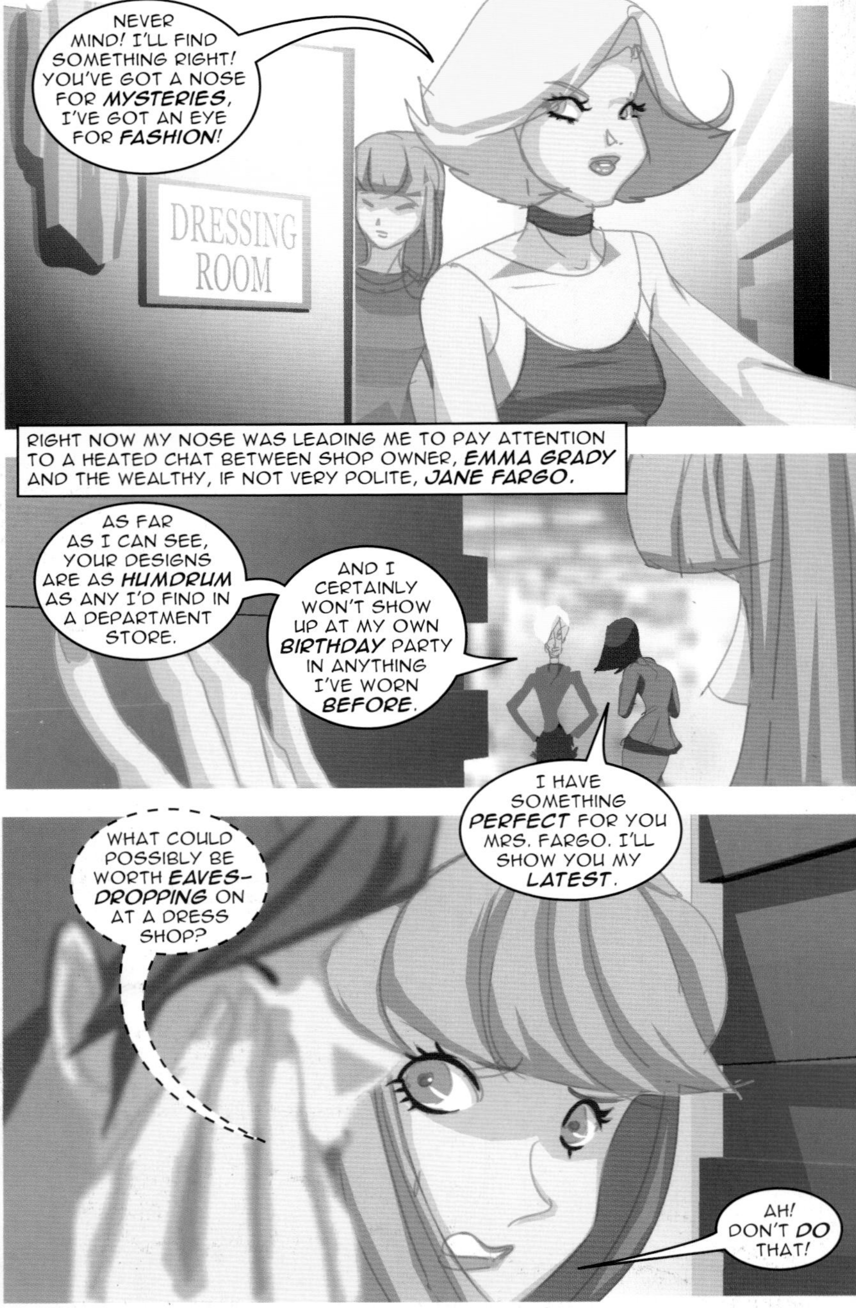
NEVER MIND! I'LL FIND SOMETHING RIGHT! YOU'VE GOT A NOSE FOR MYSTERIES, I'VE GOT AN EYE FOR FASHION!
DRESSING ROOM
RIGHT NOW MY NOSE WAS LEADING ME TO PAY ATTENTION TO A HEATED CHAT BETWEEN SHOP OWNER, EMMA GRADY AND THE WEALTHY, IF NOT VERY POLITE, JANE FARGO.
AS FAR AS I CAN SEE, YOUR DESIGNS ARE AS HUMDRUM AS ANY I'D FIND IN A DEPARTMENT STORE.
AND I CERTAINLY WON'T SHOW UP AT MY OWN BIRTHDAY PARTY IN ANYTHING I'VE WORN BEFORE.
I HAVE SOMETHING PERFECT FOR YOU MRS. FARGO. I'LL SHOW YOU MY LATEST.
WHAT COULD POSSIBLY BE WORTH EAVES-DROPPING ON AT A DRESS SHOP?
AH! DON'T DO THAT!

DON'T MISS NANCY DREW GRAPHIC NOVEL # 12 – "DRESS REVERSAL"

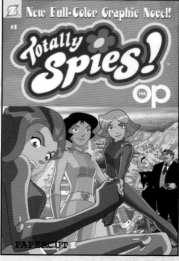
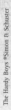

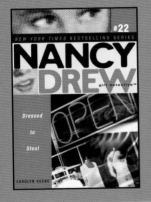

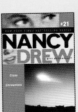

WATCH OUT FOR PAPERCUTZ

Hi, it's me, good ol' Jim Salicrup again with another jam-packed edition of the Papercutz Backpages. We've got more unbelievably shocking news, so I hope you're sitting down. Last time, we revealed that Papercutz had obtained the exclusive rights to create and publish all-new TALES FROM THE CRYPT comicbooks and graphic novels, and we're still feeling the shockwaves from that bombshell announcement! This time around, we're trumpeting the return of yet another world-famous comicbook title-CLASSICS ILLUSTRATED!

We'll fill you in on why that's such an awesome big deal in the following pages, but right now I need a moment to take it all in. You see, even though I've been in the world of comics for thirty-five years, I'm still very much the same comicbook fan I was when I was a kid! And if my partner, Papercutz Publisher, Terry Nantier, were to magically go back in time, and tell 13 year-old Jim Salicrup that he was going to one day be the editor of NANCY DREW, THE HARDY BOYS, TALES FROM THE CRYPT, and CLASSICS ILLUSTRATED, he'd think Terry was out of his mind!

Let's get real. Back then I'd see CLASSICS ILLUSTRATED comics in their own display rack, apart from all the other comicbooks, at my favorite soda shoppe in the Bronx. Each issue featured a comics adaptation of a classic novel-that's why they called it CLASSICS ILLUSTRATED. But unlike other comicbooks, these were bigger, containing 48 pages per book; cost a quarter, more than twice as much as a regular 12 cent comic; and stayed on sale forever, as opposed to the other comics which were gone in a month. Clearly, these comics were something special.

Bah, I can take a gazillion moments, but this is still way too humungous an event for my puny brain to fully absorb, so I'm going to give up trying and accept that we here at Papercutz must be doing something right to be entrusted with Comicdom's crown jewels! So no more looking back--time to focus on the future. That means doing everything we can to make sure these titles live up to their proud heritage, while gaining a whole new generation of fans. As usual, you can contact me at salicrup@papercutz.com or Jim Salicrup, PAPERCUTZ, 40 Exchange Place, Ste. 1308, New York, NY 10005 and let us know how we're doing. After all, we want you to be as excited about Papercutz as we are!

Thanks,

Jim

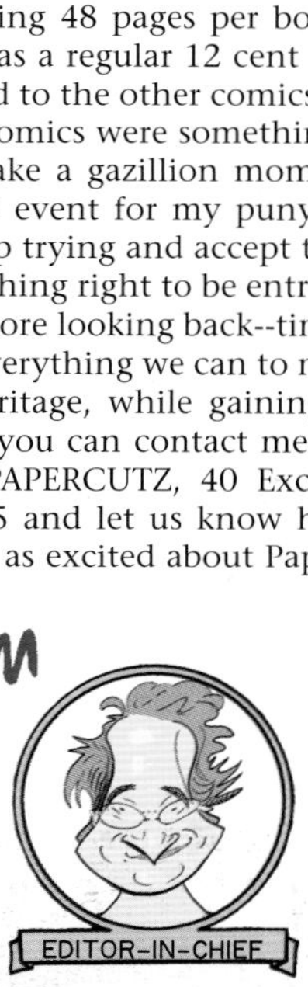
EDITOR-IN-CHIEF

CLASSICS
Illustrated

Featuring Stories by the World's Greatest Authors

Returns in two new series from Papercutz!

The original, best-selling series of comics adaptations of the world's greatest literature, CLASSICS ILLUSTRATED, returns in two new formats--the original, featuring abridged adaptations of classic novels, and CLASSICS ILLUSTRATED DELUXE, featuring longer, more expansive adaptations-from graphic novel publisher Papercutz. "We're very proud to say that Papercutz has received such an enthusiastic reception from librarians and school teachers for its NANCY DREW and HARDY BOYS graphic novels as well as THE LIFE OF POPE JOHN PAUL II...*IN COMICS!*, that it only seemed logical for us to bring back the original CLASSICS ILLUSTRATED comicbook series beloved by parents, educators, and librarians," explained Papercutz Publisher, Terry Nantier. "We can't thank the enlightened librarians and teachers who have supported Papercutz enough. And we're thrilled that they're so excited about CLASSICS ILLUSTRATED."

Upcoming titles include The Invisible Man, Tales from the Brothers Grimm, and Robinson Crusoe.

FULL-COLOR GRAPHIC NOVEL ADAPTATION

CLASSICS *Illustrated* Deluxe

THE WIND IN THE WILLOWS

By Kenneth Grahame

Adapted by Michel Plessix

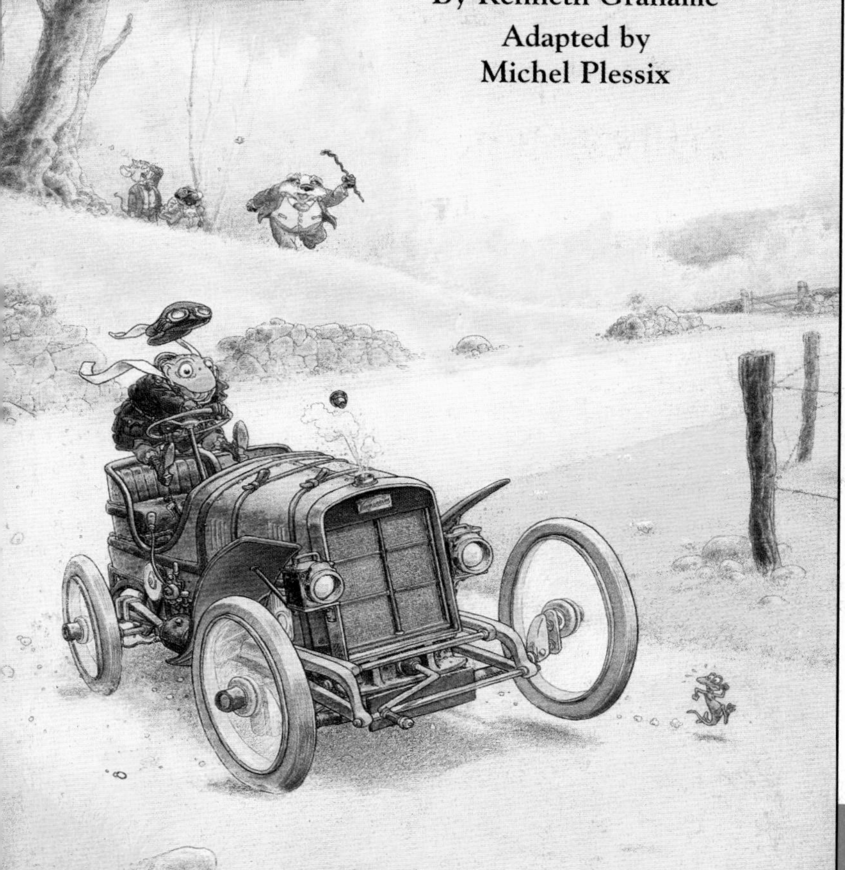

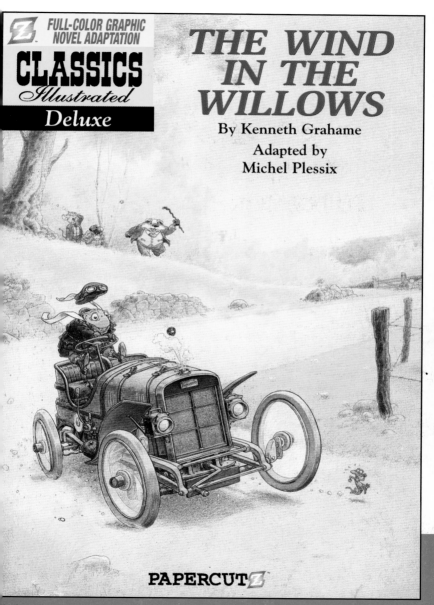

PAPERCUTZ

A Short History of
CLASSICS ILLUSTRATED...

William B. Jones Jr. is the author of Classics Illustrated: A Cultural History, which offers a comprehensive overview of the original comic-book series and the writers, artists, editors, and publishers behind-the-scenes. With Mr. Jones Jr.'s kind permission, here's a very short overview of the history of CLASSICS ILLUSTRATED adapted from his 2005 essay on Albert Kanter.

CLASSICS ILLUSTRATED was the creation of Albert Lewis Kanter, a visionary publisher, who from 1941 to 1971, introduced young readers worldwide to the realms of literature, history, folklore, mythology, and science in over 200 titles in such comicbook series as CLASSICS ILLUSTRATED and CLASSICS ILLUSTRATED JUNIOR. Kanter, inspired by the success of the first comicbooks published in the early 30s and late 40s, believed he

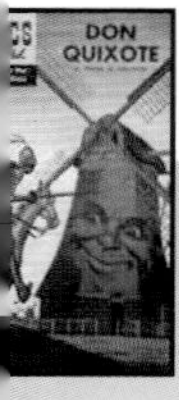
DON
QUIXOTE
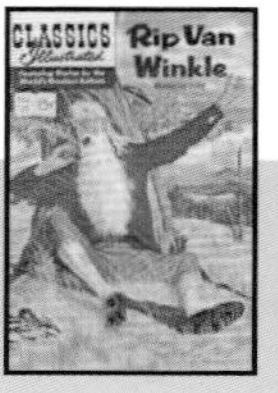
CLASSICS Illustrated
Rip Van
Winkle
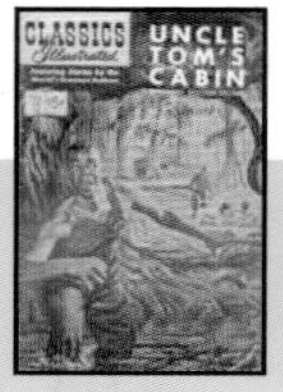
CLASSICS Illustrated
UNCLE
TOM'S
CABIN
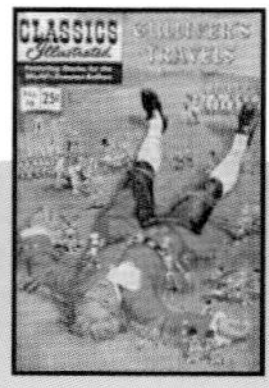
CLASSICS Illustrated
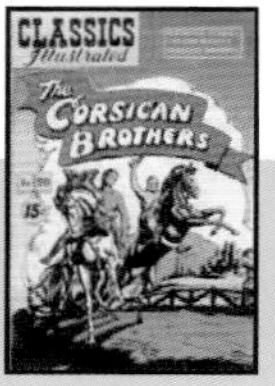
CLASSICS Illustrated
The
CORSICAN
BROTHERS
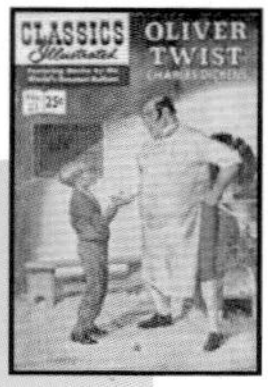
CLASSICS Illustrated
OLIVER
TWIST

could use the same medium to introduce young readers to the world of great literature. CLASSIC COMICS (later changed to CLASSICS ILLUSTRATED in 1947) was launched in 1941, and soon the comicbook adaptations of Shakespeare, Stevenson, Twain, Verne, and other authors, were being used in schools and endorsed by educators.

CLASSICS ILLUSTRATED was translated and distributed in countries such as Canada, Great Britain, the Netherlands, Greece, Brazil, Mexico, and Australia. The genial publisher was hailed abroad as "Papa Kassiker." By the beginning of the 1960s, CLASSICS ILLUSTRATED was the largest childrens publication in the world. The original CLASSICS ILLUSTRATED series adapted into comics 169 titles; among these were Frankenstein, 20,000 Leagues Under the Sea, Treasure Island, Julius Caesar, and Faust.

Albert L. Kanter died, March 17, 1973, leaving behind a rich legacy for the millions of readers whose imaginations were awakened by CLASSICS ILLUSTRATED.

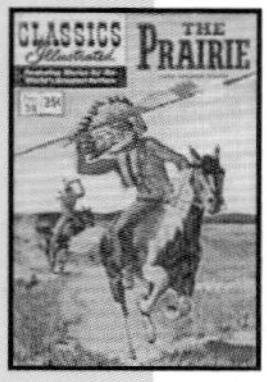
CLASSICS Illustrated
THE
PRAIRIE
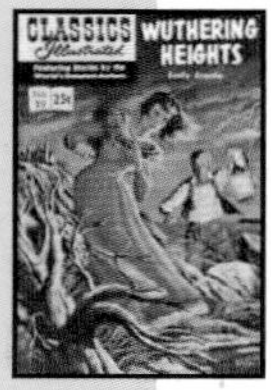
CLASSICS Illustrated
WUTHERING
HEIGHTS
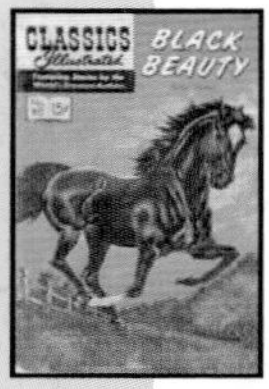
CLASSICS Illustrated
BLACK
BEAUTY
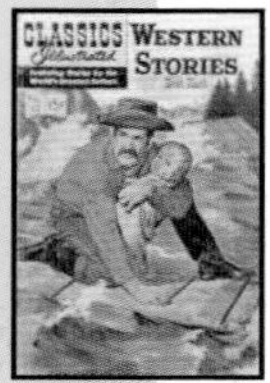
CLASSICS Illustrated
WESTERN
STORIES
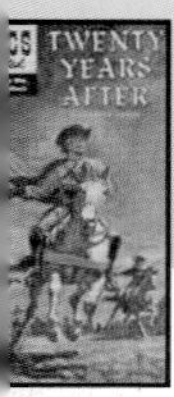
TWENTY
YEARS
AFTER
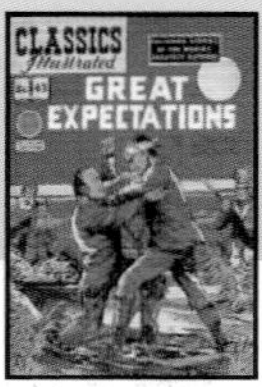
CLASSICS Illustrated
GREAT
EXPECTATIONS
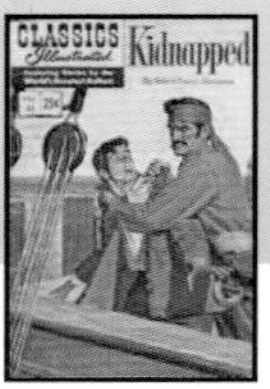
CLASSICS Illustrated
Kidnapped
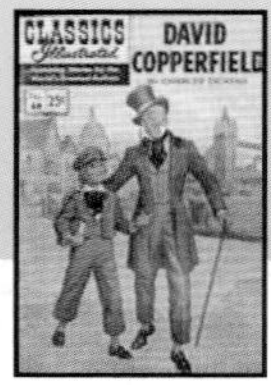
CLASSICS Illustrated
DAVID
COPPERFIELD
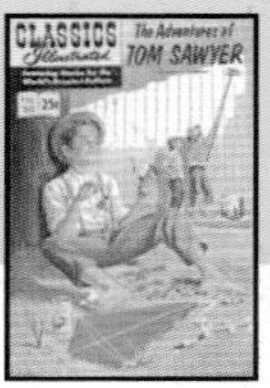
CLASSICS Illustrated
The Adventures of
TOM SAWYER
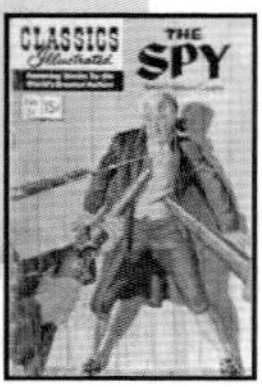
CLASSICS Illustrated
THE
SPY

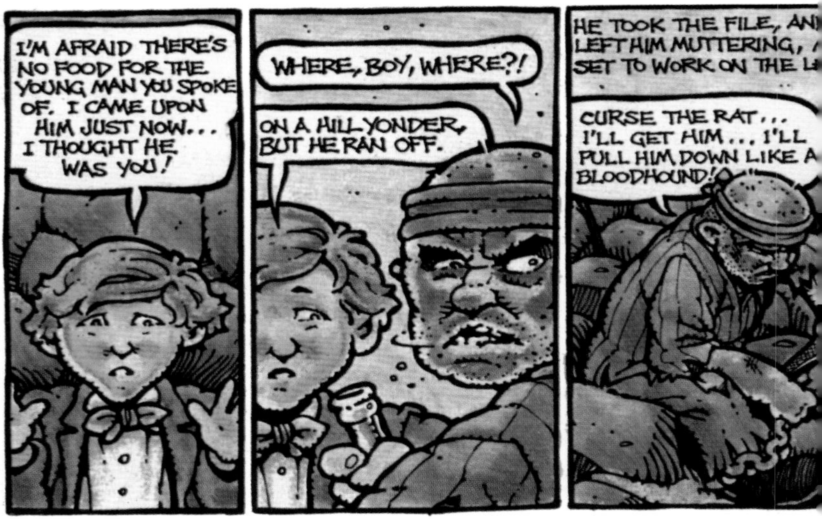
I'M AFRAID THERE'S NO FOOD FOR THE YOUNG MAN YOU SPOKE OF. I CAME UPON HIM JUST NOW... I THOUGHT HE WAS YOU!
WHERE, BOY, WHERE?!
ON A HILL YONDER, BUT HE RAN OFF.
HE TOOK THE FILE, AN
LEFT HIM MUTTERING,
SET TO WORK ON THE L
CURSE THE RAT... I'LL GET HIM..., I'LL PULL HIM DOWN LIKE A BLOODHOUND!

CLASSICS ILLUSTRATED was re-launched in 1990 in graphic novel/book form by the Berkley Publishing Group and First Publishing, Inc. featuring all-new adaptations by such top graphic novelists as Rick Geary, Bill Sienkiewicz, Kyle Baker, Gahan Wilson, and others. "First had the right idea, they just came out about 15 years too soon. Now bookstores are ready for graphic novels such as these," Jim explains. Many of these excellent adaptations have been acquired by Papercutz and will make up the new series of CLASSICS ILLUSTRATED titles.

The first volume of the new CLASSICS ILLUSTRATED series presents graphic novelist Rick Geary's adaptation of "Great Expectations" by Charles Dickens. The bittersweet tale of one boy's adolescence, and of the choices he makes to shape his destiny. Into an engrossing mystery, Dickens weaves a heartfelt inquiry into morals and virtues-as the orphan Pip, the convict Magwitch, the beautiful Estella, the bitter Miss Havisham, the goodhearted Biddy, the kind Joe and other memorable characters entwine in a battle of human nature. Rick Geary's delightful illustrations capture the newfound awe and frustrations of young Pip as he comes of age, and begins to understand the opportunities that life presents.

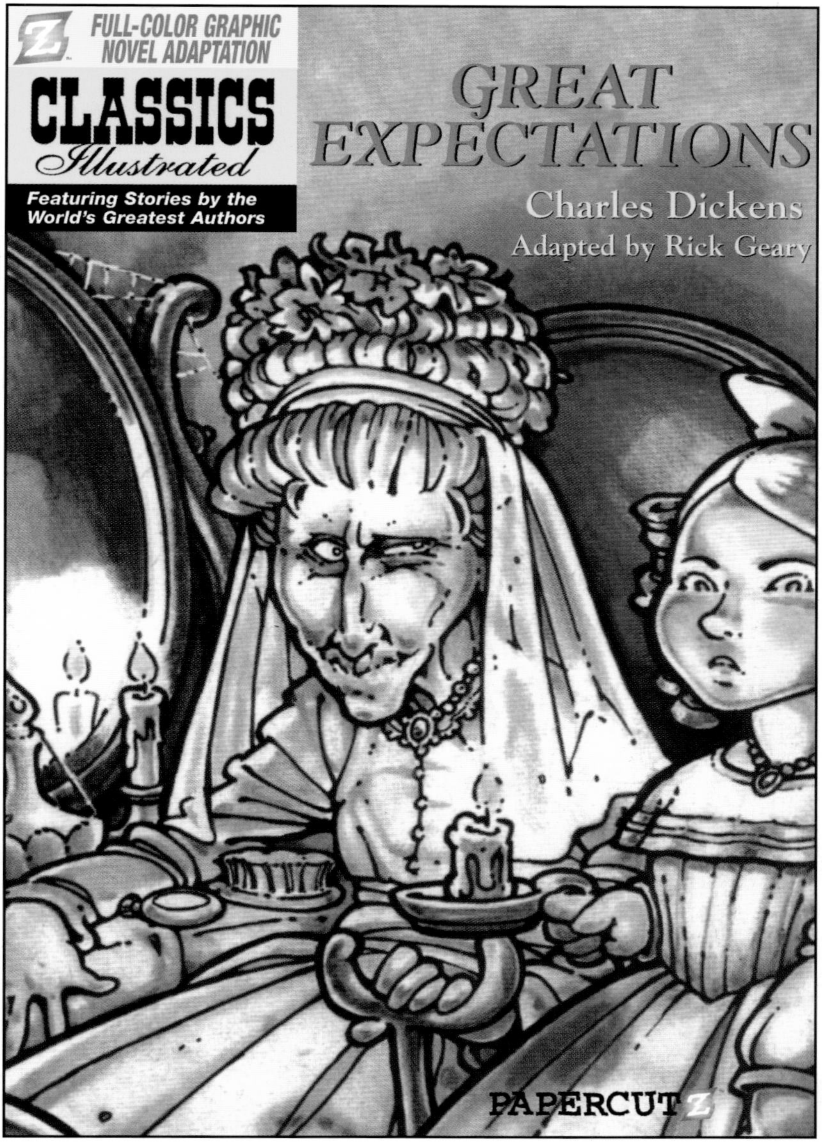
FULL-COLOR GRAPHIC NOVEL ADAPTATION
CLASSICS Illustrated
Featuring Stories by the World's Greatest Authors
GREAT EXPECTATIONS
Charles Dickens
Adapted by Rick Geary
PAPERCUTZ

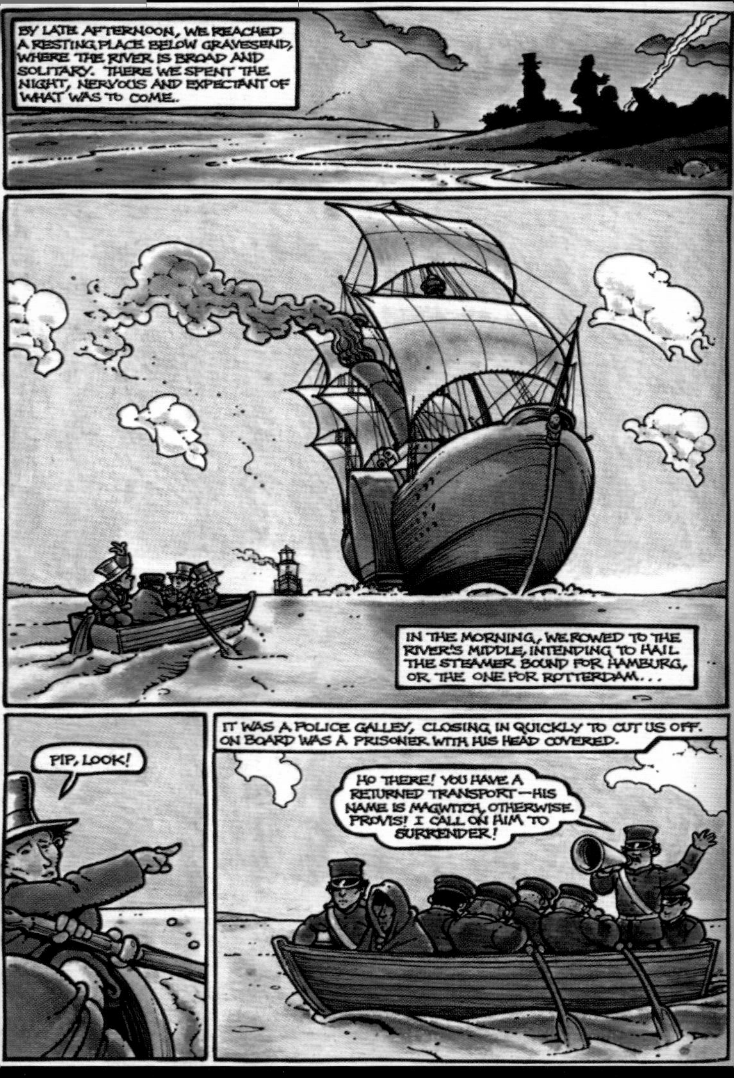
BY LATE AFTERNOON, WE REACHED A RESTING PLACE BELOW GRAVESEND, WHERE THE RIVER IS BROAD AND SOLITARY. THERE WE SPENT THE NIGHT, NERVOUS AND EXPECTANT OF WHAT WAS TO COME.
IN THE MORNING, WE ROWED TO THE RIVER'S MIDDLE, INTENDING TO HAIL THE STEAMER BOUND FOR HAMBURG, OR THE ONE FOR ROTTERDAM...
PIP, LOOK!
IT WAS A POLICE GALLEY, CLOSING IN QUICKLY TO CUT US OFF. ON BOARD WAS A PRISONER WITH HIS HEAD COVERED.
HO THERE! YOU HAVE A RETURNED TRANSPORT—HIS NAME IS MAGWITCH, OTHERWISE PROVIS! I CALL ON HIM TO SURRENDER!

Iere are two preview pages of CLASSICS ILLUSTRATED #1 "Gre
xpectations" by Charles Dickens, as adapted by Rick Geary. (CLA
ICS ILLUSTRATED will be printed in a larger 6 1/2" x 9" format, s
he art will be bigger than what you see here.)

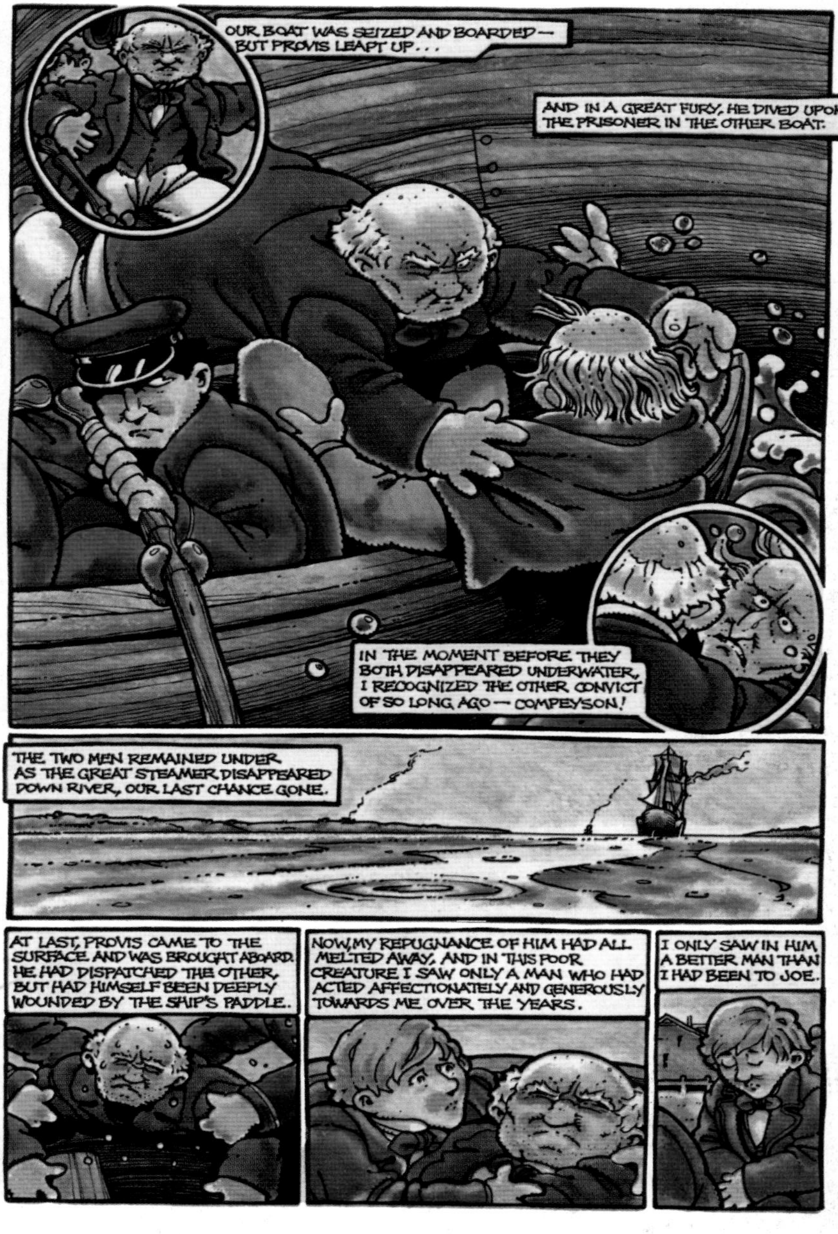
OUR BOAT WAS SEIZED AND BOARDED— BUT PROVIS LEAPT UP...
AND IN A GREAT FURY, HE DIVED UPON THE PRISONER IN THE OTHER BOAT.
IN THE MOMENT BEFORE THEY BOTH DISAPPEARED UNDERWATER, I RECOGNIZED THE OTHER CONVICT OF SO LONG AGO — COMPEYSON!
THE TWO MEN REMAINED UNDER AS THE GREAT STEAMER DISAPPEARED DOWN RIVER, OUR LAST CHANCE GONE.
AT LAST, PROVIS CAME TO THE SURFACE AND WAS BROUGHT ABOARD. HE HAD DISPATCHED THE OTHER, BUT HAD HIMSELF BEEN DEEPLY WOUNDED BY THE SHIP'S PADDLE.
NOW, MY REPUGNANCE OF HIM HAD ALL MELTED AWAY, AND IN THIS POOR CREATURE I SAW ONLY A MAN WHO HAD ACTED AFFECTIONATELY AND GENEROUSLY TOWARDS ME OVER THE YEARS.
I ONLY SAW IN HIM A BETTER MAN THAN I HAD BEEN TO JOE.

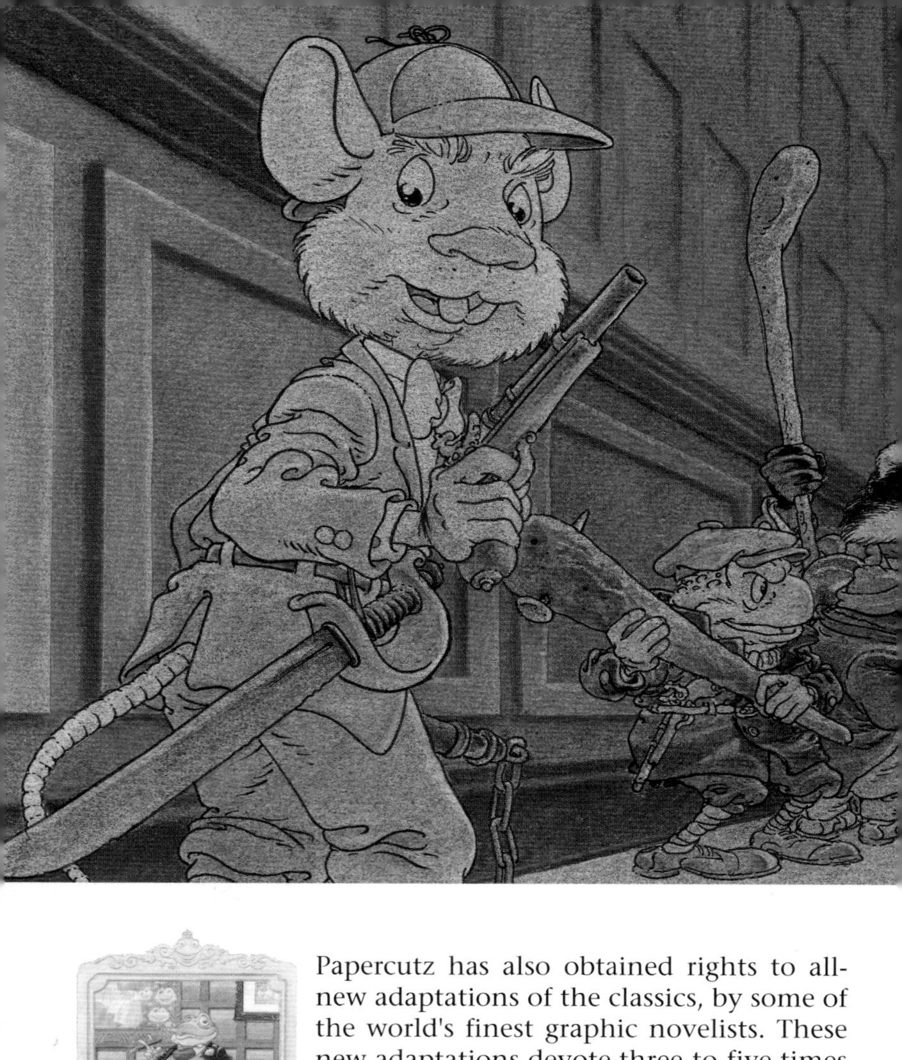

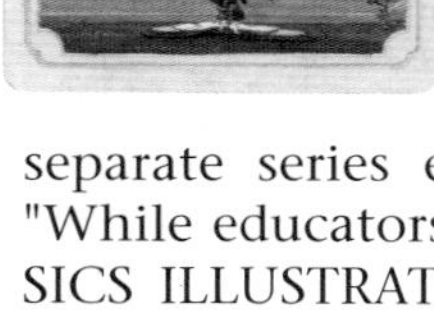

Papercutz has also obtained rights to all-new adaptations of the classics, by some of the world's finest graphic novelists. These new adaptations devote three-to-five times as many comics pages as the previous series to more fully capture the depth of the original novels. These adaptations will run as a separate series entitled CLASSICS ILLUSTRATED DELUXE. "While educators are thrilled that we're bringing back CLASSICS ILLUSTRATED, comic art fans are going to appreciate just how beautiful these books are," Jim opines.

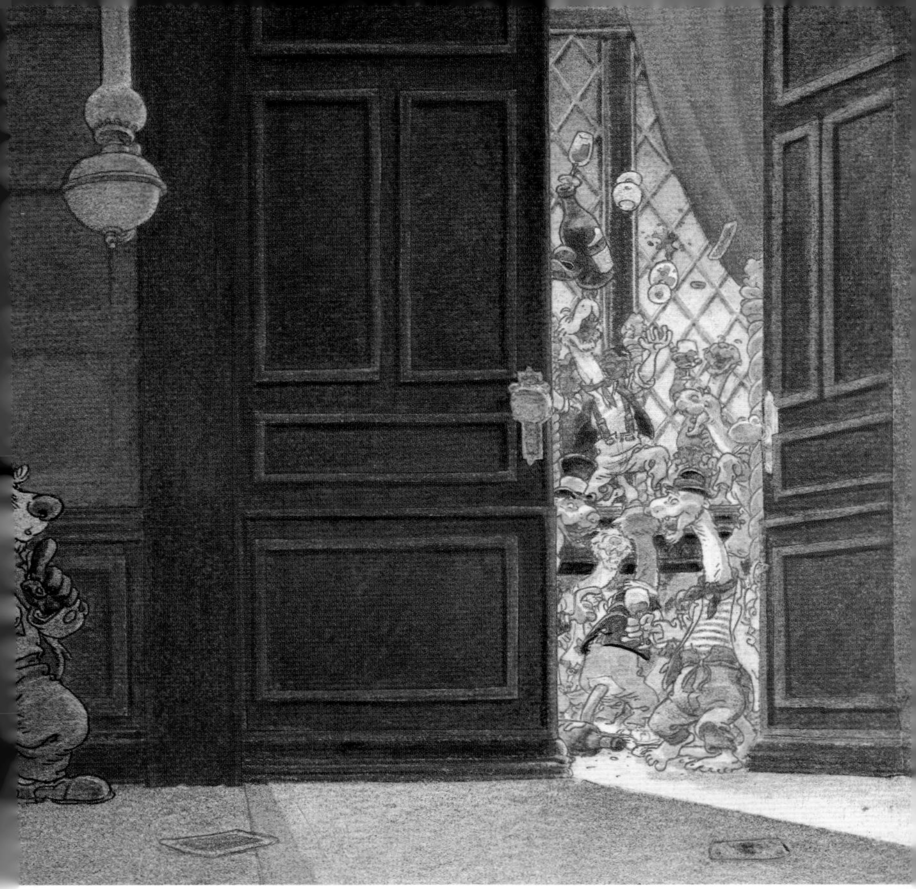

CLASSICS ILLUSTRATED DELUXE #1 presents graphic novelist Michel Plessix's lush adaptation of "The Wind in the Willows" by Kenneth Grahame. The artwork is in aquarelle, with thin, precise, detailed lines. In “Wind in the Willows,” Plessix breathes life into Mole, Rat, and Toad (of Toad Hall) as they picnic on the riverbank, indulge in Toad's latest fad, and get lost in Wild Wood. The pacing is masterful: each panel lingers just long enough to make you appreciate the simple pleasures of life. Originally published in four volumes, Papercutz is proud to collect the entire series, for the very first time, in one affordable volume.

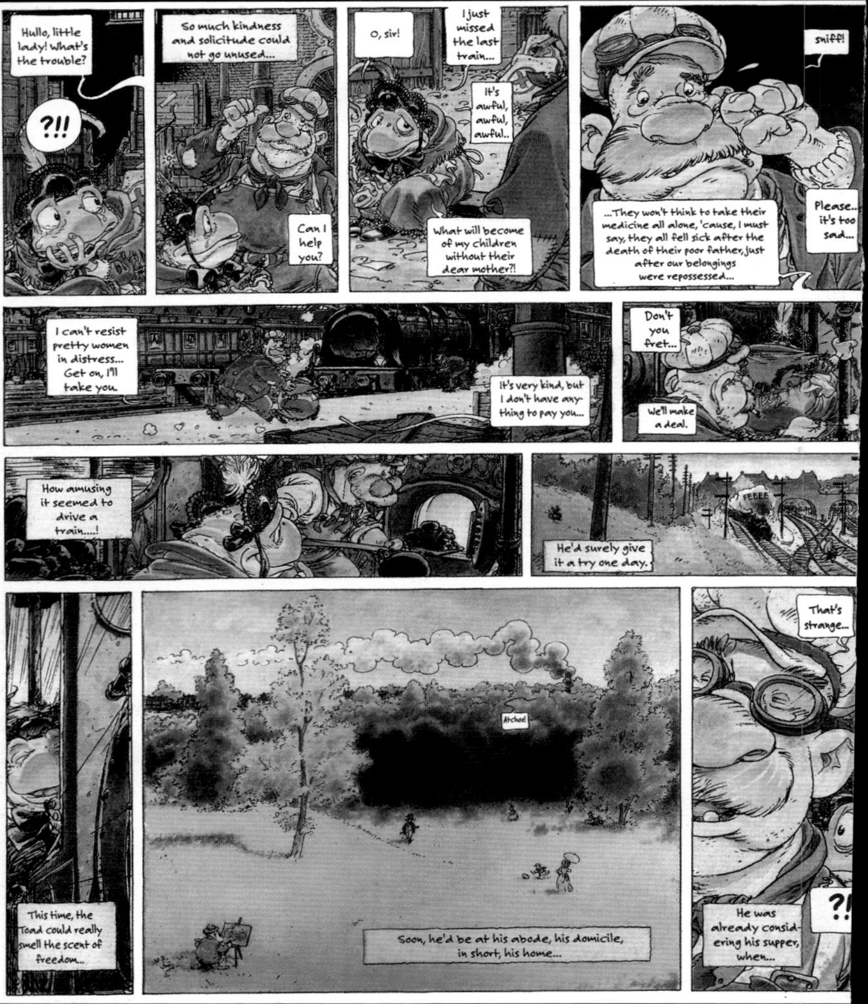
Hullo, little lady! What's the trouble?
?!!
So much kindness and solicitude could not go unused...
Can I help you?
O, sir!
I just missed the last train...
It's awful, awful, awful...
What will become of my children without their dear mother?!
sniff!
...They won't think to take their medicine all alone, 'cause, I must say, they all fell sick after the death of their poor father, just after our belongings were repossessed...
Please... it's too sad...
I can't resist pretty women in distress... Get on, I'll take you.
It's very kind, but I don't have any-thing to pay you...
Don't you fret...
We'll make a deal.
How amusing it seemed to drive a train....!
FEEEE
He'd surely give it a try one day.
This time, the Toad could really smell the scent of freedom...
Atchoo!
Soon, he'd be at his abode, his domicile, in short, his home...
That's strange...
He was already consid-ering his supper, when...
?!

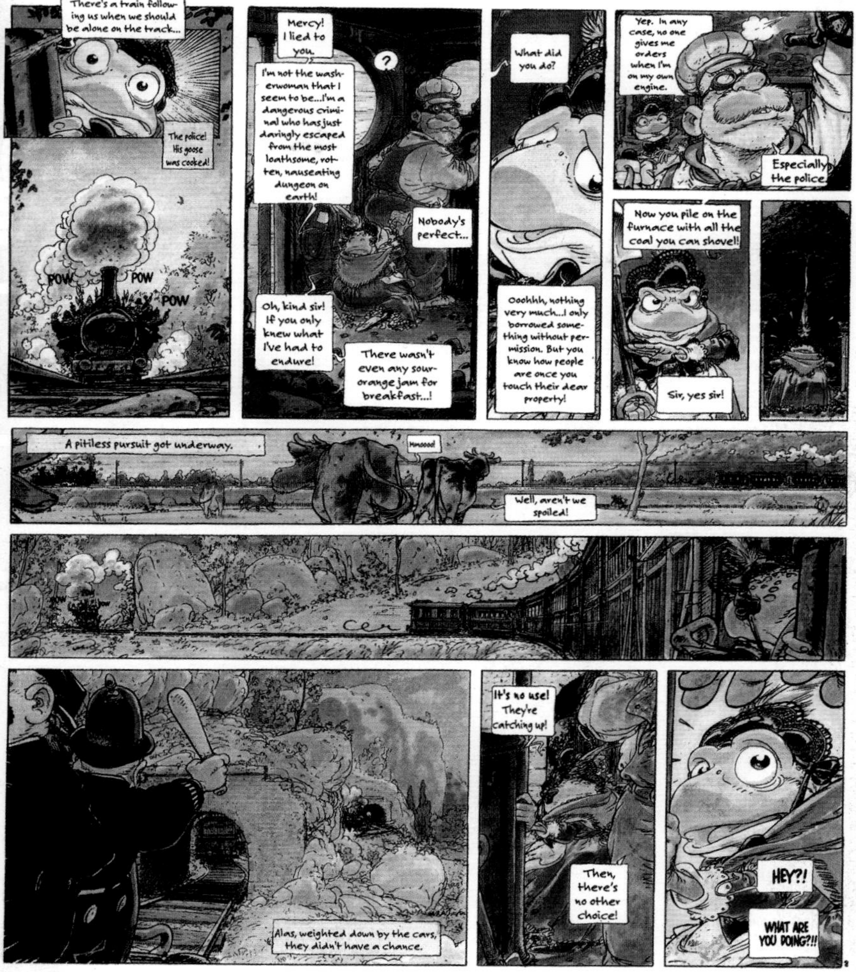

There's a train following us when we should be alone on the track...
The police! His goose was cooked!
POW
POW
POW
Mercy! I lied to you.
I'm not the washerwoman that I seem to be...I'm a dangerous criminal who has just daringly escaped from the most loathsome, rotten, nauseating dungeon on earth!
?
Nobody's perfect...
Oh, kind sir! If you only knew what I've had to endure!
There wasn't even any sour-orange jam for breakfast...!
What did you do?
Ooohhh, nothing very much...I only borrowed something without permission. But you know how people are once you touch their dear property!
Yep. In any case, no one gives me orders when I'm on my own engine.
Especially the police.
Now you pile on the furnace with all the coal you can shovel!
Sir, yes sir!
A pitiless pursuit got underway.
Mmooool
Well, aren't we spoiled!
Alas, weighted down by the cars, they didn't have a chance.
It's no use! They're catching up!
Then, there's no other choice!
HEY?!
WHAT ARE YOU DOING?!!

PAPERCUTZ Feedback

Thanks for
Nancy D.
+
Mystery

Dear Sirs:
I am sending you a thank you note from a student. I bought NANCY DREW, HARDY BOYS, and ZORRO at Comic Con in San Diego this summer. I can not keep these books on the shelf. Students check them out from the shelving cart before I ever get to put them away. The best part of the Papercutz series of books is that my reluctant readers are READING! I was tentative about getting graphic novels, comicbooks, in the library, but no more.
Keep up the good work. I need more HARDY BOYS and NANCY DREW books in the library, so write and draw faster.
Thank you,
Laura Boston
Librarian
Briarmeadow Charter School
Houston, TX

Thanks for your letter, Laura. While our main goal is to produce the most entertaining graphic novels we possibly can, it's also great to hear that our Papercutz graphic novels are helping kids improve their reading skills. We've heard similar reports from many other librarians and from many teachers as well. We're thankful for the support we've been given, and that's one of the reasons we're launching CLASSICS ILLUSTRATED. While everyone is sure to enjoy these comic art adaptations of stories by the World's Greatest Authors, they're especially compelling for reluctant readers.

As for speeding up production on our HARDY BOYS and NANCY DREW graphic novels, writers Scott Lobdell, Stefan Petrucha, and Sara Kinney, and artists Sho Murase and Paulo H. Marcondes are all working as fast as they can to create new stories and art, but we all want to make sure that each new book is even better than the last. That means sticking to our current schedule of a new NANCY DREW and HARDY BOYS graphic novels every three months.

Dear Editor,
I am a big fan of the HARDY BOYS. So when I heard of the HARDY BOYS comics, I immediately began to collect them. My favorite so far is #7 "The Opposite Numbers..." I think that Paulo Henrique is your best artist yet. I think the cars and trucks could use a little more work and I thought that the Hardys might have a case in Europe. Also I know you were looking for new characters, so I suggest Tom Swift Jr., young inventor published by Aladdin Paperbacks.

Hardy Boys fan,
Benton Hammond

Great idea, Benton! What does everyone else think about adding Tom Swift Jr. to the Papercutz lineup? The name of this section is Papercutz Feedback—and that's what we need right now. Let us know if you want to see Tom Swift Jr. in a Papercutz graphic novel series or not!
And hey, we're big fans of the super-talented Paulo Henrique (now credited as Paulo H. Marcondes) too, and are thrilled with his great work in HARDY BOYS graphic novel #10, "A Hardy Day's Night," on sale now at your favorite bookstore. There's one little bit we'd like to take this opportunity to share with you, just because it's so darn cute. Due to miscommunication, Paulo thought that Frank and Joe Hardy were to be drawn as youngsters in both the first and last panels on the following page. Well, it was just supposed to be in the first panel, so Paulo corrected the last panel to make Joe and Frank the correct ages. But, he drew little Joe and little Frank so adorably, we just had to share it with everyone on the very next page…
Tell us what YOU think about Papercutz! Love us or hate us, we want your Feedback! Send it to our bleary-eyed editor at salicrup@papercutz.com or Jim Salicrup, Papercutz, 40 Exchange Place, Ste. 1308, New York, NY 10005. We may not be able to answer or publish every letter, but we read every single one. You've got the best opinions and advice, so that's why we love getting your feedback!

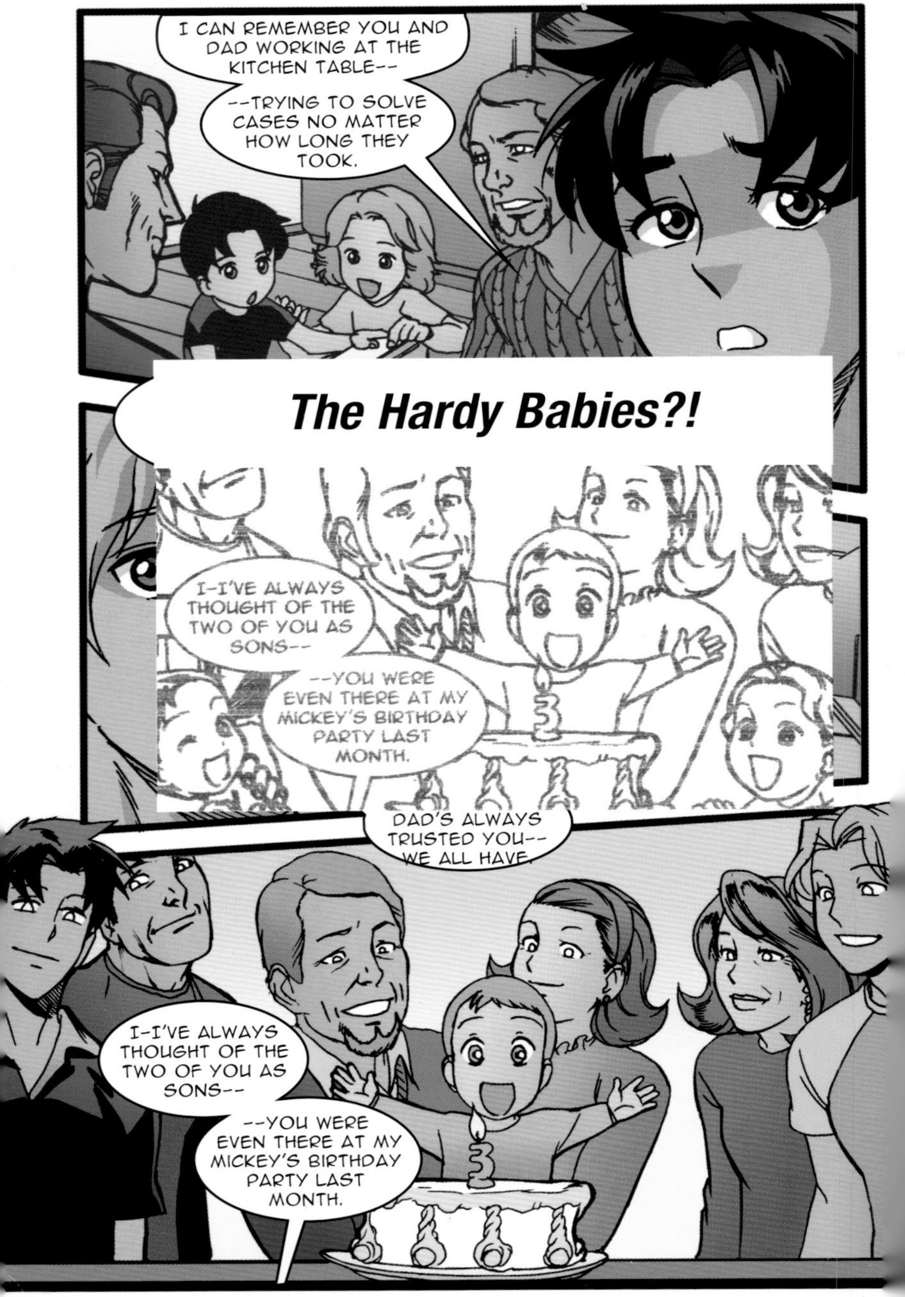
I CAN REMEMBER YOU AND DAD WORKING AT THE KITCHEN TABLE--
--TRYING TO SOLVE CASES NO MATTER HOW LONG THEY TOOK.
The Hardy Babies?!
I-I'VE ALWAYS THOUGHT OF THE TWO OF YOU AS SONS--
--YOU WERE EVEN THERE AT MY MICKEY'S BIRTHDAY PARTY LAST MONTH.
DAD'S ALWAYS TRUSTED YOU--WE ALL HAVE.
I-I'VE ALWAYS THOUGHT OF THE TWO OF YOU AS SONS--
--YOU WERE EVEN THERE AT MY MICKEY'S BIRTHDAY PARTY LAST MONTH.